BEDLAM
IN THE
BAILIWICKS

BEDLAM
IN THE
BAILIWICKS

Desmond Walker

ALAN SUTTON

GUERNSEY PRESS

ALAN SUTTON PUBLISHING
BRUNSWICK ROAD · GLOUCESTER

THE GUERNSEY PRESS COMPANY LIMITED
VALE · GUERNSEY

British Library Cataloguing in Publication Data

Walker, Desmond
Bedlam in the Bailiwicks.
I. Title
823'.914[F]   PR6073.A39/
ISBN 0-86299-366-0

Typesetting and origination by
Alan Sutton Publishing Limited.
Printed in Great Britain by
The Guernsey Press Company Limited,
Guernsey, Channel Islands.

*To all those who have found
enough time, between gin and tonics,
to weigh politicians in the balance and
to find them wanting*

DESMOND WALKER

*The author spent the war years as a pilot in
the Royal Air Force and has visited Jersey many times.
After the war he spent some years in the Far East.
More recently his work has brought him into
contact with politicians and the Whitehall 'machine'.
He has lectured widely and contributed articles
to a number of professional journals.
This is his first novel.*

CHAPTER ONE

'Ever since I learned that my mother used on occasion, no doubt absentmindedly, to hang a shoe on my father's John Thomas I knew that I came of unusual stock.'

Sir Arthur Crabbe sat back from his hard used Victorian kneehole desk and wondered whether those words would make a sufficiently arresting opening for his novel. Neither the desk, which was pine, nor the worm-ravaged country Chippendale elbow chair that went with it would, he knew, ever be changed. Although originally they were intended to be temporary, to serve only until there was money enough to replace them with more finely made and aristocratic counterparts that moment, Sir Arthur now knew, would never come. Not that his wife, Constance, could not have changed them for him at any point during their thirty-odd years of marriage, had he so wished, for Constance was rich. But he had not so wished. He had, as he saw it, indulged her in every other way. He had agreed to retire to the lovely home which she had inherited in Jersey. He had allowed her to pay for their expensive motor cars, he was content that she should pay his bills in Savile Row and he raised no objection to her meeting the household expenses.

Only in this matter of his desk and chair had he shown the obstinacy of which small weak men are occasionally capable. They were his, a relic of his pre-Constance past, more personal to him even than his clothes and he would not part with them, so he had reasoned, until he, out of his

1

own money, was ready to replace them. The bulk of his salary over the years less the prudent 15% savings, though savings for what it would be hard to say, had gone into his stamp collection, itself another form of saving and investment. When he had judged, some years back, that he at last had money enough to make the change he had found that he no longer wished to do so. Not only would it have been a gross extravagance but he had become accustomed to the scratches, the cigarette burns and the ink stains, all a bequest of some previous owner, and had come to feel that the yellow of the old pine went well with the light coloured mahogany of the chair. Besides, the seat of the chair was rather fine, a triumph of gros point with a petit point centre.

But, as Sir Arthur knew, it was more dangerous to become wedded to words than to furniture. Words could be changed and the matter at issue now was whether his should be. He knew from long experience of minute writing that on re-reading, a paragraph which one had crafted with the greatest care and which seemed at the moment of writing to express one's meaning to perfection often seemed to upset the balance of the whole. Sir Arthur had found it necessary on those occasions, painful though it might be, to summon all his courage and to strike out the admired yet offending words however resonant, seductive or memorable they might seem. Was this. he wondered, such a time?

Sir Arthur attempted to address the question but his mind, though disciplined and trained by 38 years in the Civil Service, proved recalcitrant. This phenomenon, this unwillingness of his mind to accept its instructions without question and to set to with promptitude on the given task had been occurring with increasing frequency in the past two years, ever since he had retired, in fact, and he found it most vexatious. It could, he thought, when he allowed himself briefly to consider the matter, even become a matter of concern. It was as though his mind, as it were, had a mind of its own.

2

This time his mind had been seduced into consideration of the form feminine in the person of Prudence Simpson who, with her husband, Brigadier Podger Simpson, would soon be arriving for midday drinks. Sir Arthur admired Prudence greatly. Had he come from a less sheltered and less introverted background he might have recognised that he was what is known in cruder circles as a 'bum man'. As it was his mind, basically Victorian but Edwardian in its wilder moments, would never contemplate such vulgarity and would allow him only to recognise that Prudence had a fine figure which he found most attractive. Not, of course, that Constance was not a queen among women. But she would, he thought, be extremely vexed if ever she detected his feelings for Prudence, and he resolved that this should never happen and that his admiration should continue to remain hidden.

His mind's undisciplined wandering had come up with a trigger word – 'Drinks'. In true Pavlovian fashion Sir Arthur poured himself a large gin and tonic from the drinks trolley which, as an extremely functional piece of furniture, graced his study. Not, he told himself, that he was an alcoholic. No, no, far from it. He was one of those shy people, born one drink below par, for whom alcohol, always of course in moderation, was necessary if he was to face the world. And, of course, he had to face the world every day. With practice, and with a judicious increase in dosage, he had found it easier and easier to do so.

The action of pouring a drink brought Sir Arthur back to his problem. He continued to muse. Anyone looking in on the scene would have been hard put to it to recognise that what they were seeing was a moment of crisis. All they would have been aware of would have been a small, rather ineffectual looking white-haired man, cradling his pale unlined face in one hand and an oversized gin and tonic in the other while his eyes, dreamy and unfocussed, peered aimlessly over his half moon reading glasses. Suddenly his

3

demeanour changed. His eyes refocussed and took on what, in a stronger character, might have been taken for a purposeful look. He permitted himself a small smile, and then he sighed. But it was not a sigh of ennui or despair but the sigh of one who, when put to the test, has not been found wanting and is justifiably pleased with his own performance. Sir Arthur had taken a decision. He savoured his gin and tonic in celebration of this rare, indeed almost unique event.

Never once in 38 years had he had to take a decision professionally. It had been his task to proffer advice, and his advice had been nothing if not even handed. No recipient of one of Sir Arthur's minutes, be he minister or senior official, could ever be quite sure what course of action, if any, was being advocated. They would seize upon a key phrase such as 'The balance of advantage would therefore seem to lie in . . .' and would feel, briefly, that a recommendation was about to be made until they came up against a key sentence which might read 'However, it would be unwise in the extreme to overlook the fact that the seeming merit of this course of action could at a stroke be nullified by any one of a number of factors'. And so on. But no one could deny that Sir Arthur had a certain facility as a minute writer. He enlivened what was inevitably jargon, much of it coded so as to be understood by senior officials but not by ministers, with an occasional touch of style and imagination. His minutes, though useless, were often a pleasure to read and he ensured that, if a minister were to take some disastrous decision, no blame could ever be attributed to the department.

He had been regarded by his seniors as sound. He was thorough, he was cautious and had an ability to confuse ministers which had proved invaluable on more than one occasion. He had spent the major part of his service in the Ministry of Defence, having started as a Principal in what was then the War Office. This choice on the part of his

4

seniors was deliberate. It had been clear to them, right from the beginning, that the young Arthur Crabbe was not Permanent Secretary material. But they recognised that he had quite a good mind and what looked like a real talent for identifying genuine difficulties and for manufacturing spurious ones in the interests of delay. In their view these talents could best be employed in slowing-up, if not actually reducing, defence spending. And the military to whom even a third rate mind appeared brilliant, and Arthur Crabbe's mind was far from third rate, failed to recognise a Trojan horse in the person of this likeable, mild mannered and apparently wise official.

In the fullness of time they were happy to endorse the Permanent Secretary's recommendation that Arthur Crabbe's long and valuable service should be recognised by the conferring of a knighthood on the occasion of his retirement. Constance had accepted the award with an outward display of pleasure although she felt it was both too little and too late. In her view Arthur was worth more than that and although she attempted to disguise the fact, she considered it a self-evidently inadequate recognition of her own worth and of her influence on affairs, albeit at second-hand. Arthur had no such illusions. He was lucky, and he knew it. He was glad also that his father's parsimony had resulted in him having only one Christian name and that, as a result, he was spared any difficult decision as to his future style of address.

In his private life, similarly, he had not been overburdened with the need for decision making. Constance had decided that she would marry him, and had told him so. He had been happy to concur. Had he found the prospect less than agreeable it would have made no difference. Constance was a lady of great determination and could have been described as wilful. Certainly she would brook no interference in any plan that she might make. He loved her dearly. Decisions were sometimes

5

needed in connection with his stamp collection and these invariably took the form 'Should I buy this rarity, or that one?' Sir Arthur showed boldness and incisiveness in these moments of crisis and invariably resolved the dilemma by buying both. Only in the matter of his desk and his chair did he run other than true to form.

The decision which Sir Arthur had taken, and which had so cheered him, was that he would confide in Podger Simpson and would seek his advice in the matter of that opening paragraph. His instinct told him that an opening paragraph could be critical, if not all-important, so far as a publisher's reader was concerned. Failure to hold his attention or to quicken his interest in those first few lines would lead inevitably to a rejection slip. Sir Arthur felt too close to the problem to be able to form a reliable judgment as to whether his opening words could stand as drafted, or whether amendment was called for. Certainly they had impact, though of a vulgar kind. They were arresting and they even had authority of a sort. Best of all they provided perfect cover as no one would dream that they came from the pen of a civil servant, retired and of a certain standing. On the other hand, on re-reading they seemed less plausible and convincing than he had at first thought.

On the related matter of output he had no such qualms. Thirty key words represented a good day's work and Sir Arthur was well content. If the tiresome thought intruded that at that rate a novel of 100,000 words would take him nine years to write, by which time he would be 67, Sir Arthur gave no sign. The knowledge that this was by no means the first time that he had started a novel was similarly suppressed, or at least given little weight. He told himself all that had been lacking on those earlier occasions had been time, and now he had time in abundance. And there was yet a further and more compelling reason why he should not falter on this occasion. Although Constance was a pearl beyond price and although he would yield to

6

no man in his admiration of her many qualities, there was no doubt that there were times when it was necessary to give a reasonably convincing show of being occupied, otherwise one soon would be on tasks not of one's own choosing.

Sir Arthur's reverie was interrupted by a sound that North American Indians in days gone by might have confused with that of a bull bison calling to its mate. He knew that he was wanted, indeed that his presence was commanded. He knew also that Constance could shatter a wineglass at thirty paces if provoked and he made haste to call 'Coming my dear!' just as a second cry of 'Arthuur!' with a long drawn out and rising cadence on the second syllable sent the swallows skittering. Pausing only to empty his glass he proceeded with all despatch to answer the summons of his beloved.

He had quite a long way to go as his study was upstairs at the far end of the house. Like many old Jersey houses it was long and low, built gable end into a hill to gain as much shelter as possible from the prevailing wind with only the minimum loss of sun. In the middle decades of the 15th century it had been a small farm house. Later it had been added to extensively and had become one of the show houses of the island.

Built of rose coloured granite it had been re-roofed with slate in the 18th century, a sign of prosperity in the island in those days. Many of the original French pantiles now graced the roofs of the extensive outbuildings. Nothing on the outside of the house could be dated as later than 1750. Inside it was different.

The Tissards had been people of substance as far back as the family records went in any detail, but it was old Amos Tissard who founded what was to become a considerable fortune. He had been a privateer in Napoleonic times and some said that, following the peace with France, he and his sons turned to the even more profitable trade of smuggling.

7

All that was known for certain was that by late Georgian times the Tissards had become carriage folk and had built a most imposing mansion on the outskirts of St Helier. This had had to be sold to pay the gambling debts of Aloysius Tissard who, disowned by his father, had repaired to Australia where, it was thought, he would not lack for like-minded company.

Luckily, the damage wrought by Aloysius was not fatal to the Tissard fortune, nor was it even very serious in the long run. Constance's great grandfather soon put matters to rights. True, they no longer had the Town House, but in any event to later generations the old family home in the country had come to seem more attractive, and three generations of Tissards spent considerable sums of money in heightening that attraction.

The result now, for example, was that alone in its generation of houses in the island, it was dry. This in a house built with no damp-course, with a stone flagged ground floor and with four feet thick walls filled with rubble and sea sand, was not far removed from a miracle. A miracle might have cost more, but probably not much more. It would have been one of the higher quotes, turned down in the interests of economy.

But of course that was just the shell. Inside, the house was a delight, the mahogany of the Town House finding its place harmoniously and complementing rather than clashing with the oak that was natural to the original building.

As Sir Arthur moved rapidly to take his place, as consort, at the scene of action he took pleasure from the serenity, the essential 'rightness', of the furnishings, the rich tribal rugs and richer Persian carpets, the good oils, the rare local prints and maps, the wink of Georgian silver and the soft allure of calf bindings in row upon row in the elegant low-ceilinged library. He moved his feet quickly in short steps. When he was older he would shuffle. Remembering to duck his head, although he was only five feet six, he

8

passed without incident through two Tudor doorways in the long passageway, one of them measuring only four feet ten from floor to lintel.

He came quickly down the tourelle, the circular stone staircase that was one of the classic features of the old house, and turned right-handed into the dining room and into the eye of whatever storm might be brewing. But it was only a mild blow although his greeting was blustery enough.

'For Heaven's sake do something! Do you expect me to do every single thing on my own?' the object of his lifelong affection enquired in what an impartial observer might well have construed as a hostile, if not actually threatening manner. 'That fool of a girl must have put the Hoover on "Blow" rather than "Suck" so far as I can see. Have you forgotten that we have guests coming in less than fifteen minutes?'

Sir Arthur forbore to tell his wife that she could well have afforded three living-in servants had she wanted them and that the choice of the aforesaid 'fool of a girl' was hers and hers alone. Instead he fell back on his 'irrelevant remark' gambit which he had often found efficacious in similar moments of tension. 'I'll just see if the shrimping nets are dry yet, my dear,' he said, and moved into one of the nearby barns with an agility that surprised even himself.

He had found that the time spent by his spouse in attempting to assess whether his words had a hidden meaning and, if so, what that meaning might be, often had a calming effect. And so it proved on this occasion. By the time he returned and began to busy himself with fetching ice and lemon and with checking that everything else he might need was already in the dining room and within easy reach, Constance had made the transition to a state of minor remorse.

'Poor dear Arthur,' she thought, 'I am so unkind to him sometimes, and he really doesn't deserve it. He's so

9

brilliant, too. I wonder what he meant about the shrimping nets? I daren't ask or he'll think me a fool.'

Emboldened by the silence Arthur followed up with what he thought of as the 'Current scandal' gambit, virtually guaranteed in his experience to heighten feminine interest and, at the same time, to turn away wrath.

'I say, Connie. Do you think they'll have anything new on Ernest?' he asked, well knowing that the carryings-on of the said Ernest were a matter of the greatest fascination to Constance and her immediate circle of women friends. Her slightly harassed and reflective look disappeared. A gleam came into her eyes and she passed her tongue experimentally over her lips, like a lizard that has just sighted a particularly well set-up and luscious fly.

'Oh, I do hope so!' she said.

Further speculation was cut short by the noise of Podger and Prue's arrival. 'Here they come' said Constance somewhat unnecessarily as a car door slammed and the sound of Podger 'What whatting' was carried on the breeze.

Brigadier Percy Simpson CBE, DSO, known as Podger to his many friends, was the same age as Arthur Crabbe and so had been just too young to serve in the war of 1939–45. But he had made up for it since. Commissioned into a famous line regiment he had fought either with his battalion, or on secondment, in the so-called Malayan emergency, in the Korean War, in the Mau Mau rebellion in Kenya and in Cyprus at the height of the Troubles. He had spent a lot of time in intelligence and had served 'on loan' in some remote and little known parts of the world.

He could speak Urdu, Malay and Swahili and could get by in Arabic. He was, on his own admission, 'not bad at those native lingoes', but the same could not be said for his command of English. In this mother tongue any communication that he sought to make was invariably prefaced and accompanied by snorts, barking noises and a positive barrage of 'what whats?'.

10

How he had ever passed into Staff College was a mystery to Podger's friends and, to be fair, it was equally a mystery to Podger himself. Privately he felt sure that the papers must have got mixed up. Once admitted he was safe, as no member of the directing staff would ever disclose that he found one of his students in effect unteachable lest it reflect on his own ability as an instructor.

So, in the fullness of time Podger became a Staff College graduate, entitled to the magic letters p.s.c. after his name. While this widened his promotion horizon it also inevitably led to a tour in the Ministry of Defence. It was there, as a lieutenant-colonel, that Podger had first met Arthur Crabbe, then himself a very junior assistant secretary.

Podger was thought by some to have originated the ploy of hurrying down corridors with an earnest expression on the face and a pile of files under the arm. This was said to impress one's seniors with one's industry even if the point of departure was one bog and the destination another.

What is to be surmised is that Podger had some good young majors in his office and that his role was largely confined to that of front man. In that capacity he attended many of the same committee meetings as Arthur Crabbe and, on these occasions, he made a considerable impression on his colleagues, including Arthur. His technique was to look knowing and to say absolutely nothing unless directly asked for an opinion, which seldom happened as most of those present were too busy airing their own. On the rare occasion that he was cornered and addressed directly he invariably came up with the discussion stopping formula of 'I'm afraid I must reserve my general's position'.

His air of maturity, his very wide practical experience, his known gallantry and his lack of communicativeness all served to heighten Podger's image. He was variously thought of as deep, sound, devious, subtle and sharp. Nobody, except Podger himself, thought of him as thick. Arthur Crabbe predictably had difficulty in making up his

11

mind. He could not decide whether the social persona which Podger presented to the world of a bluff, simple soldier was genuine or whether he had deliberately set out to parody first the colonel and now the brigadier of fiction and had overdone it a bit. He suspected the latter as, from time to time, he thought he had detected something vaguely resembling a keen mind behind Podger's protuberant blue eyes. But he was not sure. The pose, if it was one, was of such long standing that it had become second nature.

Prudence was first over the threshold and Arthur thought, as he always did when he saw her, what a handsome woman she was. Although slighter than Constance she had a fine athletic build. You could almost see the hockey stick in her hand, Arthur thought to himself. He feasted his admiring eyes upon her for the few seconds taken up by Connie's welcome. He saw again the striking fair hair cut in such a becoming style. Constance maintained that it was dyed, or rather rinsed, but privately he felt sure she was mistaken. Prue had a tendency to snort, possibly as a result of having lived with Podger for so long, and she was snorting now – little warm melodious snorts indicative of pleasure, a sound that was music to Arthur's ears. He knew that at any moment her lip would assume a curious curl and that, with any luck, she would show the whites of her eyes, like a horse, an expression which Arthur found positively enchanting.

He beamed his welcoming and admiring gaze upon her, as soon as Constance turned to Podger, and was rewarded by a fusillade of little rippling snorts, by a cry of 'Arthur darling' and by a warm embrace. As she stepped back the lips, that had been pressed to his cheek but a second or so before, began to curl and just for the briefest moment she flashed the whites of her eyes. In a transport of delight Arthur remembered that he would need to take care to conceal his admiration lest Constance should become vexed.

Constance had made Podger welcome and had received an answering barrage of 'What, whats? Jolly day, by Jove eh?' as well as miscellaneous snorts of a martial nature and a somewhat muffled 'say Connie old girl!' the latter occasioned by his tripping as he entered her embrace and becoming enfolded momentarily in her more than ample bosom. Released, he hid his confusion and embarrassment in a large spotted silk handkerchief and blew his nose with a loud wailing sound by way of apology. Connie and Prue exchanged private glances of amusement and began to chatter. Podger continued to mutter to himself, his 'Bad show, bad show, what, eh?' repeated with slight variation of formula, providing a rumbling background.

Arthur prepared the drinks. He knew what everyone would have and wasted no time on enquiry, of however ritual a nature. The very cold Martini, nine tenths gin with a sliver of lemon peel was, he knew, exactly how Prue liked it. He always poured gin freehand as he hated the idea of being tied to measures. Why should one, he asked himself, be tied to a single or a double or perhaps, on rare occasions, a triple or even a quadruple? With practice he had found that he could pour any measure he wanted with a high degree of accuracy. His usual measure was $2\frac{1}{4}$ and he poured one of these for Podger and one for himself. Mindful that Constance might need to be kept in a good mood he poured her a stiff $2\frac{3}{4}$ to which he added twice the amount of Dubonnet, and then put in ice and lemon. To Podger's drink he added tonic, ice and lemon and to his own just tonic and ice.

He knew that in a matter of moments Podger would need a refill. Of Podger's many qualities none was perhaps quite as remarkable as his ability to absorb alcohol. He could at will create an arid zone centred on his own glass, and this Arthur encouraged as it made him feel that his own alcoholic intake was no more than medicinal, a judicious quantity that was the legitimate requirement of ageing arteries.

Having demonstrated his particular skill Podger was two-thirds the way through his second drink by the time that Connie and Prue moved out into the garden intent on assessing at first hand the relative merits of various types of compost. Podger finished his second gin and tonic and, having moved his glass casually but purposefully in Arthur's direction, ceased to snort and began tuning-up preparatory to speech. He accepted the new gin and tonic absentmindedly, looking at it with an expression which could almost have passed for surprise, and finished his tuning-up with a final authoritative 'Harrumph!'.

They had moved to chairs on the lawn and Podger, his embarrassment forgotten, settled himself comfortably, stroking his grey, carefully trimmed moustache which, obedient to its owner's command, defied gravity and grew sideways.

'I don't like the smell of it, Arthur old bean, what what?' he started without preamble. Arthur, still in a Prue-induced daze, was not immediately seized of the drift of his friend's thought.

'What?' he said.

'What, What?' countered Podger immediately, not to be outplayed at his own game. 'Why, the Election of course. Looks to me as though those damned Socialist wallahs will get in in spite of the frightful balls-up they've always made in the past. The great British electorate looks set to put us all straight up the creek once again.'

If Arthur privately shared Podger's misgivings he gave no sign of it. Thirty-eight years of neutral facelessness are not lightly put aside and his response was the product of his training as a young man and of the belief to which he had adhered over the years.

'But, Podger,' he remonstrated, 'if the vote should go that way you really can't complain. 1 mean, that would simply be democracy in action, and the Conservatives have had a very long run, you know, and, arguably, not a

14

lot to show for it. Perhaps the time is ripe for a change.' He faltered to a finish, aware that his words were unlikely to gain him a standing ovation.

Podger looked at him with a mixture of pity and disbelief, much as he might have looked at a particularly retarded recruit. 'You can't be serious Arthur old bean. Mean to say, you're joking, having me on, what, what? Eh? Surely you can't look on these present perishers as in any way fitted to govern? The last half-way sensible Socialists went to the wall when that Welsh cove Kinnock lost the election of 1987. Since then they've been nothing but a rabble with envy as their motivation and levelling down their aim.' This unusually long sentence, uninterrupted by a single snort, testified to Podger's depth of feeling on the subject.

Arthur was unwilling to give more than grudging and reluctant credence to Podger's view. In one particular though he was certainly right. If Labour were to win, the individuals who would then be on the front bench would undoubtedly be of a new order of awfulness. They would merit that strongest of Civil servants' condemnatory words – 'Unacceptable'. But they would have to be 'Accepted' because unquestioning loyalty to the duly elected government was still the rule in the higher echelons of the Civil Service in spite of the awful let-down by that young man Ponting some years back. Arthur took some comfort from the thought that the electorate, however wayward and perverse, surely lacked an order of stupidity sufficient to put Labour in power. But, in spite of himself, he was uneasy.

He sought, if not to terminate the discussion, at least to steer it into safer channels. 'Well, Podger,' he said, 'whatever the result the effect over here can be no more than marginal. The reserved powers of the British Government only extend to foreign affairs and defence, remember. I'm sure the last thing they'd want to do would be to tamper with the constitutional relationship.'

'Rubbish,' rejoined Podger. 'I tell you I know their type

15

better than you do Arthur, for all your time in Whitehall. What? Its a matter of knowing men and I know their breed well enough, by Jove. So far as competence goes I wouldn't trust 'em not to shoot themselves in the foot with a blank cartridge, but when it comes to helping themselves to your money then they're mustard. Mustard, Arthur. You mark my words, mark 'em, I say, if that lot get in they'll have one hand on their heart and the other in your pocket before you can say 'About Turn', constitutional relationship or no constitutional relationship. What, what!'

Arthur thought that in the face of Podger's evidently passionate views some limited concession, without, of course, sacrifice of principle, might make for a lowering of temperature. 'I'm prepared to concede, Podger,' he began in his most urbane and placatory tone, 'yes, I think I could go so far as to concede, that they might well set up a working party, or even a commission, to see if there is any way under the Law in which taxes could be levied, for the benefit of the Exchequer, on individuals living in this Bailiwick or on companies based here. So far as companies are concerned it is arguable that, with a change in the Law, they could do so, but they would find, and sooner rather than later, that they lost thereby. So far as taxing individuals is concerned there is no way in which they could do that without coming slap up against the constitutional relationship. Surely you remember, Podger, don't you, that a Labour backbencher called Foulkes or Fowkes or something of that nature raised the issue some years ago? They must have concluded there was nothing in it because nothing more was heard of the idea after a while.'

'Poppycock, Arthur! Fiddlesticks!' rejoined Podger. 'Who taxes my service pension, Arthur? And who taxes your Civil Service one, eh? eh?, tell me that, Arthur old bean. The Inland Revenue, isn't it? And who are they acting for if not the British Government? Tell me that, Arthur and, harrumph! while you're at it old man tell me how that squares with your constitutional relationship, eh? You know me Arthur, I'm basically a simple soul', here Podger assumed an innocent look and gazed directly at Arthur with untroubled, if somewhat protuberant and bloodshot blue eyes, 'but in my book that's taxation without representation and they got in a bit of a mess last time they tried that caper, Eh? What? didn't they, by Jove.'

He chuckled, though Arthur was not quite clear why. 'It's a serious point, Arthur old man. Think about it. You and I haven't got a vote in the U.K. not that I want one, what? Eh?' he added quickly, 'and we get no benefit from that taxation which is applied without Allowances and levied at a much higher rate than would apply over here, isn't it now? If they can ride roughshod over your precious constitutional relationship in that way you can bet your boots they'll find some way round it to clobber everyone else over here if they make their minds up to it. You know, Arthur. You know, Arthur, what? Eh?'

Podger rested what he clearly felt was an unanswerable case, and looked thirstily about him. While Arthur refilled Podger's glass he explained patiently that there was per- haps a case to be made for the United Kingdom's taxation policy as it applied to Podger and to himself.

'I don't think its quite as unreasonable as all that, Podger, you know,' he said. 'It's a Government pension and it's open to them to elect to pay it in the United Kingdom under United Kingdom taxation rules. You and I don't have to live in Jersey. The fact that we've decided to do so is our own business and irrelevant so far as the taxation authorities are concerned. After all, we earned the pension in the United Kingdom and it's surely not unreasonable that it should be paid there. It certainly, in my view, could not be held to be a precedent for taxing Channel Islanders as a whole.'

Podger was determined not to allow the issue to be smoothed over in this way.

'That's bosh, Arthur, and you know it. Sheer rubbish, however you try to rationalise and excuse behaviour that would land a private individual in clink. No better than a lot of pirates, you know, what? You may have earned your pension in the U.K., Arthur, but I certainly didn't. Most of mine was earned, and damned hard earned even if I say it myself, in the Middle and Far East fighting for the Queen, not for some bunch of politicians. Harrumph!' he ended aggressively.

Arthur had a strong feeling that there was nothing to be gained by taking the argument further. So, doing no more than murmur 'Deemed to have been earned in the United Kingdom, Podger, deemed to have been so earned', he fell back on his grandmother's formula which had never failed to put an end to childish argument. 'Well, we'll see, shan't we?' he said sagely and then moved swiftly to forestall any further disagreement from Podger.

'Podger,' he went on, almost in the same breath, 'I know it's an abrupt change of subject but Connie and Prue will be back soon and I'd much appreciate your advice on a small matter which is exercising me somewhat.'

Podger was immediately all attention, and his features assumed what could easily have been mistaken for an alert look. 'Yes, yes, of course. Certainly, old bean', he said.

'I of course wouldn't wish it to become generally known' Arthur went on in a confidential tone, 'and I know I can rely on you to keep it to yourself, but I've started a novel and I'm a bit worried about the appropriateness of the opening sentence. I'd like your honest opinion when you've heard it.'

'Harrumph!' said Podger with evident interest. 'Novel, did you say, Arthur? Novel, Eh? What d'you want to do that for? Surely there're enough long haired fellahs around doing that already?'

This was a fair question and Arthur recognised it as such. He also knew that he had no answer that would make sense to Podger, and wasn't at all sure that he had one that made sense to himself. It wasn't a matter of money, he had no burning message to transmit, it wasn't vanity, in the normal sense at least, as he intended to publish under an assumed name. Perhaps, though, it was vanity of a sort. He had always been a wordsmith but he had never had to write more than a few hundred polished words, crafted and balanced to perfection. Could he write 100,000 and, furthermore, 100,000 that would sell? He liked to think he could. And surely, he told himself, the cracking thirty word start augured well?

'I don't know, Podger' he answered truthfully, if somewhat unsatisfactorily, and then added vaguely 'Something to do, I suppose.' Podger remained mystified. 'Something to do, Arthur?' he repeated in an incredulous tone. 'But I mean to say there's golf and the garden, eh? Wouldn't have thought you'd be stuck for something to do with Connie around, what? Well, perhaps that's not what I mean, but you know what I mean, what, what?'

Arthur took advantage of his friend's momentary confusion to read his opening paragraph. Now that he came to read the words aloud for the first time, pride of authorship asserted itself. He felt that the words had a good ring to them, that they were essentially right, and all he now wished to hear from Podger was enthusiastic confirmation of this judgment. He waited expectantly.

'Well,' said Podger at length, his tone sounding rather doubtful, 'isn't it going it a bit, Arthur old chap? I mean to say, respected ex-civil servant and all that, knight and so on? Might even be read by ladies. After all more than half the population are women you know and some of them must read. I mean, Prue does for one, what?'

Arthur explained that he intended to ensure the strictest anonymity. Podger was evidently relieved. 'Ah, well, that's a bit different then,' he conceded. 'But I don't think John Thomas will do, you know,' he said, and then went on before Arthur could register either a protest or an enquiry, 'When I was cramming for Staff College entrance, cramming y'know, read a book called, I think, Fowler's English Usage. Might even have been written by a cove called Fowler, I suppose, what?' he said, as if struck by a new thought. 'Yes, well this Johnny Fowler, or whoever wrote it, was held to be quite an authority as I remember it. And one of his big points,' here Podger broke off, convulsed by private mirth. 'Hah! Hah!' he exploded. 'Just thought of it, Arthur, wouldn't have done for your lot, eh? What? What? One of his major rules was something like "Never use a long word if a short one will do."'

There was a short dramatic pause and then, his timing perfect, Podger suddenly leant forward. 'What about "cock"?' he said, his blue eyes protruding in a questioning mode. Was this, Arthur thought, an example of the keen trained mind at work? Had Staff College honed Podger's critical faculties to a pitch that could be trusted to provide a reliable, if not indeed unerring, guide in anatomical matters of this sort? He resolved to probe the matter further.

'What about prick?' he said tentatively.

Podger's response was immediate, that of a master in sure and complete command of his chosen field. 'No, no, not prick, Arthur. Wops and dagoes have pricks. Englishmen have cocks!'

Arthur could not find it within himself to contradict. Podger had obviously researched the subject thoroughly.

CHAPTER TWO

Meanwhile, in the garden, Connie and Prue were twittering happily. Prue, like Connie, was Jersey born and they had been friends for as long as either of them could remember.

'Arthur's so sweet,' said Prue. 'He's an absolute poppet. You did better than you knew when you grabbed him, Connie. He's so dreamy and intellectual, and house-trained into the bargain.'

'Yes, he really is a darling,' Constance agreed. 'And he's so funny. He actually believes I don't notice when he gives you or Pussy or any of the others the glad eye, so I have to make sure he thinks I'm looking the other way. Killing, isn't it?' She gave what, in a younger woman, might have passed for a girlish giggle.

'Podger isn't half as gallant, I'm afraid,' said Prue. 'He's an absolute duck, but a non-starter with other women. The only thing I've ever known him to make eyes at was a horse, which makes me wonder sometimes what he saw in me. But he's biddable and under control. Most of the time anyway.' She smiled at her old friend. 'In fact, Connie', she said impulsively, 'I think we can both consider ourselves jolly lucky. I've no complaints really except that Podger drinks like a fish. It doesn't seem to affect him though, except that he's liable to fall asleep in unusual places, sometimes standing up.'

'Yes, you're right, we are lucky,' Constance agreed. 'Though it would never do to let them know that we thought so,' she added, a sterner note creeping into her voice. 'Arthur drinks too much as well though I don't really mind. It stops him from pestering me all the time, if you know what I mean.'

'Yes, I do indeed,' said Prue. 'The small ones are always the worst, aren't they? I mean, just look at Charlie Chaplin! My dear,' she said, as though one thought led naturally on to the next, 'what's the latest about Ernest? The last I heard Maureen seemed to be the likely choice.'

Ernest was a recently retired Captain R.N. with a beard, a deeply seamed and tanned face and a way with the ladies. With at least three ladies, anyway, who were busy competing for his favours. All three were widows. Maureen was red haired, Irish of course, and enough to scare the pants off most men. She didn't scare Ernest however, although whether or not his pants had come off on her premises was a matter of continuing interest to her friends.

'Oh, really?' said Connie. 'I hadn't heard that. What's happened to Maggie and to Isobel, then?' Maggie was a loose-limbed, amiable creature, happy and disorganised, whose attraction Connie found hard to see. But, as she told herself, you could never tell with men. Isobel was dark, sultry and mysterious. She always claimed, coquettishly, that she was at her best at three o'clock in the morning by the light of a guttering candle. But had Ernest accepted the implied challenge of her words? That was something which her friends longed to know.

'Do you think he's, you know, doing it to them, Prue?' asked Connie, her tongue flicking out unconsciously to moisten her lips. Her breathing quickened almost imperceptibly as she leant forward.

Prue showed the whites of her eyes, a sure sign of excitement, and she too leaned forward conspiratorially. 'Well!' she said, 'I don't really know, but they all look suspiciously sleek and contented, rather like cats who've been at the cream. If I had to make a guess I'd say he was doing it to all three of them, and doing it rather well.' Her lip curled in its

22

curious, almost sensuous way.

'Do you really think so?' breathed Connie, entranced by the scandalous possibilities implicit in her friend's words. But then she was struck by doubt. 'Surely you can't be right, Prue. Not all three of them. I mean I don't think any man could have the stamina. Could he?' she asked curiously, the note of enquiry seeming to throw doubts on her professed disbelief.

'I'm not so sure,' said Prue. 'If you think about it, it could happen. Say the average man of Ernest's age has 200 shots in his locker for a year. And say he's at sea, as Ernest has been for eleven months, then he might well, indeed probably would, be able to use those same 200 shots in thirty days. That's better than six a day, or two apiece all round.' Her eyes, just for a moment, showed dazzling white.

Connie was convinced. 'Why didn't we all marry sailors?' she sighed dreamily.

They walked back to the house together, each busy with her thoughts. For both of them the subject of fertilisers came a bad second to the subject of Ernest, and the magical properties of various types of compost, normally of consuming interest, received scant attention and was pushed to the back of the mind for later review. Each was occupied with the saga of Ernest and it was images of him and his three women that filled the small screen behind their eyes.

Thus pleasurably occupied they arrived at the lawn, Constance having decided on the way to seek out another of her close friends, Pussy Fox, at the earliest opportunity, and see what she made of Prue's theory.

The men came to their feet, Podger with a welcoming snort and a murmured 'Good show, good show.' Arthur took their empty glasses and reappeared a few moments later with refills.

'And what have you two had to say?' Constance enquired, more in politeness than in a genuine search for

23

enlightenment. Arthur briefly sketched in their political qualms and then, to forestall another outburst by Podger, moved hastily to safer ground. 'And what about you two? Have you taken Ernest to pieces yet or have you been totally taken up by fertilisers?'

'Fertilisers, I'm afraid,' said Connie without hesitation. 'Though we were just about to get on to Ernest, weren't we Prue? Didn't you say you'd heard something?'

Prue had not played centre forward for nothing. She gathered up this fast ball effortlessly, the more so as, by great good fortune, she had indeed heard something.

'My dear!' she said. 'I certainly have! He's gone into a Chinese phase and they're all buying woks and besieging the Red China Emporium for bean curd and buffalo horn! Wouldn't it be funny if he couldn't make up his mind any other way and decided to marry the one who cooked Chinese food the best?' She gave a little snort of amused pleasure at the thought.

Arthur turned this new intelligence over in his mind and inclined to the view that Ernest knew when he was well placed and would be in no hurry to seek a resolution. As things stood he was getting nothing but honeyed words and three times the number of dishes of his choice, for the moment oriental, as he would have done had he been so careless as to plight his troth.

But instinct told him that these musings would not be well received. 'Really?' he said. 'What an old rotter he is, to be sure.' From the look that Constance cast in his direction he was not at all sure that his comment had carried conviction, and he sought hastily to change the subject.

'What . . .' he began, but Podger was there before him. 'Hah! Hah!' he exploded. 'All that stuff about old Ernest and his Chinese phase has just reminded me of a really frightfully good story. Perhaps a trifle gamey, but you gels are broadminded enough, aren't you, eh? What? What? It's really frightfully funny!'

24

'Perhaps, Podger, you'll allow us to be the judge of that, after you've told it,' said Prue, her tone distinctly discouraging. But Podger was past danger signals and pressed ahead with some involved story about a Chinaman and a Greek, pausing every now and then to underline some point by way of a 'Damned clever that, eh? Eh? Ha! Ha!'

There was not exactly silence, because any silence there might otherwise have been stood no chance in the face of Podger's mirth, but gradually it seemed to dawn on him that his view might not command unanimity and that, indeed, he might be in a minority of one. Becoming confused, he lost his thread and began to gabble, anxious only to reach his punch line. That delivered he collapsed into his handkerchief and blew his nose loudly with a note indicative of distress and, by dint of a plaintive tremolo, even managing to communicate that its owner felt unjustly used.

Serenely, Prue surveyed her mate as she might have looked at a naughty little boy, covered in jam. She even managed a somewhat wintry smile. 'Very funny, Podger dear,' she said. Podger plunged desperately. 'Once commanded some Chinese irregulars in northern Burma. Good troops! Good troops!' His voice tailed away, somewhat sadly.

The hostess in Constance took over at this critical moment and she steered the conversation on to safe ground of her own choosing. She was a fine looking woman, big by any standards, but built in proportion and she carried herself well. She had kept her figure and with her thick dark hair, lightly tanned complexion and even, sparkling teeth she made a striking, if slightly formidable, picture.

Not for nothing had she been an unofficial and unconscious pin-up girl for Arthur's junior staff many years ago. They had used to joke among themselves about the discrepancy in size between their boss and his wife, likening Arthur to Sherpa Tensing and Constance to Mount Everest. Indeed their nickname for Arthur was The Sherpa. Constance they called Mr Universe, some wag almost always adding, sotto voce, words descriptive of her sex, a simple witticism that, however often repeated, never failed to reduce the outer office to helpless laughter. But this banter did nothing to hide the fact that they recognised that she was a magnificent woman. The years had been kind to her and she still was. But even the most ardent admirer would have found it impossible to claim that her build was other than substantial.

And so it came as something of a surprise to those few people who knew her well enough to discover, as they inevitably did in time, that she held beliefs more usually associated with frailer and more sensitive seeming beings. She believed totally in the spirit world. She had no doubts at all about reincarnation and even at times fancied that she detected signs which, if not hard evidence of previous existences, were sufficiently unusual to reinforce an already strongly held belief.

She was convinced by those signs that she had been present at the court of King Charles the First. Before that time, when Europe had been cold and uncomfortable, she had had the good sense to spend a life as a maharani and, much earlier, as a Hittite noblewoman at the height of that empire's sway. From her silken tent she had viewed the Battle of Kadesh when Hittite arms had crushed the power of Egypt in 1296 B.C.

Strong and vivid memories of the backwoods of Tennessee, of poor white trash and of the brutal and often incestuous life in the mountains, she attributed to some film, now forgotten, rather than to reincarnation. She was not a snob but, she told herself, there were limits.

It was in pursuit of this interest that she now turned the conversation. 'Prue, dear. Have you heard anything new about the strange happenings at the Hall?' she enquired.

The Hall, which was owned by mutual friends, Group Captain Richard Fox and his wife Pussy, was a vast rambling structure which had once been fortified and still had battlements, and towers slitted for bowmen. Parts of the building, which had been added to over the years, dated to the 11th century and it had its own chapel, long disused as such, standing at a little distance from the Hall itself. By repute the house, and more particularly the chapel, had been haunted for centuries and there were well authenticated reports, some of them of quite recent date, of chanting coming from the chapel and of monks having been seen, both singly and in procession.

For most Channel Islanders the existence of ghosts is not a matter of scepticism, or even debate, but is accepted as a well known and often self-evident fact. Prue, and of course Constance, were no exception. Podger was never quite sure whether the strange things he sometimes saw were ghosts, or just a trick of light or shadow, so he had no firm view. Of the four of them only Arthur, in spite of Constance's conviction, could be classified as a sceptic. He had no real conviction in the opposite sense but inclined to a verdict of 'Not Proven' or, as he might more probably have expressed it, he 'reserved his position.'

Nonetheless, he had privately to admit to himself that what he thought of as a rational stance had to a degree been undermined by the recent disclosure that, in any given year, more exorcisms were carried out in the Channel Islands than in the whole of the rest of the Diocese of Winchester. And so there was no disposition to dismiss or even, for the most part, to question vague reports that the Hall was in what might be described as an active phase.

Richard Fox, as a Jerseyman, accepted his ghosts of long standing with equanimity and tolerance. Just as he would never have wished to challenge the validity of a long-established right of way across his property, so he would have felt it in some way unsporting to attempt any interference with what he regarded as legitimate and time-honoured hauntings. So it must have been something quite out of the ordinary if, as was rumoured, he now felt some disquiet. This, Prue now confirmed.

'Yes, indeed,' she said. 'It all sounds very queer, and Pussy was telling me that Richard's getting a little worried.'

Constance was agog. 'But what exactly's happening?' she asked, her eyes alive with interest.

'Well,' Prue answered, 'I don't know exactly as I didn't see Richard, and you know how vague Pussy is. But so far as I can make out quite heavy objects, I think Pussy mentioned those brass trays they have, are being thrown about, pictures are jumping off their hooks and other things, she didn't say what, are disappearing.'

'There's only one explanation for that,' said Connie decidedly. 'It has to be a poltergeist. How thrilling!'

'Yes, I'm sure you're right and, in fact, I think Pussy did say that Richard's of that opinion. But what does one do about a poltergeist?' Prue asked the question of all three of them, but it was of course Connie who answered, unless Podger's 'Tricky, by Jove, yes, what? Tricky, eh? By Jove Yes!' could be so interpreted.

'It depends a great deal,' Connie told them, 'on the type of poltergeist you're dealing with. Most are just mischievous children but others can be more of a problem. Some few, at least I think it's only a few, have been known to be evil and malignant. It's not a subject I've looked at at all closely and I'm afraid my knowledge is rather sketchy, but I'm quite sure it's not a thing to dabble with or to treat lightly. If, as you say, Prue, the activity is enough to cause Richard concern, then he really should call in an expert.'

She pondered for a moment and then went on, 'Arthur knows, but you two may not as I've not advertised the fact, but I attended a number of Maeve O'Cork's seances during our last few years in London and know her quite well. It's just possible that she might be willing to come over if

28

Richard wanted her to. I'm sure she'd be interested in the classic hauntings, quite apart from the poltergeist.'

She bit her lip reflectively, then came to a decision. 'We'll go over to the Hall tomorrow, Arthur, and see whether Richard wants help.' She remembered the business of Ernest and added, 'I want to see Pussy anyway.'

Prue was much impressed by the disclosure that Connie knew the famous Maeve O'Cork, and would have liked to prolong the conversation, but she felt that it was past time for Podger and herself to leave. 'That sounds a marvellous idea, Connie,' she said. 'It's been a fascinating morning but we really must be off. Come along, Podger. Time we went.'

Arthur moved swiftly to circumvent what he looked upon as a premature departure. 'Oh, come on, it's still early by Jersey standards. Do have another one.'

'Yes, do,' Connie chimed in.

Podger, whose cheekbones were a little pink, was clearly willing to set his seal of approval on this scenario, but Prue would have none of it. 'No, thanks awfully, but we really must go. Do come on, Podger,' this last with just a hint of sharpness. Podger, recognising the tone, came obediently to heel and after fond embraces they set course for their car, Prue snorting with a quiet contentment to a background commentary from Podger of 'Good show, super do, what? What? By Jove, yes! Good show, good show!'

The next morning Arthur and Constance drove through the great gates of the Hall, carved with heraldic devices. Before they reached the forecourt they could see that Richard's hound, Dolly, was on hand to greet them. Dolly, or Dilatory Dido of Didcot, to give her her kennel name, was an impressive cross between a Mastiff and a Great Dane. She had inherited the solidity of the one and the height of the other and was a massive brute, if indeed such a description could fairly be applied to such a docile animal.

With her deeply furrowed brow, puzzled, rather blood-shot eyes, loose jowls and general air of solid dependability, she was an uncanny canine equivalent of her master. They differed in only one essential characteristic. Dolly, unlike Richard, was unquestionably thick. Useless as a guard dog, she appeared to be convinced that all humans were automatically friends and might, with luck, be sources of food. She was similarly convinced that the correct way to greet her master's guests was to stick her muzzle firmly between their legs and then to toss her head, wagging her tail the while. Her neck muscles were powerful and she had once succeeded in lifting a frail and elderly female relative of Richard's several feet in the air.

There is no doubt that such a habit can be unsettling if the guest is unprepared and Arthur had long thought, privately, that it would not be unreasonable to count it as a major fault in a dog of Dolly's size. However, both he and Constance were well aware of Dolly's proclivities and took the appropriate precautions on dismounting and while making their way to the side entrance of the Hall.

The front was north facing and the door was so massive that it was seldom used. On those occasions the daylight was sufficient to illuminate the outer hall but did little for the vast inner hall that loomed beyond.

The Butler, though he had not known the precise time of their arrival nor been warned of their approach, had the sixth sense of his profession and was on hand to open the door.

William Henry Itch was something of an enigma. He was suave, but this was simply an outer skin. Underneath there was something that was much harder to identify, a product of his wide and diverse experience of a world not always sympathetic, and of his origins and upbringing about which he would furnish only the barest particulars, the minimum needed to ensure employment. It seemed curious that a man of his evident sensitivity had never taken steps to change his name as, inevitably, he was known as Scratcher. Only on the most formal of occasions was he addressed as William, the alternative possibility of Itch having been discarded by mutual agreement.

He received the Crabbes deferentially but with a cordiality reserved for old friends of his employer. 'Good morning, Sir Arthur. Good morning, Lady Crabbe,' he intoned. 'Good morning, Scratcher,' Arthur replied cheerfully. 'How are you today?'

His well fleshed face assumed a doleful cast. 'Not too good Sir Arthur, I'm afraid. "It is better to live in a corner of the housetop than in a house shared with a contentious woman." Proverbs 21 Verse 9. Need I say more?' He finished on a quiet and fatalistic note, his voice that of one who knew his limitations.

This was not entirely new ground and Arthur and Constance were aware that Scratcher had problems from time to time. Capable though he had shown himself to be of withstanding the buffets of fortune and of outwitting the un-Godly, he had met his match in Mrs Itch. A very small, almost minute woman, she had the tenacity of a terrier and the aggressiveness to match. If Scratcher was content to do as he was told then, metaphorically, she would wag her tail, emitting only a low warning growl from time to time. If, either by accident or design, he acted contrary to Mrs Itch's clearly expressed wishes then, if detected or apprehended, he could expect to be bitten in the ankle, the severity of the bite corresponding to the magnitude of the offence. Judging from his demeanour, Scratcher had been found guilty of a fairly substantial deviation from the true and laid down path and, by terrier standards, had been severely mauled.

'The Group Captain is expecting us, isn't he, Scratcher?' said Arthur, not wishing to probe further into the Itch matrimonial affairs.

'Yes, Sir Arthur, I think that's him coming now.'

As if on cue Richard came bustling forward to meet them. 'How lovely to see you both. Do come in. Dolly, for Heaven's sake get down!' he exclaimed almost in one

31

breath. Then, turning his head slightly, 'Where's my wife, Scratcher? Do you know?'

'In the conservatory, I think, Mr Richard. Shall I tell her that Sir Arthur and Lady Crabbe are here?'

'Yes, please do. And then see if you can charm Mrs Jones into making us some coffee, will you?'

'Very good, Sir', and with that recognition of the charge placed upon him Scratcher retired, grateful for the opportunity of wielding a little brief authority over Mrs Jones. The relationship between Scratcher and Mrs Jones was not an easy one. Mrs Jones was the resident cook, a practitioner of imperious mien, outstanding talent and even more outstanding temperament. She was the sole living-in member of staff. Scratcher had a cottage in the grounds, as had both gardeners, and none of the maids would have been willing to live in even if Richard had offered to double their wages. But Mrs Jones was both deaf and shortsighted and, as she only believed in things which she could see and hear, she was dismissive on the subject of ghosts and remained happily oblivious of the phantoms by whom she was visited from time to time.

Mrs Jones, unlike her counterparts of bygone days, did not have help in the kitchen. She did not command the same forces as Scratcher, to whom the maids were answerable, so that she could not sit down with him to drink their employer's port with a sense of equality, even had she so wished.

The lack of help was of her own choosing. Richard, and more particularly Pussy, had tried many times to persuade her to accept some underling, but she would have none of it. She had always run her own kitchen and she would continue to do so. 'So long, that is, as I give satisfaction,' she would say to Pussy with a glower whenever the subject came up.

So Mrs Jones remained in possession of the field, and her kitchen, much to Scratcher's chagrin, remained an independent command, in no way responsive to his otherwise unchallenged authority. He welcomed the opportunity to give orders to Mrs Jones, all too rare an occurrence in his view.

Having alerted his employer's wife to the arrival of the Crabbes he advanced on Mrs Jones' stronghold, determined to stand no nonsense and to make the maximum impact with his brief authoritarian appearance in enemy territory. Sir Francis Drake, about to send his fire ships against the Spanish fleet at Cadiz, must have had similar thoughts. Scratcher drew himself up to his full height and, having opened the door without ceremony, made an impressive entry. With head thrown back, and with lidded eyes, he looked down his nose at Mrs Jones and gave his instructions in a commanding voice. 'Coffee for four, Mrs Jones.'

Mrs Jones was quick to react. She played her deaf card. 'Polish the floor, did you say, Mr Itch? I'll have you know there's nothing the matter with my floor. Polish it yourself!'

To say that Scratcher was taken aback would be no exaggeration, but he returned to the offensive. 'Coffee for four, Mrs Jones,' he repeated loudly, drawing out the four into two syllables.

Mrs Jones sensed an opening. 'I'll thank you not to call me a whore, Mr Itch, and certainly not in my own kitchen!'

Scratcher was made of stern stuff but this was too much. He was unwilling to expose himself to this counter-battery fire for a third time. Seizing a piece of chalk he wrote the instruction on the slate normally used to tell the milkman how many pints were required that day. Thrusting the slate into Mrs Jones' hands he left abruptly, not trusting himself to further speech. Mrs Jones gave a smile of grim satisfaction.

When Scratcher arrived with the coffee soon afterwards, he had recovered his poise. His features had regained their usual impassive mould and gave no hint of the turmoil which had raged within as a result of his defeat at the hands of Mrs Jones. His voice and his hands also gave no hint of the emotional storm through which he had just passed. Both were steady. He had never liked Mrs Jones and now, more than ever, he felt that the psalmist must have had earlier versions of Mrs Jones in mind when, in Psalm 58 Verse 4, he wrote: 'They have venom like the venom of a serpent, like the deaf adder that stops its ear'.

The reflection helped both to comfort and to calm him. He set the heavy silver tray down on a graceful early Georgian coffee table. It was heavier than it might have been because he had, as he would have put it, anticipated Mr Richard's wishes. This was something that Scratcher often did.

Richard indulged him in this respect, as in many others and, on occasions such as this, when only close friends of the family were present, Scratcher tended to abrogate to himself some of the privileges of a host.

There were two plates on the tray, one of delicious almond flavoured biscuits and the other of miniature cheese scones, both the product of Mrs Jones' genius. But there were also three bottles and an array of glasses. At the sight of these Arthur's eyes lit up as he thought, not for the first time, that Scratcher was the perfect servant.

Scratcher came centre stage. 'I thought, Mr Richard, that you might all like something with the coffee. There's cognac or Armagnac, of course, but I took the liberty of bringing the sloe gin. I thought on a lovely crisp morning like this that might be best. It's five years old, made from the sloes you picked in the Massif Central, if you remember, Sir.'

Scratcher hovered. The ladies made little noises which Scratcher was free to interpret as being indicative of delight, anticipation or congratulation or, more probably, all three. Richard said quietly 'Good show, Scratcher, perhaps you'd see what everyone would like.'

34

Arthur felt privately that this calm acceptance of genius at work was quite inadequate. Had he been the host the word he would have used, he told himself, was capital. 'Capital, Scratcher,' he would have said, 'Capital.' What a pity it was, he reflected, that Richard's vocabulary should have been so stunted by his long service in the Royal Air Force.

When they had all been served and Scratcher had withdrawn, Constance made haste to enquire of Richard and Pussy's daughter Ursula, known as Urse, whom she knew was the apple of their eye. She was well, Pussy said, and would be bringing their twelve-year-old grandson Johnnie over to stay in the summer. He was apparently still mad on soldiers and all things military and had a particular interest, so Pussy said, in the Roman legions.

Arthur, musing, found it hard to believe that Urse could have a twelve-year-old child. It seemed only yesterday that as a high spirited, not far removed from delinquent schoolgirl, she had managed seriously to embarrass him in church by contriving, from the pew immediately in rear, to tie his shoe-laces together. This, Arthur had found, made it difficult to move with aplomb to the lectern when the time came for him to read the second Lesson. He had never since felt quite the same about Ursula, and his enthusiasm at the prospect of her forthcoming visit would not have read high on any scale designed to measure that emotion. Urse and Johnnie were subjects of compelling interest to the other three and Arthur was free to disengage conversationally.

He feasted his eyes on Pussy. What an absolutely superb little thing she was, he thought, and not for the first time. Small, black haired and brown eyed, she was an enchantress. Beautiful as a girl and beautiful still, thanks to the fine bone structure inherited from distant Spanish ancestry of some distinction, she carried her years with ease. Her eyes were perhaps her greatest asset. Many men had fallen under their spell, believing that the eyes into which they gazed with such longing held a message for them and for them alone, seemed to speak of soul mates and even to hold out a hint of promise. Arthur was one such and, whenever she turned her great warm eyes upon him, his admiration reached fever point, a reaction which he was at pains to conceal from Connie, of course.

There was no doubting that by any standards Pussy was a smasher. She dressed dashingly, except when the occasion demanded discretion, and favoured bright colours and striking patterns. Jewellery of heavy gold, as often as not from the souks and bazaars of her and Richard's extensive travels, added to her exotic air. This air of exoticism was further accentuated by the fact that she was seldom escorted by fewer than three cats. This extreme fondness for cats, so her friends liked to think, was the origin of her nickname, and the possibility of an alternative RAF derivation, though fascinating, was not seriously entertained.

At the time of Arthur and Connie's visit she had eight cats on the ration strength. Picasso, a many hued tom, overly fond of fish and females; Aneurin Bevan, a self-important but effective ratter; Arthur Marshall, a portly humourist, smiling, sleek and worldly-wise; and, to complete the male roll call, the three of alleged Spanish ancestry, El Thinco, El Thico and Donkeyshot. To hold the balance, in the ratio normally considered adequate in the feline world as in the human, were two females, Emma and the Ranee. Emma was small but made to look larger by her luxuriant coat of black, trimmed becomingly with white. Her whiskers were of an astonishing elegance and she had eyes only for Pussy. The Ranee was all black, in nature as in fur. An effective killing machine she had no weakness except for Richard, of whom she was inordinately fond. To that extent she was in competition with Dolly, if any cat would acknowledge such a possibility, but as Dolly was either too placid to object, or too stupid to notice the relationship between the three of them remained equable.

When Pussy had made her entrance earlier she had been accompanied by the cats-in-waiting for that morning. They had inspected Constance and Arthur with a supercilious air and with what could only be described as a certain lack of respect. One of them, Aneurin Bevan, Arthur had fancied, had been rude enough to yawn, but at least all three of them had realised that Connie and Arthur, if not notably fond of cats, were at least not actually allergic to them. They had not therefore sought to jump up on the newcomers' knees. When Dolly had ambled in and knocked two of them flying with her tail, Arthur was not overly sympathetic.

Arthur's thoughts reverted to Pussy and he knew that his admiration for her, indeed something more than admiration, his fondness for her exceeded even his fondness for Prue, at least when Prue was not there. He gazed at Pussy's thick sleek black hair. It had the sheen of youth and there was not a grey hair to be seen.

He found himself wondering whether in the privacy of her bathroom she could sit on her hair, and the mental picture that that thought conjured up caused him to take a quick sip of his sloe gin. He recalled that when he had been unwise enough to mention Pussy's hair to Connie, he had been told that he was astonishingly naive in those matters and that the appearance of her hair owed much to artifice. Arthur had preferred to believe that, for once, Connie was in error but, naturally, he had not argued the point.

To Arthur's eyes Pussy seemed peerless, and he wondered idly while the conversation rumbled on whether in fact she fell short of perfection and if she had some trait that would seem less than desirable were one to live with her. Perhaps, he reflected, there was one. When, earlier, Pussy had come in late to greet her guests she had welcomed Constance and Arthur with total impenitence, and utter charm.

'I'm terribly sorry I wasn't here when you arrived,' she had said and then, turning to Richard: 'Richard darling,

37

would you be a dear and ask Scratcher to find my glasses for me? I think they're beside the bed or, if not there, on the dressing table. Or possibly in the bathroom,' Pussy finished with a fetching smile. 'I really am so silly about my glasses,' she said to Constance as though confiding some totally new intelligence.

In fact this trait in her otherwise estimable, and indeed flawless character, was widely known and was something which she exploited with panache and style. It became Pussy to have men running here and there at her lightest behest. And run they did. Richard and Scratcher had both been known to lose pounds in one of Pussy's more forgetful weeks. Having briefly considered this as a possible drawback to cohabitation Arthur dismissed the thought. He needed more exercise and if this were to take the form of a near continuous search for glasses or other mislaid belongings he would count it a small price to pay.

Arthur's thoughts were interrupted and his attention momentarily engaged by what his subconscious had registered as an apparent aberration in the others' conversation. The talk had just moved from Ursula, and Pussy had said that the situation was a pidad. Arthur boggled momentarily and then he remembered. Years ago Pussy and Richard had discovered in the course of their travels that in Spanish any word ending in 'dad' ended in 'ity' or 'itty' in English. They had seized on this new found knowledge with childlike pleasure and what had at first started as a game and also occasionally as a code when they wished to keep something from the young Ursula, had become a habit of speech to which their closest friends had been made privy.

What they had not foreseen was that their daughter, and now their grandson in turn, would crack the code with ease. Johnnie had indeed done much more and had used his newly acquired knowledge greatly to increase his standing at his prep school. To mark the arrival of their new form master Johnnie had inscribed on the blackboard in bold letters 'There's an old Spanish didad runs, isn't it a pidad she's only got one tidad'. The new master, somewhat nervous and anxious to make a good start with his young charges, addressed them as soon as he came into the room. Standing with his back to the blackboard he could not understand why his carefully thought out words, or was it his appearance, were inducing such hilarity. He made a surreptitious check of his flies and stumbled on, but he was a broken man. The result was judged highly satisfactory and the ploy voted jolly widad.

Johnnie continued to exploit this initial success and coded rude words rang merrily down the corridors from time to time to the great contentment of the young cognoscenti.

Arthur ceased meditating just in time to pick up the thread of the new conversation. The situation which had been pronounced a pity was that surrounding and springing from Richard and Pussy's decision to put the Hall on the market. Arthur knew that this was an area of conflicting emotions and, listening to the arguments surfacing once more, he found himself wondering yet again how strong their commitment to sell really was. He knew money was not a consideration. The main factor driving them, and it was surprising in someone seemingly as placid and equable as Pussy, appeared to be frustration on her part.

Within the house she was everlastingly embattled with Mrs Jones, and the constant feud between that talented virago and Scratcher, though kept always within bounds, got on her nerves and she found herself almost counting the hours to Mrs Jones' next day off.

She suffered a similar frustration in the garden where demarkation disputes were the hallmark of a somewhat tempestuous relationship with Sayers and the gardener's boy Bert, a stripling of fifty-two. Pussy seldom managed to get her own way in the garden, despite constant effort. Only in the greenhouses and in the conservatory was her reign absolute, as in those two places the installation of self-watering had allowed her to mark out an inviolate territory.

Pussy, while Arthur listened, had just contracted the essence of this argument within two short sentences. 'I'd quite honestly like to have somewhere where we could manage with very little help. The staff here are sweet but they really are quite tiring, particularly in the garden and in the kitchen,' she said.

Then, as though aware that this on its own might be considered a less than adequate reason for seeking to sell this unique and historic property, she deployed the second line of reasoning, again in skeleton form. 'We don't have a son, as you know, and Urse of course has her husband's house that Johnnie will inherit in due course; so there's simply no point in us hanging on.'

Arthur doubted the validity of this on at least two grounds. Firstly Ursula might have another son even if Johnnie didn't grow up, as he well might, to prefer the Hall to his father's house. But perhaps more importantly, there was every point in 'hanging on' if the alternative was, as well it might be, a sale to some buyer whose wealth far exceeded his taste and who could not necessarily be relied upon not to inflict some near mortal blow on the interior of the old house which, unlike an exterior, could be altered at will.

Richard had been nodding his head while Pussy spoke and it was clear that he had great sympathy for her point of view although, Arthur guessed, he was not himself being driven on a parallel course and might at times even have felt that the matter could more readily be resolved by a change of cook and gardener. But he was far too devoted a husband not to be giving his full support to Pussy and he was genuinely irritated at the turn of events.

As Richard proceeded to explain, the spirit world seemed to have taken a collective view that a sale of the Hall would not be in their best interest and had taken, and were continuing to take, active measures in support of that view. What he told them confirmed the rumours they had heard.

'The snag is,' he said, 'the Hall's virtually unsaleable as things stand. It's not the traditional ghosts that are written up in all the books. Any would-be purchaser knows about them and accepts them, otherwise they wouldn't arrange to view in the first place. It's this wretched poltergeist, if that's what it is, that's doing all the damage.'

Richard paused and looked at his guests ruefully and Arthur remarked, not for the first time, on his uncanny resemblance to a mastiff and, at this particular juncture, to a mastiff with a problem. Connie leant forward eagerly and addressed herself to Richard.

'We've heard rumours of course, but what actually happens?'

He smiled apologetically. 'Nothing much really, I suppose, as these things go, but a bit off-putting to prospective purchasers. And there's another thing,' he said half to himself, 'how on earth can it, whatever it is, tell who's a would-be buyer and who isn't? Why did nothing happen when you two came in this morning?'

His puzzled look deepened still further and then, as though shaking off his thoughts, he turned back to Connie. 'Two main things, I suppose,' he carried on. 'Pictures falling off the walls or, more properly, jumping off the walls, as their picture hooks remain in place and the wire is unbroken, and a barrage of trays, and sometimes plates, all centred on or coming from the inner hall.'

A new thought seemed to strike him and he turned to Pussy with a half-questioning, half-accusatory look. 'I'd no idea we had so many trays,' he said.

'Well, darling,' Pussy flashed him a radiant and explanatory smile, 'you know how these things happen. One simply forgets from one posting to the next. Rosemary Potter found she had twenty seven teapots when the Admiral retired, so I don't think you can really complain about a few old trays. Or about our seventeen salt cellars,' she added quietly.

Connie jumped in before Richard could reply. 'Rumour has it that things are disappearing as well. Is that right?' she asked.

Richard nodded. 'Yes, that's so,' he said. 'Of course one can't be sure that there's a link, although I must say it seems probable. What makes me doubtful is that it's not only would-be buyers' belongings that disappear. The odd casual visitor has lost things too.'

'What sort of belongings?' asked Connie with a look of suppressed excitement. 'It's just possible that what's being stolen, if there's a pattern to it, would give a lead as to what's disturbing the poor earthbound spirit.'

Richard considered this and, from his expression, it was not immediately apparent that any poor earthbound spirit would be wise to count on an unlimited supply of sympathy and understanding from that quarter.

'Well, er, yes,' he said at length. 'What can you remember about it, Pussy? All woollen things, hasn't it been, so far?'

'Yes, I think you're right.' She paused in an effort to remember. 'Certainly the Sykes and the Robinsons lost scarves and those American people, the Hargreaves, lost those curious woollen waistcoats that they wore under their overcoats.'

'No fur?' interjected Constance. 'I mean, no mink, or anything like that? That could give us a lead to the spirit personality as well.'

'No, definitely no fur, I'm delighted to say,' Richard assured her. 'In fact, nothing of any real value, although nonetheless extremely annoying and frightfully embarrassing for us. You could see some of them looking and

42

wondering whether either of us might be a kleptomaniac.' His jowls shook. Clearly it was not among his favourite memories.

'Well!' said Connie, with an air of excitement and finality, 'One can't, as you say, Richard, be too certain about the thefts, but the rest of it has the stamp of a poltergeist all right. What are you thinking of doing about it?'

Richard's expression changed slightly from that of a mastiff with a problem to that of a mastiff who has just been asked a difficult question.

'That's just it,' he said. 'What can one do? We've thought of calling in the Dean but this doesn't strike either of us as a matter for exorcism. I mean, there's nothing malignant about it, it's just a thundering nuisance. I suppose we could just carry on, but it's getting to be too much of a worry. We were discussing it last night and I think that by the time we went to sleep we'd pretty much agreed that the only answer was to take the Hall off the market for a while. Isn't that right, Pussy?' he asked.

'Yes,' she said. 'I think Richard's right. We'll just have to try again later.'

Constance waited until the silence that followed Pussy's remark had had time to settle. Then, very quietly, she said, 'There could just be another way, if you two would like to try it.'

Pussy's and Richard's looks urged her on.

'I'm in touch with Maeve O'Cork from time to time and I'm sure she'd be willing to come over and take a look at things. In fact, knowing the Hall's history and reputation I think she'd be eager to come.'

'Oh, do you really think so?' breathed Pussy. 'That would be simply wonderful.'

'Yes, absolutely wonderful,' Richard chimed in, with dutiful backing. 'But who's this O'Cork bird?'

'Oh Richard!' Pussy's tone of exasperation showed that even her devotion to her mate had its limits. 'You must

43

have heard of Maeve O'Cork! She's probably the most famous medium of all time!'

'Well, er, no, actually,' said Richard. 'But don't let that worry you. I expect there're a lot of people around I haven't heard of. If she's mustard, by all means let's sign her up.'

Pussy shrugged impatiently and turned back to Connie, a warm smile returning to her face.

'Oh, do try and get her, Connie! Please! If anyone can sort this thing out, she can.'

CHAPTER THREE

Maeve O'Cork entered the Hall a few days later to a positive frenzy of spirit activity. It was as though the poltergeist, or perhaps poltergeists, recognised that this was tantamount to a royal visit and that it was incumbent on them to rise to the occasion and to put on a show commensurate with the visitor's standing in the spirit world. There was a deep hush full of expectancy as the famous medium was admitted by Scratcher, a hush broken only by one or two pictures apparently jumping off their hooks and crashing to the floor, rather as nervous athletes so often jump the starter's gun.

Once the visitor had been welcomed by her host and hostess and Scratcher had withdrawn, a positive barrage opened up. But not for long. With closed eyes and with her right hand held high, palm outwards, the O'Cork spoke in a deep and resonant voice:

'Cease unquiet spirit, cease!' she commanded. And cease the unquiet spirit did, except in the matter of two further pictures, over which it seemed to have somewhat tenuous and uncertain control, which jumped their hooks as though ignorant of the fact that the cease fire had been sounded.

Maeve O'Cork's features arranged themselves as best they could to convey her pleasure and satisfaction at the speed with which her orders had been received and obeyed. The effect was as though a vulture had essayed a smile and had not quite brought it off. For, apart from the

45

fact that she had thick red hair, cut with a fringe and in a sort of bob, her resemblance to that bird was most marked. Her piercing eyes gleamed over her huge hooked nose and her Adam's apple bobbed up and down in her long scrawny neck, setting her beads a-quiver as she turned her gaze first on her hostess and then on Constance who, as sponsor, had been invited to witness events. Richard and Arthur were in attendance.

'See,' she said. 'It is not a malevolent spirit, just wayward like a naughty child, but one which recognises and perhaps half craves the voice of authority.'

The effect of this speech was, at least for Arthur, somewhat spoilt by the fact that its termination was accompanied by a sound that resembled a large brass tray impacting on a stone floor. Maeve O'Cork gave no sign that this sound, reading high on the decibel scale, so much as penetrated her consciousness.

'Now,' she said, addressing herself to Pussy but this time signalling subtly that her message was also for Richard, 'I have a feeling that this—' she paused momentarily as if in search of the exact word '—this unusual happening, though deeply interesting, will not prove so intractable a case as I at first feared. In particular I already feel confident that there will be no need for exorcism, with its attendant risk of disturbance to the haunting patterns of the long-established and recognised spirits. That would of course be lamentable and must, as I'm sure you agree, be avoided at virtually any cost.' She directed a beady and interrogatory glance at each of them in turn.

Pussy nodded in agreement and Richard, seeming to find the O'Cork somewhat overpowering, managed only to muster an affirmatory gulp.

This seemed to satisfy his interrogator. 'Quite so,' she said. 'Now, please give me all the facts as you know them, omitting no detail however apparently trivial. I know that Lady Crabbe is well aware of the importance of this.'

46

Constance flushed and gave the nearest approach to a simper that Arthur had witnessed in the whole of their married life. 'But possibly the rest of you are not,' she finished in an understanding and gracious tone.

Richard and Pussy did their best to lay all the facts before Maeve O'Cork, even calling in Scratcher to see whether he had observed anything which they had overlooked or forgotten. To Arthur, listening intently, there was little new, and that seemed of no importance. There had been only minor material loss in terms of pictures because, immediately the manifestations began, and they had started slowly, Richard had had the foresight to replace the original pictures with others which were normally stored in attics and in cellars. The trays, which sounded so numerous when in action, in fact numbered only eight.

They had been collected by Pussy in the Middle East, were made some of copper and some of brass and were normally displayed, together with weapons from the same area, on the walls of the inner entrance hall. Like the pictures, they jumped their hooks but, unlike the pictures that travelled essentially vertically, the trays moved fast and with some accuracy in the horizontal plane over a distance greater than any human hand could hurl them.

Finally it was established that only woollen things had disappeared and that anything placed on a hanger, even if woollen, had not been touched.

'That seems all perfectly of a piece,' said Maeve O'Cork, her beak wagging sagely. 'I think after I have had the time to tune into and to become one with the vibrations with which we are immediately confronted there will be no need for further concern.'

She hooded her great eyes and gave a secret, self-satisfied smile, her beads clanking in approbation. Constance raised her head quietly and looked at the O'Cork as a nun might look at a particularly dressy cardinal. 'And when shall we hear from you then?' she asked softly.

47

Maeve O'Cork was not only a celebrated medium; she was also a woman with a large frame who had heard tell of the artistry of Mrs Jones. She felt that her judgment would be all the sounder if her faculties were fuelled and sharpened by a leisurely sampling and appreciation of the other's skills.

'Should we say the day after tomorrow, in the morning? I really feel'— and here she addressed Pussy directly — 'that I must not become a burden to you, but I'm sure also that you wouldn't wish me to give anything but a considered judgment.'

'Of course not,' said Pussy. 'We're so immensely grateful to you for coming. Richard and I both hope you'll stay just as long as you possibly can. We're simply thrilled to have you here.'

This endorsement from the chair was received by a gracious inclination of the O'Cork head.

A picture fell from the wall, whether in defiance or in resignation it was hard to say. The meeting was adjourned.

CHAPTER FOUR

Arthur was prevented by a previous engagement from accompanying Constance to the Hall on the morning that Maeve O'Cork was due to give a summary of her conclusions and, who knew? perhaps also to make recommendations. Constance, who was greatly looking forward to what she felt sure would be a masterly and fascinating exposé by the great medium, promised faithfully to give Arthur a detailed account of proceedings on her return.

Arthur's engagement was with Podger, who was due at eleven o'clock. He had insisted that Podger go to his house rather than the other way round, as Podger had kindly suggested, for two reasons. The first was that he wanted no risk of Prue interrupting what he felt instinctively would be a critical consultation, one on which his future reputation as a novelist might well come to depend. The second, even more vital to his scheme of things, was that there should be no chance of Prue controlling, metering or, worst of all, cutting off the supply of gin which he knew to be essential to Podger's thought processes. Arthur knew that, just as oil is necessary to the smooth running of machinery, so was gin necessary to Podger if his cerebral equipment was to give of its best.

That it should give of its best that morning was, Arthur felt, of the highest importance, as the successful completion of his novel could well rest on the outcome of their meeting.

The crisis had arisen because after days of worry and

uncertainty and nights of increasing sleeplessness, Arthur was no longer content with the opening paragraph of his novel. The trouble lay, he felt, in the words 'no doubt absentmindedly'. Apart from what might perhaps be termed a doctrinal difficulty, whether anyone performing that action could be absent-minded at that particular juncture, whether the choice of those words did not impart a certain lack of realism to the scene, there was the matter of his mother's character.

He felt the use of those words would commit him irrevocably to making her a fey, delicate and dreamy creature, and he was sure now that this was not what he wanted. He wanted a mother of spirit and one who knew what she was about at such moments.

He had accordingly re-drafted his opening paragraph to read: 'Ever since I learned that my mother used often, no doubt playfully, to hang a shoe on my father's erection I knew that I came of unusual stock.' That seemed to Arthur to hit it off nicely. It immediately gave his mother a blither, lighter, more believable character and avoided the use of the coarse word 'cock'. He thought it had an authentic ring though he was a trifle anxious as to how Podger would react to the loss of his 'cock'. Arthur remembered he had set great store by it at their last meeting.

Podger arrived a few moments late in a great bustle. 'Hello Arthur, sorry I'm late. Bad fault. Bad fault. Wouldn't allow it in my junior officers, now I'm doing it myself. Bad show! Bad show!'

He paused momentarily for breath and then went on to explain how it was that he had come to offend against his own code.

'Trouble was, Arthur old man,' he said, 'couldn't get rid of Prue and the dogs. By the time they'd set off for the cliffs I was a bit pressed to manage the couple of snifters that I felt were an essential preliminary to this meeting. Critical, you did say, Arthur, didn't you? Critical, you said? Critical, eh? Sounds a bad business, I must say, what, what? I mean to say, what? Eh? Thanks old man, steady on the tonic,' he added hastily, giving his moustache a warning sideways brush to signal that a glass, plus contents, would soon be on the way up, and should be given safe conduct. 'What's the trouble?' he concluded.

Arthur spoke eloquently, indeed movingly. He explained how he had wrestled with the novel for five days and nights, and how he was convinced at last that he had found the precise words that he wanted for the opening paragraph, those all important few words by which what was to be his life's work might be judged and by which it might ultimately stand or fall. All he needed now was his old friend's endorsement of his judgment in this critical matter.

Having explained the reasoning behind the abandonment of his first draft, Arthur read the re-drafted paragraph and tried delicately to persuade Podger that, if only for reasons of symmetry and balance, 'cock' would no longer do and that 'erection' was le mot juste.

Podger automatically drained his glass as a preliminary to addressing himself to the question. Then, realising that as a result of this reflex action his glass was now empty, he moved it towards his host with the words 'Thirsty work, Arthur! thirsty work!'

With the means of staving off dehydration once more to hand he went into contemplative mode, snorting and harrumphing quietly to himself from time to time. At last, the judgment was handed down. 'Won't do, Arthur old man; won't do, I'm afraid.'

Arthur's heart sank. The absence of a single 'What?' or 'Eh?' brought it home to him that this was no lightly given opinion but was a considered and final verdict.

'But why, Podger?' Arthur almost pleaded, his disappointment adding poignancy to his tone.

'Two things, old man,' said Podger. 'Two things, you know, what? What? That "Playfully" makes your Mother sound like a cockteaser. I mean to say, you wouldn't want that Arthur, would you? Gives a no doubt wrong impression and lets the side down a bit, what? Eh?'

Momentarily Arthur wondered whether Podger was confused as between the identity of his real mother and the fictional mother of his novel but he dismissed the thought on the instant. Podger was far too shrewd for that.

'And the second thing, Podger?' Arthur heard himself enquiring calmly, the tone of his voice giving no hint of his inner turmoil as he refilled Podger's glass.

'Well, this "often" and "erection" makes it sound as though your father had a permanent horn. I mean to say, hardly likely, old man. Not permanent, you know. Makes him sound like a foreigner. You didn't have a foreign father, did you, Arthur?' said Podger suddenly, subjecting Arthur to a keen glance.

Then, as though reassured by recollection of Arthur's pedigree, he went on 'No! No! of course you didn't! Stupid of me. What? What?'

Doubts as to whether there was confusion in Podger's mind flickered intermittently, only to be dismissed by Arthur. Podger was far too clear minded for that. Arthur took stock and, amid the ruins of his hopes, attempted a realistic appraisal and, perhaps even, who was to say, the salvage of a favourite phrase or two.

'But Podger,' he said, 'if you re-draft it on the lines you suggest you'll be left with "Ever since I learnt that my mother used to hang a shoe on my father's erection I knew that I came of unusual stock."'

'I mean, it lacks all impact,' he continued. 'There's no symmetry and there's no clue to character!' The frustration which he felt added force to his words and, Arthur fancied, he might even have raised his voice a trifle.

'See what you mean, Arthur. See what you mean,' Podger answered after some short reflection. But that Johnny, Fowler would've approved, you know,' he

52

rallied. 'No unnecessary words. Short. Anglo-Saxon. Says just what you mean it to say – Leaves everything else to the reader's imagination. What sort of a woman was your mother? How did she hang her shoe? Gaily? Boldly? Surreptitiously? In hope? In exhaustion? I mean, the possibilities are endless and it gives you a totally free hand in the development of her character.'

Podger warmed to his work and he exuded enthusiasm and conviction.

'And as for your father,' he continued, 'once again the reader can form his own conclusions. How frequent an event was this? Was this the second erection that morning, or was it the first erection that year? Nobody knows, and that's the beauty of it. Any suspicion of a possibility of his having beastly foreign tendencies is greatly reduced, if not eliminated.'

Arthur heard Podger. He could not fault what he had said, and yet his heart was heavy. The artist in him was rebuffed and affronted. His mood was black and he poured himself a second gin and tonic, this time a large one, in the hope that alcohol would dull the pain that he felt at Podger's rejection of his so carefully chosen words. Podger said nothing, but his eyebrows signalled his thirst.

As Arthur poured an even larger one in response to that mute plea, Constance came in, hot from the Hall.

'My dears!' she said, 'you'll never believe it! A simply wonderful exhibition of psychic skill by that marvellous woman! You should have been there, Arthur! I'm sure this meeting between you two could have waited.' The touch of asperity in her tone was slight but unmistakable. But then her enthusiasm took over once again.

'She had analysed and accounted for everything. The poltergeist's motivation is that it does not want Richard and Pussy to sell the Hall. It feels at home with their persona. She's sure that it will only become active when it perceives a threat to their continued ownership. She attributes the performance two days ago to sheer enthusiasm engendered by the arrival of so eminent and sympathetic a psychic personality, and therefore as a-typical.'

Connie's eyes gleamed with enthusiasm and remembered excitement as, looking at Arthur, she pointed commandingly at the gin bottle. 'I think I will, Arthur, please. It's not every day that one is privileged to listen at first hand to the immediate on-the-spot findings of a great authority.'

She rammed her point home in case its significance had been missed by either of them. 'This case may well become a classic and be required reading for students of the occult in years to come.'

Not waiting for prompting or interrogation, she poured out her story in a steady stream. 'Yes, and do you know what the poltergeist was in its former life, or lives actually, since it remembers two of them?' she enquired.

Podger and Arthur simultaneously signalled the expected blank negative.

'Well, it's so obvious really, a child might have known it instinctively, but it takes a medium of Maeve O'Cork's knowledge and experience to set the seal of certainty upon it. It was a Roman artilleryman in Hadrian's siege train, as I understand it, accustomed to the operation of catapults and well versed in ballistics. Hence the trays, hurled with skill and accuracy. In a later life it suffered a regression and passed a singularly uncomfortable and cold sixty years or so as an Eskimo, which explains, of course, its instinctive urge to purloin and to hide articles of warm clothing.'

That was too much for Podger, whose belief in the spirit world was, at the best, tenuous.

'Well,' he said, 'well, Connie old trout, that's all very well but, I mean to say, dash it, things can't just disappear, you know. What? Eh? Eh? Stands to reason, they've got to go somewhere.'

She gave him a look which, had he not been an old friend, might have been mistaken for the 'withering glance' beloved of fiction. 'Naturally, Podger,' she said, laying down the cosmic banana skin, 'of course they go somewhere.'

'Oh, good,' he said, and then as an afterthought, 'where?'

'Into the great cosmos, to become one with all matter,' she replied, triumphantly and with conviction.

'Oh, ah!' said Podger.

CHAPTER FIVE

The General Election resulted in a Labour majority. It was not a landslide nor, in terms of votes, did it indicate that more than one in three of the voters were in favour of the Government which, actively or by default, they had called into being. Nevertheless, the Government felt that it had a clear endorsement of its policies, in some areas ill-defined if not downright muddled, and what it called a clear mandate for the most unlikely, unreasonable and plain stupid propositions that its least sensible elements had advanced prior to the election.

When Kevin Pratt took office as Prime Minister and began to exercise his power of patronage the electorate sensed that something was wrong. Initial puzzlement gave way first to bewilderment and then to anger. It had been expected that he would allocate the great offices of state, and those of only somewhat lesser importance, if not strictly on a basis of merit and suitability, at least as close to those ideal criteria as the internal politics of the party would allow. But he did not do so. Very few of the Shadow Cabinet were given office. The 'talking heads' that the public had become familiar with on their television screens, seemingly moderate men propounding comforting and caring policies, disappeared at a stroke and their place was taken by hardliners who emerged from under the stones where they had lain hidden during the run-up to the election. Fraudulent? Yes. Criminal? No. The great British electorate had brought it on their own heads. And, in Kevin

Pratt's book, when it came to junior posts, the influence of minorities and extremists was absolute.

Thus it was that a Militant Tendency member, Ernest Twite, came to be appointed as junior minister at the Home Office. Any political party inevitably has elements it would rather be without, at least in opposition. Elements which it finds embarrassing and would rather not have to acknowledge and reward, elements of which the party leaders are secretly ashamed, but dare not say so, elements which bring politics into disrepute and keep voters away from the booths, disgusted by the mountebanks who ply for their favours.

Ernest Twite was one such mountebank. A mean, cowardly little creature whose natural posture was a cringe, and whose driving force was envy, Ernest Twite had become a force on the back benches. Encouraged at the success of his dour, waspish, nonetheless apposite interjections, he had gradually developed a public persona in which the cringe gave way to an arrogant strut and in which his cowardice showed only as the swagger and bluster of a bully. To be fair, which was difficult when called upon to consider anything which pertained to Ernest Twite, he had the excuse of a deprived background.

But his upbringing had left him not so much with the desire and the determination to better the lot of the least fortunate but rather, by whatever means, so to regulate affairs that those who had money, whether earned or inherited, should soon have a great deal less of it.

Was it pre-ordained, he wondered, that he should be given this particular post in government with special responsibility, under the Secretary of State, for the affairs of the Channel Islands and the Isle of Man? For there was more money, ripe to be tapped for the Exchequer, in those islands than ever existed in El Dorado.

Ernest Twite knew little of the Isle of Man, and was prepared to leave proposals concerning its future to officials, but he knew about the Channel Islands. He had once spent a weekend in Jersey. He had seen enough to know that here he would find his 'killing ground'. He resolved that his first action on moving into his new office would be to call for background papers on the constitutional relationship. Only after he had mastered that would he feel able to make the move which he felt was crying out to be made.

CHAPTER SIX

Sir Humphrey Bowcester, or His Excellency Lieutenant-General Sir Humphrey Bowcester, KCB, MC, to give him his full style and title, having breakfasted in leisurely fashion, cast his eye over his day's programme. Yes, it was as he had remembered it. The chairman of the Methodist Conference and his wife were due for tea and there was a fund-raising dinner which couldn't be avoided that night. An easy day, he thought, unless the Bailiff sprang any surprises.

Sir Humphrey, known as Bragger to his friends, considered the curious twist that his life had taken. Retiring as a lieutenant-general at 57, as was normal, he had had no particular plans or ideas as to what he and Cecily might do for the next few years. He had been asked casually whether he would be interested in being considered for appointment as Lieutenant-Governor of Jersey. Just as casually he had said 'Yes', never dreaming for one moment that anything would come of it.

Suddenly, it had all happened and here he was, now, wondering why the Bailiff, Sir Frederick Marais, had elected to call at 1000 hours.

The appointment was of the Bailiff's seeking and Sir Humphrey reviewed in his mind those subjects which he felt might possibly be raised. He concluded that none of them would in themselves justify the Bailiff seeking a meeting at such short notice and at such an early hour.

Sir Humphrey was relatively new in his appointment and

still found much in the Bailiwick to surprise him. Before
appointment he had, like most Englishmen, vaguely known
that the Channel Islands were just off the coast of Normandy, were famous for their Jersey and Guernsey cows
and, for some reason or other, were not part of Hampshire
like the Isle of Wight.

In fact, as a serving soldier he had known slightly more
than that. He knew that they were the other side of the
Cotentin Peninsula away from the D-Day beaches, and he
had known also that they had been occupied by German
forces during the War, the only bit of Great Britain, or indeed
British territory, to suffer that fate.

When, on the recommendation of the Secretary of State
for Home Affairs, acting as Privy Councillor with special
responsibility for the Channel Islands, Her Majesty The
Queen had been graciously pleased to appoint him to the
extremely ancient Office of Lieutenant-Governor and
Commander-in-Chief of the Bailiwick of Jersey, Sir
Humphrey had set to to brief himself and had read a number
of books on the history, constitution, customs, economy,
geography – including flora and fauna – archaeology and
folklore of the island. He was a walking compendium of facts
and dates but, he realised only too well, he was a mile away
from understanding a Jerseyman.

He knew that the Channel Islands, or Les Iles Anglo-
Normandes as the French called them, had formed part of
the Duchy of Normandy and that their allegiance to the
Crown of England dated from Duke William's conquest in
1066, an allegiance which in Jersey's case had never
wavered over the centuries in spite of frequent punitive raids
and several periods of French occupation.

The Bailiwick of Guernsey had not been so steadfast and
had favoured the Great Protector though only, so it was said,
because of the unpopularity of the Governor of the day.

Sir Humphrey knew that this difference between the
islands, going back well over 300 years, still left its mark

today. Although the common misfortune of the German occupation had done something to bridge the gap and to give a sense of common identity, the islands were too similar ever to get on together and each took pleasure in emphasising its superiority and looked down upon, and even pitied, its less fortunate neighbour.

Jersey was bigger, brasher, more go-ahead and, above all, richer than Guernsey, and saw this as conclusive evidence of its greater importance.

Guernsey saw this as a fault. The Guernseyman moved at a slower pace, and liked it that way. He saw no need to hurry. He learnt from Jersey's mistakes and avoided its worst excesses. He did everything on a smaller scale. He might not be as rich, but he held other values to be more important, liked things the way they were and was reluctant in the extreme to change the pattern and the rhythm of the ways he knew.

Privately, Sir Humphrey felt that there was a good deal to be said for the Guernsey way of looking at things. Certainly Guernsey did not attract the football hooligan type that flocked to Jersey in the summer.

But he knew such thoughts must never be allowed utterance. Custom demanded that, as Lieutenant-Governor, his loyalty to Jersey must be absolute. And yet, not quite absolute. He pondered the constitutional niceties.

As Lieutenant-Governor he had two distinct roles. Firstly, as the Queen's personal representative, he acted for the Crown whenever occasion so demanded. But, secondly, he had a less well defined role which was to act as the channel of communication between Her Majesty's Government, as represented by the Home Office, and the insular authority, as represented by the Bailiff. Here again, however, all was not as it might seem on the surface. The Home Office, or its officials, had only the power vested in them by the Privy Council. The House of Commons and Her Majesty's ministers had no power whatsoever, other than in the matter of defence and foreign affairs, and that was a matter which the States had been at pains to affirm and indeed to reaffirm in the past when a greedy Treasury had sought to cast illicit glances to the south.

But all that was in the past and successive United Kingdom Governments had continued to respect the financial independence of the islands, although the Conservative Government of a few years ago had come close to blurring what had been a clear cut line by inviting the islands to make a 'contribution' to the cost of Defence and representation abroad. Had Sir Humphrey been in office at that time it would, he knew, have fallen to him to interpret the qualms and misgivings of the insular authorities to a no doubt unsympathetic Home Secretary, under pressure from the Chancellor. In that role it would have been his duty to remain neutral although, in practice, he realised that such neutrality was next to impossible.

He had already discovered after a very short time in Jersey that you could not help but share the enthusiasms of the people you governed. Or didn't govern, he reflected wryly. Here was another paradox. The Lieutenant-Governor had no power. He might, and indeed usually did, have influence, but he had no direct authority. He was even that supreme anachronism, a commander-in-chief without troops to command.

It was all dashed odd, Sir Humphrey ruminated, not really English. And of course it wasn't. It was British. And the dashed oddest thing of all was this office of Bailiff, existing since medieval times. By unbroken tradition the Bailiff was a Jerseyman and the office was a Crown appointment. He had to have been called to the English bar and to have French legal qualifications from Caen university in addition. He usually, though this was not an absolute requirement, served first in the offices of solicitor-general, attorney-general and deputy Bailiff before appointment as Bailiff. As Bailiff he spoke for the island

and was the first man in the Bailiwick after the Lieutenant-Governor.

He was not dependent on votes either for his appointment or for his continuance in office, which was normally to the age of 70. His office had no English equivalent. It did not equate to that of Prime Minister, as there were no political parties in Jersey and legislation was enacted by the States, the rough equivalent of the House of Commons, voting on propositions laid before them by committees of their fellow deputies.

The Bailiff, though steeped in politics, was not therefore a politician in the normal sense of the word, and exerted his political power indirectly. His overt role equated to that of Mr Speaker on the one hand and to that of a High Court judge on the other.

It was all very strange, Sir Humphrey reflected, and strangest of all was that it worked, and in fact worked much more effectively than Westminster. Because there were no political parties there was no party political programme, and therefore things moved more slowly than on the mainland. But, with no ideological commitment, fewer mistakes were made. There was a welcome lack of rhetoric, and deputies voted on the merits of the proposals before them. The final and most marked difference was that the business of the States, in sharp contrast to that of the Mother of Parliaments, was conducted with unfailing courtesy.

As this was to be an official call, Sir Humphrey prepared to receive the Bailiff in his office. He let himself out of the front door of Government House, an elegant late Georgian, early Victorian building, and walked the few yards through the extensive grounds to where his office block was situated. Here he was met by his secretary and ADC, a retired commander R.N.

Commander Geoffrey Point was 57 years old, some six months younger than Sir Humphrey. He had been appointed in his thirties and Sir Humphrey was his fifth Lieutenant-Governor. He felt that Sir Humphrey would do.

'Good morning, Your Excellency,' he said. 'The mail's on your desk and the Bailiff has left his chambers and is on the way here. I couldn't get anything out of his office on the reason for the call, in fact I got the impression that they themselves don't know. I've assumed you'd like coffee as usual?' Geoffrey ended in his brisk naval fashion.

'Yes, fine, jolly good, thank you, Geoffrey,' Sir Humphrey responded absently, his mind still busy on the possible reasons for Sir Frederick's unexpected call. 'Show him in as soon as he arrives, please.'

A few moments later Geoffrey opened the door and announced 'The Bailiff, Your Excellency.'

The Bailiff was older than the Lieutenant-Governor and the two men had no background or experience in common. In spite of this, or even perhaps because of it, they respected one another and had rapidly got on close terms.

'Hullo, Fred. Morning. Come in and sit down,' said the Governor. 'Geoffrey's organised coffee. Does that suit you?'

'Morning, Humphrey. Yes. Fine. Thank you,' said Sir Frederick, sinking into the comfortable chair which had been indicated. There was an exchange of small talk while a uniformed maid brought coffee and poured it from a fine Georgian coffee pot.

When she and Geoffrey had withdrawn Sir Humphrey looked at the Bailiff questioningly. 'What's it about, Fred?' he said.

'Twite,' said the Bailiff.

Sir Humphrey was momentarily nonplussed. 'Twite?' he said vaguely. 'You did say Twite, didn't you?'

Sir Frederick puffed out his cheeks. He was a man of ruddy colouring which tended to give him a choleric appearance. This was quite misleading. He had sparse white hair and was clean shaven but for some luxuriant, some were unkind enough to say over-luxuriant, side whiskers. He was a man slow to anger, excitement or agitation, but he gave signs of agitation now.

'Yes,' he said, 'Twite. Frightful little man. Godfrey rang me late last night to say that Twite was going to the Home Office as Junior Minister. And you know what that means?' his voice shook slightly. 'It means he'll have special responsibility for Channel Island affairs.'

The Lieutenant-Governor considered. He knew that the Godfrey referred to was a senior official and would have been unlikely to have telephoned the Bailiff without due cause. On the other hand he found it difficult to believe that any one member of Parliament could possibly warrant the concern which Sir Frederick was only too plainly displaying. Recognition slowly dawned.

'Twite,' he said. 'Twite, yes I'm with you now. You mean that impossible little bounder who makes such an intolerable exhibition of himself at Prime Minister's question time?'

'The same,' the Bailiff acknowledged glumly.

'Good God. I see what you mean, Fred,' Sir Humphrey responded. 'What do you have in mind?'

The Bailiff drank some coffee and steepled his fingers. 'Nothing very precise at this stage when we don't know which way he may be thinking, but I felt we should consider the possibilities open to us, which is why I wanted to see you this morning.' Sir Frederick gave every indication of depression.

'You're really worried, Fred, are you?' enquired the Governor.

'Yes, I am, Humphrey,' the Bailiff admitted. 'Any other Government, or even any other individual in any other Government, wouldn't have given me a moment's concern but, quite frankly, this frightful little toad Twite scares me to death because I think he might really go for our jugular.'

'You mean, might try to bring the Bailiwick within the United Kingdom tax structure?' enquired Sir Humphrey.

'I don't know, Humphrey,' came the response. 'I just don't know. But I don't like the smell of it one little bit.'

'But he couldn't do that, surely, could he?' Sir Humphrey found himself pleading the island case with spirit and conviction.

'I wouldn't have thought so, Humphrey,' he replied. 'But you never know with these impossible little buggers.' Sir Frederick's descent to the vernacular betrayed the depth of his feelings. 'Anyway, the reason I wanted to see you this morning was to suggest that it might disarm Twite to some degree if we were to invite him to visit the Bailiwick – sort of get our blow in first, if you know what I mean.'

'Yes, that would be a good idea.' Sir Humphrey turned the matter over in his mind. 'I think you're right, Fred. How soon do you think we should ask him?'

'Well,' the Bailiff resumed a more normal business-like tone. 'With anyone but Twite I would have assumed a two or three month period of grace for the new man to find his feet and read himself in. But I've a feeling that friend Twite will think he knows it all and could well be thinking of imposing himself on us much sooner, perhaps even within a month.'

The Governor looked at his diary. 'Umm,' he said. 'We'd best get moving fairly fast then. We'll have to co-ordinate with Guernsey and they'll have to consult Alderney and Sark, as I suppose Twite will want to make a complete tour of both Bailiwicks while he's at it. Have you spoken to Bill Dumaresq yet?' Sir William Dumaresq was the Bailiff of Guernsey.

'No,' said Sir Frederick. 'I thought on the whole it would be best if the approach came from you to Havelock as the invitations will after all have to come from you and James.' Vice-Admiral Sir James Havelock was the Lieutenant-Governor of Guernsey. 'You can, of course, tell him that

I'm very much in favour, and I'm sure he'll find Bill Dumaresq will think the same.'

'Yes, I agree with you, Fred. I think they'll both see the advantage of taking the initiative, but I'm afraid there's a considerable snag as far as I'm concerned. There'll be major work going on in the kitchen at that time and I can't very well put the little bounder up in Government House if I can't feed him.' Sir Humphrey looked worried. 'If we were dealing with the Secretary of State, he'd be more likely to understand, though I'm not even sure of that in this particular Government. But an awful little johnny-come-lately like Twite would be sure to think we'd done it on purpose and to take the most frightful umbrage.'

The Bailiff's face set in morose lines. 'I'm afraid you're only too likely to be right but, as there's nothing we can do about it, he'll have to make do with an hotel. A suite at,' and here he mentioned one of Jersey's leading hotels 'is likely to provide a higher standard of comfort and service than he's ever seen before, and that might just satisfy him.'

Sir Humphrey shook his head. 'Not if I know his kind. I've seen too many of 'em overseas on those all-party fact-finding tours they're so fond of in the long recess. Nothing's ever right for the Twites of this world, and there are always a few Twites on those tours. If you don't put down the red carpet for them and push out a fair sized boat they get frightfully slighted and huffy and, if you do, they're liable to report that the standard of living is too luxurious and that allowances in the theatre should be reviewed downwards. Old Tom Bowdler once told me that when he was C-in-C in Singapore he used to stick as close to bread and water as he dared in the hope of getting his allowances reviewed upwards. Didn't work, of course.' He chuckled reminiscently.

'You know, Humphrey, I've just had a thought,' said Sir Frederick, showing signs of animation. His face could not exactly be said to have lit up, but his expression had become a trifle less morose and, for the first time, there was what might have been taken for a gleam of hope in his eye.

'I know it would be a frightful imposition but I was just wondering whether the Foxes would be prepared to put him and his retinue up in the Hall. It's the only other house in the Island I know of that's adequately set up and staffed, and Richard's very helpful, and so's she. Awkward subject to raise, though.' The Bailiff's voice lost something of its newly acquired optimism. 'On the other hand, would be difficult for them to refuse once they'd been asked. Not that one wants to lean on them in any way,' he added hastily. 'You know them better than I do, Humphrey. How do you think they might respond if things were explained to them?'

The Governor passed his hand absentmindedly over the back of his head and reflected irrelevantly, but with satisfaction, that his hair was a great deal thicker than that of his visitor who, he noticed for the first time, was beginning to show signs of his age.

He liked and admired Sir Frederick but wasn't he, he wondered, taking this whole business of Twite a good deal too seriously, almost showing signs of panic in fact, before the chap was even in office? On the other hand, the Bailiff would take the brunt of any offensive that Twite might launch while he, as Lieutenant-Governor, would be on the sidelines. And he had no reservation on the tactic proposed. It was the civil equivalent of 'taking the battle to the enemy', usually a sound course of action.

Sir Humphrey addressed himself to the question. 'Yes, Fred. As it happens we saw quite a bit of one another at one time. I always thought Richard should have gone on, you know. Don't know what happened. Perhaps he didn't want to, but he's a jolly good chap and she backs him up splendidly. I'm sure they'd help out with friend Twite if we asked them to. Probably even be curious to see what the frightful little fellow's like. I think they might be quite keen to help. Would you like me to ask them?'

'Yes, that would be excellent if you think they'd agree, Humphrey, just excellent.' Sir Frederick blossomed like a parched mountain flower that feels the rain of spring. 'Once you've got Guernsey's agreement, of course,' he added.

'Have some more coffee, Fred, or is it cold?'

The Bailiff considered. 'No, thank you, Humphrey, I don't think I will. I should really be getting along to the office. I've asked Arthur Crabbe to call at 1130. It occurred to me that he could be most helpful over this Twite business.'

'Oh,' said the Governor, 'How?'

'Well, he knows Whitehall inside out, something that none of us over here do. He's had a lot of experience of ministers of one sort or another and might be able to help over Twite. He might even, as he's still a lot of contacts, be a source of intelligence and what I think you, Humphrey, would call "early warning".'

Sir Humphrey looked unenthusiastic. 'Dare say you're right, Fred. Don't really know him but can't say I'm much impressed. Not mad about the way he sums you up over those half-moon glasses of his. And I can't abide her. She terrifies me. Tell me why it is, Fred, that mild little men like Arthur Crabbe always go in for vast Rhine maidens, twice their own size. Is it ambition, or a sort of death wish?'

The Bailiff looked slightly startled, but held to his view. 'I don't know the answer to that curious phenomenon but I think you're underestimating Crabbe. I think he's likely to prove most helpful.'

The Lieutenant-Governor declined combat. 'I hope you're right, for all our sakes, Fred,' he said.

CHAPTER SEVEN

Scratcher ruminated as he worked away in the small cubby-hole off his pantry which served as a workshop, primarily for the minor maintenance tasks which were a recurring feature of life at the Hall.

But today no thought of maintenance was in his mind. He was working on a scale model of a Roman ballista which he intended should be finished by the time young Master Johnnie came to stay.

Scratcher had already completed one such engine, and was well satisfied with its performance. He felt that Johnnie, of whom he was very fond, would be delighted with the surprise present, and even more delighted with two engines which would double the rate and intensity of fire. Two ballistae would also, of course, mean that it would be both legitimate and permissible for Scratcher to take his place alongside Johnnie in the firing line.

The thought cheered him for a moment, but not for long as his heart was heavy. He did not so much ruminate as brood and felt much as Joel must have felt when, perhaps overstating it a bit, he claimed that: 'The sun and the moon are darkened, and the stars withdraw their shining.'

The cause of his being at one with Joel in general terms was women, and in specific terms the apparent determination of the Foxes to sell the Hall. If that were to happen the consequences for Scratcher would, in his view, be little short of cataclysmic. If, as he knew to be his employers' intention, they were to move to a smaller house, there would be no further place for him, and this he could scarcely bear to contemplate. He had become so fond of the family and of the children, first Ursula and now Johnnie, that a severance of daily contact would be similar to amputation in terms of pain and the difficulty of re-adjustment.

At the thought of the unbroken and unrelieved company of Mrs Itch, Scratcher became so unmanned that he lost concentration and hit his thumb a nasty blow with the hammer he was wielding, adding to his already acute distress. And no more verbal battles with Mrs Jones? It was unthinkable, the very spice of life withdrawn.

There was no doubt about it that Mrs Fox was the prime mover behind this disastrous decision which, if not reversed or at least frustrated, would bring distress and unhappiness to them all, and most of all to him, Scratcher. He knew very well that the Group Captain did not really want to sell and was only indulging his wife whom, as Scratcher had observed over the years, he adored.

So, he reasoned, it was women again who were the cause of the threatened disaster. Mrs Jones because she exasperated his mistress almost to the point of no return and Mrs Fox herself because she was not able to see that her remedy for the present malaise was totally out of proportion.

Scratcher knew very well, or thought he knew, that the Group Captain's wife was seriously in error and should be thwarted in her purpose if reason failed and if no other remedy could be found. He had, he felt, a heavy responsibility, but one from which he would not shrink, and in the execution of which he would not be found wanting. The poltergeist was a great help, or had been so far, but Scratcher knew that in itself it could be considered only as a temporary reprieve. Sooner or later some prospective purchaser of the Hall would turn out to be a poltergeist aficionado, if not addict, and would sign up on the spot, even waiving a surveyor's report in his or,

71

perhaps more likely her, eagerness to complete a deal which threw in an earthbound spirit at no extra cost. Possibly some transatlantic lady, a widow perhaps, Scratcher fancied.

But what, he wondered, would be the position if, after the sale had gone through, the poltergeist failed to polt, or was it polter? Would that be the equivalent of a non-consummation of marriage and grounds for annulment or cancellation of the conveyance? Scratcher tended to the view that a legal precedent was unlikely and that, should events take that course, the matter would have to be resolved in court.

Scratcher put aside his tools and turned to his daily exercises, which never failed to relax him and to bring him solace. He flexed his fingers and, on the instant, held a pack of cards deployed as a perfect fan. As he brought his other hand into play, the cards took on the aspect of a concertina leaping and rippling from one hand to the other in perfect symmetry and formation. Then, just as suddenly, they vanished and it was as if they had never been. Warming to his work, Scratcher increased the tempo. Cards, billiard balls, coloured scarves, pound notes in sealed envelopes, came and went in a whirl of multi-coloured bravura.

Suddenly the pace slowed; in the imaginary audience the tension would have risen. With the eyes of this audience upon him Scratcher advanced on two portraits which, because they were so badly executed, had been banished from wherever they had hung in the Hall and had ended up in his sanctum. The one was of a lady dressed in the manner of the 18th century, amply bosomed and markedly decolletée. The other was of a gentleman of the same period whose main characteristic was his ears. These were of such prestigious dimensions that the viewer fell to wondering whether he might not have been the victim of selective breeding for some purpose now hidden in the mists of time. If this was so, it was not likely to have been for the purpose to which Scratcher now put the portraits. Advancing first on the lady, he encouraged a large dove to climb out from between her breasts and perch on his finger. Then, having seemingly vaporised the dove in mid-air he plucked two large and somnolent white mice from the right ear of the male portrait. 'No great trick', someone who wished to sell Scratcher short might claim; and he might indeed have been right had not Scratcher, split seconds before, introduced the two mice into the male portrait's left ear. But all this was nothing to the Scratcher finale. He positioned himself behind a contraption which simulated a seated man wearing, essentially, a jacket, trousers and braces. Scratcher appeared merely to lean forward for a few seconds, as though communicating some confidential information into an imagined ear and then stood back, waving the braces to his wildly enthusiastic imaginary audience.

His workout complete, Scratcher let reminiscence hold him in thrall for a brief moment. He was no longer William Henry Itch, a respected member of the Magic Circle, but Fingers Itch, the most gifted and talented member of a gang of young pickpockets on whom much care had been lavished. He was being carefully groomed for higher things by his mentor, one Albert Grimes, known to the underworld as Farting Fagin, when disaster struck.

Or perhaps, and more probably, it was salvation. Young Fingers Itch, one of a large East End family, had been copped and had only been saved from the consequences of his arrest by the intervention of the Reverend Simeon Smythe. This good and good hearted man had seen something of worth and worth salvaging in the person of the young apprehended Itch and had volunteered to stand guarantor for his future good behaviour.

Young Itch had responded to this kindness and trust, something so far unknown in his young life, and had remained with the Reverend Smythe for a number of years, in the course of which he had acquired an extensive knowledge of the Bible. During that same period he had gone straight, or almost straight, only exercising his fingers from time to time in the interest of ensuring that the offertory plate did not become too heavy for the Reverend Smythe to raise aloft.

By the end of their time together his conscience had got the better of him and he had resolved never again to use his particular skills for financial gain other than legitimately. But he practised regularly and in time became an accomplished illusionist.

At first, when he left the Reverend Smythe, it was with the thought that he had a vocation and that there had been divine purpose behind his rescue from what would undoubtedly have been a life of crime. So he served for a while with a mission in Africa where he soon found himself, somewhat unsuitably, in competition with the local witch doctor. He was of course a dab hand at turning water into wine and, as his stay among them coincided with an eclipse, he was able to give a convincing demonstration of his power over the sun. This was conceded by the locals to be big medicine indeed, very much in the first league and, when he followed up that success by plucking seventeen toads from the witch doctor's navel in as many seconds, he had advanced the cause of Christianity to an unparalleled degree.

Unfortunately, his method of spreading the word was not acceptable to his more conventional and senior colleagues and what had promised to become a spectacular success story was smothered at birth by the dictates of orthodoxy.

Scratcher saw little difference of substance between what he had been doing and what was being done, quite openly and with a marked degree of success, by Catholic missions in the same part of Africa. For them it was results, as represented by the tally of souls saved, that counted. The methods employed to achieve those results were not necessarily of the first order of importance. Scratcher believed that they showed good sense and were certainly far better psychologists than his own superiors.

It would not exactly be true to say that Scratcher was disillusioned by this experience, but it did nothing to relieve the doubts with which he was increasingly beset as to whether he had not been mistaken in thinking that he had a vocation. Gradually the doubts increased until, in sum, they became certainty and he recognised, not without regret, that he was not fitted for the work to which he had aspired.

But, as he soon found, it was one thing to know what you were not fitted for but quite another to discover what you were fitted for. The Reverend Smythe had ensured that his education was sound, if somewhat heavily weighted towards religious learning but, as Scratcher realised, it would not be reasonable to expect a prospective employer to offer him more than a menial position. And Scratcher did not want a menial position.

The only answer, he felt, was to emigrate, and where better to go than to Australia which, from everything Scratcher had read, was a land of promise, opportunity and equality. Although he felt sure that Australia would suit him, he nonetheless also felt that it would be prudent to see the country and its people at first hand before deciding to become one of them. And so he signed up as a steward on an Australia-bound liner, was given a crash course in the basics of his new trade and ultimately joined his ship shortly before she was due to sail.

The Purser was a kindly man, as was the chief steward, and they were only mildly surprised, and not at all affronted, to find that Scratcher was not a homosexual. But Scratcher's fellow stewards, whose fraternity anticipated by many years the Gay Liberation clubs of the Greater London Council, were not so tolerant, and opinion was divided as to what attitude should be adopted.

At one extreme it was felt that the signing-on of a heterosexual set a precedent which could not easily be ignored, and a body of opinion led by the Shop Stewards argued that an immediate walk-off was mandatory. At the other end of the scale it was felt that it might be ever such fun to have one of them around, just for a change, and that his presence among them would present a challenge.

But it was the middle ground that carried the day by arguing, purely as a matter of self interest, that all single ladies would soon come to require the services of Scratcher and that the workload of the remainder, which was all of them, would thereby be reduced.

The voyage was a great success. Scratcher soon endeared himself to the first class passengers by his unique method of serving the 11 o'clock beef tea on the boat deck, where they sat on their long chairs. Instead of serving the steaming cups from a tray, as would be normal, Scratcher introduced a novel effect by advancing with an empty tray and serving the spellbound passengers with cups apparently plucked from his left ear. Soon the single ladies' bells were ringing a merry tune and the prophesy of a reduced workload for the remainder of the stewards was fulfilled.

On arrival in Australia Scratcher found to his surprise and disappointment that to be a pom was not an immediate passport to the affection of the populace. Rather the reverse, in fact, and although Australia might remain a country of promise, opportunity and equality were in short supply and only grudgingly granted.

To graduate from pommy bastard to mate, on whom the final accolade of 'Good on yer' might be bestowed, took time and the failure rate was high. Those who failed to become accepted joined the disconsolate and swollen ranks of the wingeing poms, higher than an abo but lower than a cuckaburra in terms of social acceptability.

Once he had summed up the situation, Scratcher graduated to 'Good on yer, mate' in what must have been record time by demonstrating on numerous occasions his ability to cause tubes of cold Fosters to materialise, apparently from nowhere. This was taken as proof positive that he was a 'right cobber' and should be granted the status of honorary digger straightaway. From then on all was plain sailing and Scratcher soon found himself engaged as an illusionist, initially as part of a cabaret turn.

As part of his finale he wore a bush hat with two dangling corks which he contrived to contra-rotate in parody of a stripper with her tassels. This proved to be such a popular turn that he rapidly became well known in the entertainment world and could take his pick from a number of lucrative offers.

And so for some years Scratcher travelled the country to the benefit both of his education and of his bank balance. But the life failed to satisfy him. Gradually the novelty faded and he found himself thinking with increasing frequency that life must have more to offer than cold Fosters and contra-rotating corks.

Eventually he decided to return to England, when he could get passage as a steward, with no clear idea of what it was that he wished to do but knowing only that he needed to get back to surroundings that had once been familiar before it was too late and they, by a strange inversion, became alien.

It was really quite by chance that Scratcher, back in England, but adrift and rudderless, without purpose or satisfaction in his life, came to realise that what he lacked, and what he wanted, was family, or extended family. In a pub one night he was witness to the camaraderie and warm ties, the easy going companionship and the instant loyalty one to the other of the young men of the local garrison.

He realised then that this was what he was seeking. A sense of identity, of purpose and belonging and he realised also that in the armed services this was to be found uniquely in the Army. Both the Royal Navy and the Royal Air Force were large loose-knit organisations in which the individual might, and indeed would, spend a year or so in a particular ship or in such and such a squadron, but the loyalty from the individual's point of view was to the Service rather than to the unit. In the Army, Scratcher instinctively understood, it was quite different. The Regiment was everything. It was much more personal, something in which a man could believe and take pride, and that was what Scratcher needed.

Once he had comprehended this it took little time for him to act upon the knowledge. He enlisted in a prestigious regiment and, almost inevitably because of his experience with the Merchant Navy and also partly perhaps because of his age, became a mess steward. This particular regiment was so grand that corporal stewards, before promotion to sergeant steward, served a set time during leave periods undergoing special training in the extremely grand residence of the colonel of the regiment.

So Scratcher, when he had served his time and perforce had to return to civilian life, had a wealth of experience behind him and a great deal to offer to someone like Richard Fox who was looking for a butler. His only drawback was Mrs Itch and she, after all, was a self-inflicted wound whose impact on the inhabitants of the Hall was likely to be minor indeed. As the job carried with it a tied house in the grounds, Richard and Pussy felt that the matrimonial discord, if it were to prove ongoing, if not chronic, would at least be cabined and confined, as someone once said. And they were at one in their recognition of the fact that, in Scratcher, they were taking on someone with unusual if not unique talent and personality.

Scratcher for his part was attracted by the whole ambience. He liked Jersey, he liked the Hall and, most of all, he liked the quiet retired Group Captain and his wife and their lively young daughter Ursula. In weeks they all knew that the right choice had been made, and the months and years that had passed since then had served only to tighten the bonds, bonds of affection which leaped the gap between employer and employed.

This was, Scratcher knew, what was so wrong about the projected sale of the Hall. Everything in their relationship which had been built up and forged over the years was, he felt, being recklessly hazarded. The Foxes, he realised, could not be expected to see things in the same light. For them, life in a smaller house without Scratcher would be sustainable and it would take a great exercise of imagination on their part to recognise that the reverse did not hold true. They had clearly not made this small yet simple leap in understanding, and Scratcher felt bereft that this should be so. Bereft, and beseiged and charged, at least in his own mind, with responsibility for ensuring that his employers be protected from the possible consequences of their own folly, Scratcher continued to brood.

A prolonged meow issuing from three or more feline throats warned Scratcher that Mrs Fox was in the offing and perhaps about to draw near. The fact that she should approach his sanctum in this fashion, rather than summon him by bell, gave due notice that she had something of importance to say. The additional fact that she had a feline escort, according full musical honours, added importance to the occasion.

He slipped on his jacket and, homing on the caterwauling, went forward to see whether he could be of assistance.

'Ah, Scratcher, there you are,' his employer's wife said. As an opening gambit it perhaps lacked originality but Scratcher, nothing if not magnanimous, was quite prepared to overlook this fact as he recognised that matters of moment were afoot.

'Oh good! I didn't want to ring as it's off duty time but I thought I might catch you if I came out. I've just had a telephone call from Urse, and she'll be coming in a week's time, bringing Johnnie with her. Isn't it thrilling? I hadn't expected them anything like so soon. But the real reason I came to tell you,' she went on breathlessly, 'is that Wing Commander and Mrs Phipps and Charlie are coming at the same time. You remember them, don't you? We've known them for years and of course Charlie is Urse's very oldest and most precious friend.'

Scratcher did remember them. He liked them all but he particularly liked the Wing Commander, who had been a wartime officer, and for whom his years as a pilot in the RAF had held a special magic. He had had what was known as 'a good war', as his DSO and his DFC testified. Some nostalgia for that very special period in the Wing Commander's life was evident even today in his phraseology and expressions, some of which Scratcher, in common with Sir Arthur Crabbe, was inclined to deprecate.

'Yes, of course, Ma'am,' said Scratcher. 'That's good news indeed. And will Mr Philip be coming at the same time?' He referred to Ursula's husband, who was something in the City and whose movements were frequent but not always predictable. But on this occasion at least, they were.

'No Scratcher, I'm afraid not,' said Pussy. 'He's going to be doing something frightfully important in China. Or is it Ceylon?' she added as an afterthought. Then almost plaintively she gave voice to a grievance shared by educated people over 50 the world over: 'but of course it isn't Ceylon any more is it? What's the new name, Scratcher? I can't remember. How I wish they wouldn't keep on chopping and changing. Only this morning I heard the BBC World Service calling Jesselton Kota Kinabalu and some ignoramus of an interviewer referring to Sabah as though it were an island. You couldn't have got confused when it was British North Borneo. Quite clear, then, that there were other bits of

Borneo and that not all of them were British.'

Scratcher attempted to sort all this out. 'Quite so, Ma'am,' he replied. 'Most aggravating. I rather fancy Sri Lanka is the name you were seeking.'

'Yes, of course, Scratcher,' she answered. 'How silly of me. Lot of Tamils there. Always chewing betel nut, as I remember. Yes, now, where was I? Yes, that's right. Just to give you the good news as it were, so that you can be thinking about any staff arrangements that might be necessary. I know nothing would ever persuade Ivy and Doris to sleep in, but perhaps they might be prepared to come a bit earlier and maybe leave a bit later while the house is full. I'll leave it to you to see what can be done. Oh! I'm so thrilled.'

Pussy did a little pirouette of pleasure which enchanted not only Scratcher, but also her feline escort who, recognising that the palaver was at an end and that they would shortly be required to move off in column of route by the right, snatched a brief respite to twitch their whiskers and meow their applause.

Pussy and her entourage withdrew. Scratcher, hastily, unwisely and without due thought, resolved to pass on his newly gained information to Mrs Jones, partly so that she might make an early start in menu construction but, more particularly, so that he might demonstrate his seniority and superiority in being first with this new intelligence.

Advancing on the kitchen with due solemnity Scratcher transmitted the word. 'And so,' he finished, 'I'm telling you this early, Mrs Jones, so that you can get off to a good start.'

Mrs Jones regarded him malevolently. 'If and when I feel the need to let off a good fart, Mr Itch, I'll not be seeking your permission,' she said.

Scratcher, outraged, decided to fight back. 'If and when you do, just let me know, and I'll hold a taper to your backside and blow you up, you old bag,' he fulminated.

Fortunately for their future relations his invective fell on deaf ears. 'It's Thursday tomorrow, isn't it?' she said.

81

CHAPTER EIGHT

The week passed quickly in a flurry of planning and preparation. The Hall was a mass of cut flowers, the window cleaner was called in ahead of schedule and there were endless consultations with Mrs Jones. Pussy never seemed to sit down and appeared to be in a permanent orbit of supervision. The cats-in-waiting were exhausted and their whiskers wilted.

The awaited day came and, if the island did not actually shake in recognition of the arrival of Urse and Charlie, it should have done. They had been two of the wickedest products of their particular academy for young females, an academy renowned for its steady output of high spirited young ladies who might perhaps have been adjudged a trifle fast by an earlier generation.

Ursula at 31, with a child of 12, and Charlie at 30 and as yet unmarried, looked and behaved as though they were in their teens. For them, at school, life had seemed a fascinating, delightful, exciting and hilariously funny adventure. Nearly fifteen years later it still did. Like the couple of children they still were at heart they exploded into the Hall, bringing with them all the enthusiasm and vitality of youth.

Johnnie, who adored his grandmother, had not been put down or overshadowed by his mother's powerful personality and remained a pretty balanced 12-year-old with an eye to mischief and with a well developed sense of humour. He also, of course, was a great buddy and fellow conspirator of Scratcher and he asked nothing better than

82

the opportunity to spend the maximum time possible in the great man's company.

Pussy enfolded them all, including the Phipps, in her wide embrace. 'Oh, you darlings,' she said. 'How simply wonderful that you're actually here. I can hardly believe it. And did you have a good journey, or was it all a bit awful?' she enquired. 'I know it can be simply foul.'

'No. Wizard,' said the Wing Commander making his first contribution to the cultural exchange. 'Absolutely wizard. Bang on.'

'Oh, super,' Pussy breathed delightedly and then, turning to Pansy Phipps, one of her very oldest friends, 'Pansy, love, Scratcher will do the luggage and all that sort of thing. Do let's go in and have a drinky-poos to celebrate,' she said, reverting in her excitement, as she not infrequently did, to the language of the nursery. 'I can't think what's happened to Richard,' she added in a puzzled tone.

She had no sooner said it than Richard arrived, brow creased but furrowed features nonetheless relaxing in what a mastiff would undoubtedly have recognised as a welcoming expression.

'Marvellous to see you all,' he said, kissing Urse and Charlie and Pansy, giving Johnnie a great hug and slapping Pansy's husband on the back. 'Great to see you, Pranger. How are things going?' he asked, not as a serious question but just in the accepted jargon of modern day greeting.

His friend recognised the question as purely rhetorical and automatic and, ignoring it, glided it quietly to leg with an acknowledgment in no known language but which sounded like 'woof'. They all moved in for drinks, chattering like jays or magpies.

It was a memorable occasion. The cats paraded at full strength and duly marched past the assembled company. Dolly came in and nudged a favoured crotch or two before passing a monstrous wind that might almost have been classified as a typhoon.

83

'Oh dear, Dolly!' said Pussy reproachfully. 'Farty-poos!' and then, as though seeking to excuse this display of canine excess and lack of sensibility, added, 'the poor darling is pregnant, you know.'

After a while, the initial greetings and excitements being over and something approaching normality having supervened, Richard succeeded in gathering their attention.

'Pussy,' he said, 'I haven't had a chance to tell you as I'm just this moment off the 'phone, but you might as well all know together as you'll all be affected . . .'

'What on earth are you gabbling about, Richard?' Pussy interjected. 'Have you gone totally potty?'

'Hang on a minute, old thing, and I'll tell you,' he replied. 'Just before you all arrived, old Bragger Bowcester came on the 'phone and asked if we could help him out by putting up some visiting fireman from the Home Office who's apparently arriving next week. Some new chap called Ernest Twite, I think he said. Apparently Government House is going to be out of action and, for some reason or other that I couldn't quite follow, Bragger and Fred want to lush this fellow up and are asking us to look after him rather than sending him to an hotel. I said that of course I'd need to check with you, but I thought you'd be willing to rally round, in spite of the houseful' and here he looked around with a slow all-embracing smile of pleasure and of renewed welcome. 'Went so far, in fact, as to say I was sure you'd agree and that unless I rang back this morning he could take it as settled.'

'Oh, gosh,' Pussy breathed. 'Yes, of course, Richard, we can't possibly let Bragger down, but it will be rather tight. Let me see now. How many underlings is this Twite likely to have with him, and has he got a wife?'

'I'm pretty sure the answer is "no wife" and one private secretary. As an under secretary he doesn't rate a Special Branch man, so it's a total of two, both male so far as I know.'

'Well, then,' Pussy said, 'that's no problem at all. There'll be bags of room if we open up the west wing. It could do with a good airing and there's plenty of sun now. A bit spooky, though, but I don't suppose they'll mind, because they won't know, will they?' she finished with all the childish innocence of her 50-plus years.

Richard smiled happily at her evident acceptance. 'Good, that's super,' he said. 'I only hope this Twite fellow isn't too much of a pill. I really don't know anything about him, haven't even heard the name so far as I know. Have you heard of him, Pranger?'

'No. Can't say I have,' said Pranger. 'But to be fair my reading doesn't go much beyond Private Eye or the Sun. If he hasn't appeared in either of those, and I don't think he has, then I'd think that might just possibly be a good mark.'

'I wouldn't count on it,' said Richard. 'I suppose we've got to wait and see but I can't help thinking that this new Government is a pretty awful lot and that probably Twite will turn out to be a typical representative. Anyway, we'll soon know, and I hope it'll be fun finding out,' he said with his endearing smile.

Pussy was entranced. 'Oh, how exciting,' she said. 'First of all you arrive, which is sheer Heaven, and now we're called into the front line to help out Government House. Fantastic! Who ever said nothing ever happened in Jersey and that it was dead for ten months of the year?'

'Probably some Guernseyman, I dare say,' said Richard, smiling.

Pussy ignored this. 'Right. Now,' she said, taking charge, 'we need to find out about him, what he likes and doesn't like and so on. Do you think he's in Who's Who, Richard?'

'No, I wouldn't think so,' he answered. 'He's far too junior. But the Governor's Office might have something on him. He might even have been the subject of MI5 observation,' he said, only partially in joke. 'But I'm sure I can find out anything you want to know. I've only to ask Bragger's secretary to get on to the Home Office.'

'Oh good,' she said. 'That's lovely. I'm sure we can work out a super programme.'

'Simply bang on,' said Pranger, who'd been listening to this exchange. 'A piece of cake, or even a morceau de gateau, as we used to say, as I recall. Press on regardless. If in doubt stamp on their goolies, that was the cry, I remember. Don't suppose these modern Home Office chaps have any goolies to stamp on, have they? No, I thought not, how disappointing, but no matter, the principle is what counts.'

Pussy, eager to pass on the news to Scratcher and to Mrs Jones, asked Richard if he knew anything more.

'No, I don't at this stage,' he said. 'And indeed I don't think anything is yet settled in any detail. But Bragger thought he would probably arrive on Thursday afternoon sometime and leave for Guernsey on Saturday morning and would spend one more night here, probably the following Monday, before going back to the U.K.'

'Well,' Pussy said, 'I'll need to know quite soon for guest lists and so on. In fact I think I'd better warn a few people now, and say we'll confirm later, don't you think? I'd like to make sure of getting Podger and Prue and Connie and Arthur, for example.'

'Yes. I think you can count on Fred holding an official banquet for him on the Friday night and I doubt if we'll be called on to give him lunch any day. So,' Richard said, 'that leaves us with Thursday night and probably the following Monday night.'

Pussy thought a moment. 'Perhaps it would be best if we had the dinner party on his final night and kept Thursday night small and informal, perhaps just us. On second thoughts that would mean we'd be eight, which is a bad number. Do you think it would be fair to ask Podger and Prue to come on both nights?' she asked Richard. 'Then we'd be ten, which is much better, and we'd have Podger to help with light relief if things prove at all sticky.'

'I can't see why not,' said Richard. 'I'm sure they'd be only too happy to help. Anyway, why not ask Prue?'

'Yes, I will,' she said. 'Now come on, everyone, we're neglecting you all dreadfully. Let's have another drinkies. All this excitement is making me thirsty, and there hasn't even been time yet to begin to hear all your news. I'm just dying of curiosity.'

CHAPTER NINE

Arthur read the conclusions of his report to the Bailiff, not without a certain satisfaction. He felt he had struck just the right note, not too cautious, certainly not alarmist. He read part of the manuscript again, savouring each word.

'In coming to any conclusion in this matter it is necessary to reiterate that one must constantly have in mind the mercurial temperament of Ernest Twite, a temperament which necessarily exposes any forecast of probable behaviour to a greater than usual likelihood of error. While, therefore, one may perhaps be certain that his intentions towards the Channel Islands are hostile, it is by no means easy to discern in what way he may choose to make this hostility manifest. It is not inconceivable that he may seek to disguise this hostility in a display of apparent bonhomie and acceptance of the status quo. It is even, of course, possible that he has no hostile intentions towards current institutions, notably financial, in the islands and that there is not, in fact, undue cause for alarm. But one is forced to the conclusion that any such reading of the situation might well, indeed probably would, prove false. Not that one can, of course, proceed in this matter on the basis of probability. All that can be said on the basis of certainty is that Ernest Twite, on his forthcoming visit, will have something of interest to impart.

'Proceeding from that assumption of certainty, and it is of course important to remember that it is no more than an assumption, one moves into those areas of uncertainty and

conjecture which were discussed earlier in this consideration of the salient facts. Beyond that point it is difficult to
foresee how Twite may decide to act, or what the proper
forestalling move should be.

'As to your specific enquiry, Mr Bailiff, as to whether or
not I concur in your tactic of taking the initiative in inviting
Twite early, I am forced to say that it is a difficult question to
answer. The nub of the matter is, of course, the effect that
such an invitation will have on Twite or, to be even more
specific, how is he likely to react. Will his assumed hostility
towards the Channel Islands be heightened by receiving the
invitation or will it be decreased, always of course remembering that it may not have existed in the first place? And will
the matter of interest which it has been assumed he will
impart be made more interesting, or will its assumed interest
be lessened, as a result of your letter? These are difficult
questions indeed.

'In seeking to address them I have attempted, as it were, to
put myself in Twite's shoes. As a young Militant, granted his
first taste of power, Twite might well wish to ensure that he,
and he alone, controls the timing and sequence of events. In
other words he might well wish, as our American friends I
believe say, in their colourful idiom, to call the shots. In that
case your invitation, which could to a degree be interpreted
as depriving him of the initiative, might not be altogether
welcome, might in fact, not to put too fine a point upon it, be
actually unwelcome. Alternatively, he might see your letter
as indicating a willingness, if only tentative and uninformed,
to at least listen to and perhaps even to meet him halfway in
whatever proposals he might have it in mind to make. Then,
naturally, your letter would be well received. Again, he
could interpret your letter as a declaration of hostilities, as a
gesture of defiance and as an invitation, if not a challenge, to
him, Twite, to do his worst. He would then act accordingly.

'Next, he could perhaps see your invitation as a gesture of
friendship and goodwill, not I think a likely interpretation

although it would be foolish to discount this possibility. And, of course, there is always the possibility, perhaps remote but nevertheless real, that Twite might take your invitation at its face value, as an automatic and required reaction from Bailiff to Home Office Minister, and draw no conclusions, favourable or otherwise, from the singularity of its early issuance.

'And so, Mr Bailiff, after deep consideration and exhaustive examination of all the relevant factors, I find myself in no position to make more than an interim judgment on your action in sending what might be interpreted as a premature invitation.

'Tentatively, and strictly as an interim assessment, I am, however, prepared to go so far as to say that receipt of such an unusually early invitation is likely to have made an impression on Twite and that, as I am sure you, Mr Bailiff, will agree, is the really significant point. An impression will have been made.'

Arthur felt a certain glow, the reward due to the professional and expert solution of a difficult problem. The Bailiff, he felt, could not have had better advice, nor could he possibly have hoped for a more detached, dispassionate and balanced analysis of the situation.

This, Arthur felt, was the difference between the polished professional and the unlettered amateur, the difference, to be blunt, between the civil and the military, for Podger's criticism of his opening paragraph still rankled.

In an uncharacteristic flush of determination, and with what might have passed for aggressiveness in a less passive individual, he resolved to allow Podger sight of his report, and his findings, before he presented them to the Bailiff. He felt sure Podger would be suitably impressed, would recognise the touch of a master draftsman and, as a result of this recognition, would perhaps entertain doubts as to the validity of his criticism of Arthur's work. He might even, and Arthur's pulse rate quickened at the thought, withdraw that criticism, admit that he had been hasty and in error, and ask Arthur's pardon for what was after all, Arthur reflected, a minor form of lèse-majesté.

But this mood of buoyant confidence did not long survive his encounter with Podger, who came around at about 6 o'clock at Arthur's invitation. Constance and Prue were both out at some ladies' function.

Arthur explained the circumstances which had led to the Bailiff seeking his advice and then said casually, 'Don't know if you'd care to see my analysis, Podger? There's nothing confidential or personal in it. I'm sure the Bailiff would have no objection and, quite frankly, I would welcome the views of an old friend able to consider the matter with a fresh mind.'

He sat back content, sure now that Podger would accept his offer and would be suitably impressed by his brilliant exposition.

Podger drained his second large whisky with one long practised swallow, regarded his empty glass with what appeared to be surprise, edged it gently in the direction of his host and stroked his moustache sideways, either in encouragement or in admonition to it to maintain its horizontal posture. 'What! What! Arthur, want me to take a dekko, eh? Certainly, old man. Absolutely. Only too happy, what?'

So saying, Podger began to read, watched benevolently by Arthur. The report was not a long one, and he was soon finished. His brow was furrowed and his pale blue eyes assumed a look which could, without undue exaggeration, have been described as glassy.

'Ah,' he said. Arthur felt his confidence begin to evaporate. He could scarcely credit it but, if he was reading the signs aright, Podger had some fault to find with his report, might even indeed, unbelievably, be critical of its form and content.

'What do you mean, Podger?' he enquired anxiously and

91

rather sharply. 'Did you find something you didn't agree with?'

'Jolly hard to say, Arthur, old man, because when you come down to it and cut the cackle and all that sort of rot you don't actually make yourself very plain, if you know what I mean. What? Eh? I mean it's not exactly pikestaff stuff is it, old bean? What's Fred supposed to make of it, eh?'

Arthur was dumbfounded by his friend's reaction and could make no reply. He gave a feeble gulp, like a fish suddenly deprived of water, and his eyes goggled.

Podger, not noticing the effect that his words were having, continued unabashed. 'Well,' he said, 'obviously you know what you're up to, old man. Years of experience and all that. And it's a political subject when all's said and done, so I'm sure you know how best to handle it. Not the way we'd do it in the Services though,' he concluded. 'Not the way at all.'

Arthur was outraged and only by a great effort was he able to calm himself sufficiently to speak in a near normal tone. 'Well, how would you do it in the Services? Have you some special and exclusive method?' he enquired, not quite succeeding in keeping all trace of bitterness and sarcasm out of his final words.

'Well, yes, actually, we have,' said Podger. 'Learnt about it at Staff College, you know. Can't remember too much about it now but I do remember that if you do it right, it works a treat. Every time a coconut, if you know what I mean. Nothing those Directing Staff chaps couldn't sort out by that method. Can't think why they didn't all go into the City and get stinking rich. Could have done, I'm sure, but they all wanted to become Generals. Can't have everything, what? I mean to say, what? eh?' he said, as though to make his point clearer.

Arthur, in spite of a feeling of desolation at having his lovingly crafted words thus condemned and treated with what was undoubtedly disrespect, if not something close to contempt, was nonetheless unable to control his inquisitiveness.

'How do you set about it in the Services, Podger?' he enquired, swallowing his pride and attempting to keep a certain coldness out of his tone.

'Well,' said Podger. 'It's called an appreciation, and there are two sorts, the formal and the informal. The formal is a bit complicated and frightfully long winded and has an absolutely rigid framework. It's really only used in order to get the old brain accustomed to surging down the right channels. When you've got the hang of that and the grey matter has been properly programmed, as it were, they switch you over to the informal, which is the normal thought process used in the Services in an adversary situation. And that, of course, is what you have got here, isn't it, Arthur? I should say it is, what? Certainly is, I should say!' concluded Podger.

'But,' Arthur said quickly, sensing a weakness in Podger's reasoning, 'you can't know that it's an adversary situation; that's no more than an assumption at this stage. And it would be very unwise to proceed on the basis of an assumption. Most unwise,' and Arthur tut-tutted as though to emphasise the peril and impropriety of such a course.

'Ah!' said Podger, 'but the appreciation would be written on the assumption of an adversary situation, which is pretty certainly what you're faced with. If that assumption is wrong and friend Twite is all sweetness and light then you haven't got a problem at all. But if it's right you've at least had a look in advance at what he might do and at what responses are open to you once the bounder shows his hand.'

'Yes, I see,' said Arthur judiciously, beginning to become engrossed, in spite of his wounded pride. 'I understand the principle, Podger, but surely it wouldn't work in this case. I mean, we've absolutely no idea what line the man is going to take.'

'Doesn't matter, old man,' said Podger, 'you just bung

down all the possibilities. One of them is bound to be right.'

Arthur was far from convinced. 'I still can't see it working in this case, Podger. What sort of solution would one of your bright Directing Staff come up with? I mean, we don't even know the problem yet. I can't see that it makes sense.'

Podger gave a quick barking laugh, a noise closely resembling that of an overexcited hyena. 'If I could answer that, Arthur, I would have retired as a General and not as a Brigadier! But I can give you an idea of how they'd set about it. They'd start by a short summary of the facts, so far as we know them. That the Parliamentary Under-Secretary with special responsibility for the Channel Islands will be visiting both Bailiwicks – giving dates – accompanied by his private secretary. That, in agreement with Guernsey, he has been invited unusually early in an attempt to rob him of the initiative and that, while in Jersey, he will be staying at the Hall rather than at Government House.'

Here Podger interrupted his flow of explanation to make the point that both those decisions should properly have stemmed from the appreciation itself, whereas they had been taken in isolation and were now facts rather than options. 'Probably the right answer reached by the wrong method. Anyway, we're stuck with it,' Podger concluded before picking up his main thread.

'Then there would be a potted version of what we know about Twite and his P.S., leading up to the disquiet of the island authorities and their feeling that it is possible, if not indeed probable, that Twite may be planning something to the disadvantage of the Channel Islands as a whole. What do we know about them, Arthur?' Podger interjected. 'Anything to the discredit of either of them? Any weaknesses that we know of? That's the sort of material we want.'

Podger paused, taking the opportunity, with seeming artlessness and with a skill born of long practice, to draw his host's attention to the fact that his glass was empty.

'Yes, as a matter of fact we do,' said Arthur, busy with the decanter. 'We know that Twite is unmarried and unattached but, our source says, there's nothing funny about him. Very much the reverse, in fact. He has what used to be known as a "Roving Eye" and is very susceptible to young females or, indeed, females of any age so far as I can gather. He's also a bit of a boozer. Given to taking a drop too much on occasion.'

'Bit of a boozer, eh?' said Podger. 'Bad fault that. Yes! Bad fault indeed! What? What?'

Arthur concurred.

'What about the Private Secretary?' Podger persisted.

'We know nothing about him at all, I'm afraid,' said Arthur realising, as he said it, that this was indeed an oversight.

'Not good, Arthur. Not good,' said Podger. 'Remember the old saying "Know your enemy". What? What? He could be more dangerous than Twite. Better find out about him straightaway.'

Podger returned to his explanation. 'Yes, well, after that summary of the situation they would settle on the aim, which is the sort of lynch pin of the whole thing. The aim in this case would have to be pretty broadly stated and might be something like "To ensure the continuance of the political and financial status quo in the Channel Islands". Then they would run through the possible courses of action that Twite might consider, that is to say the various forms that his threat to the status quo might take. Then there would be a section on what we might do, or the courses of action open to us under the various hypotheses, ending up with a so-called "selection of the best course" or, in other words, what we ought to do about it.'

'Yes,' said Arthur after a few moments contemplation. 'I can see how it just might work.'

'It's better than that,' Podger riposted. 'It's a sure fire winner. It never fails. Guaranteed satisfaction or your money back in full, and all that sort of stuff.'

95

Arthur felt a mounting excitement. Could there be something in this method? He doubted it. All his training and experience cautioned him to rely on fact alone, and this would be a departure from that lifetime habit. And yet, and yet, he had to admit that there just could be something in it. What Podger had to say sounded persuasive, certainly persuasive enough for Arthur to want to hear more.

'Yes, I can see that, Podger,' he said. 'I can see that it's a very sound method of dealing with most problems but I can't see it working in our present situation.'

'Why not? I've never known it not to before. It's a tricky one, I agree, as we have so little to go on,' said Podger 'but I think you'd be surprised at how much you could get out of working along the classic lines. Let's have a try, just so that I can show you what I mean.'

'How should we start, when we know nothing for certain?' asked Arthur. 'It's hopeless, it'll never work, I'm sure.'

'Well now, let's see. If you ask yourself why you perceive Twite as an adversary and as a threat, that might give us a starting point.' Podger stroked his moustache reflectively.

Arthur searched for something concrete. 'Well, as I say, there's nothing really to go on, it's just that it would be all of a piece with this Government.'

'Surely you base your feelings on a bit more than that,' Podger persisted. 'What about Twite himself, apart from his weaknesses. Doesn't his political background tell you anything? Who are his friends? Has he any powerful sponsors? How does he stand with his boss, the Home Secretary?'

'Ah, yes indeed, Podger,' Arthur said after a moment's reflection. 'Yes, of course, that's why one's worried, although I hadn't really crystallised it in my mind before. Yes, indeed. Well, he's a member of Militant Tendency, a Marxist; has been in open support, if not an active encourager, of some of the most disgraceful scenes of violent and illegal picketing in recent years and is, of course, well known for his unpardonable behaviour in the House. Seething both with resentment and with ambition. Not without talent and a certain effectiveness in spite of his odious behaviour.

'Yes, and of course, how silly of me,' Arthur went on, 'I know why one is so concerned about what he may do. It's the fact that quite obviously he's consumed with envy which, in turn, makes anything which can be represented as privilege a prime target. And, of course, there's no doubt about it that to one of Twite's persuasion the Islands must seem a hot-bed of privilege. The fact that the taxes are lower because affairs are better ordered would not of course be an explanation which he could accept or even be willing to consider.'

'Right,' said Podger. 'Now we're beginning to get somewhere. We've got the motivation. Now tell me what he could do.'

'Well, realistically, the only thing he can hope to do is to turn the screw on the financial sector to the benefit of the Treasury. It's a very delicate and dangerous business, closely akin to the goose and the golden egg, and fraught with constitutional pitfalls, but that's what I think he'll try.'

'No, Arthur, no,' Podger said regretfully. 'That's not the method. I asked you what Twite could do, that's to say what he might do, what courses of action are open to him. And you've told me what you think he will do. Not the same thing at all, you know, what? Now, if we take your forecast of his probable action as a likely middle of the road course, what might Twite possibly think of doing which you would consider less dangerous and, on the other hand, as more dangerous. Eh? That's the way to look at it Arthur, you know. If you don't and make your plans only on the basis of what you think he will do you're liable to be badly caught out if your forecast is wrong and, in the event, he does something quite different.'

'Ah yes, indeed, of course, how very stupid of me.' Arthur thought for a moment. 'I suppose,' he said at length, 'the absolute minimum that one might expect would be something akin to the 1984 invitation to contribute to Defence, a sort of submission to voluntary taxation at a level set by the islands themselves. That might be manageable financially, but would certainly be objectionable constitutionally. At the other end of the scale it is difficult to imagine how far they might seek to go, and for what purpose. Theoretically, I suppose it would be possible to seek to change the relationship between the Channel Islands and the United Kingdom, a relationship which has stood since the 13th Century, but no one would stand to gain. The finance houses would move to Bermuda or the Cayman Islands, the fiscal penalties would be severe and a large increase in taxation would be unavoidable. This would benefit no-one and would achieve nothing. The only tangible results would be a decline in local prosperity and a sharp fall in the standard of living of the better off.'

'Well,' said Podger, 'is that so unlikely an aim? Might that not be just what Twite would like to see, no one better off but a lot of people a good deal worse off, the levelling-down which has such a strong appeal for him and for people like him.'

'If you put it like that,' said Arthur, 'I suppose it doesn't seem all that impossible, but I would hope that no one, not even Twite, could be so shortsighted and could have such mean and despicable motives.'

'For the purpose of this run through, to give you a very rough idea of how appreciations work,' said Podger, 'it doesn't really matter. You've broadly stated the minimum and maximum threat and have also indicated broadly what form you expect the likely attack to take. Now you have to consider what your reaction should be, once Twite shows his hand. What is it open to you to do, in broad terms? Can you react appropriately and immediately?'

'Well,' said Arthur hesitantly. 'Any minor challenge could be contained and some sensible conclusion arrived at. But it's the higher level of threat that worries me.'

'What response could you make?' asked Podger.

'Well, of course, the natural, and indeed the only, way of disputing any proposal which threatened the constitutional relationship would lie in an appeal to the Privy Council, but their response would almost certainly support the Home Office line as laid down by the Secretary of State.'

'So. Is there any hope there?' Podger asked. 'Is it possible that the Secretary of State might take an entirely different view and overrule Twite's proposals, whatever they might turn out to be?'

'Absolutely none, I'm afraid,' came the depressing response. 'Garry Stote and Ernest Twite served together on the Inner London Education Authority and apparently saw eye to eye on the policy then being propounded. Indeed, I understand that Kevin Pratt gave Garry Stote virtually a free hand in filling the under secretary post, the only condition being that whoever was chosen had to come from Militant Tendency. So he had a very wide field to choose from and his choice of Twite must be considered significant. My contacts also tell me that, as Home Secretary, Stote is expected to concentrate initially on the police and on the prison service, for both of which, as you may imagine, he has some novel ideas.

'Twite has Stote's confidence and is expected to be given carte blanche in an area which in Home Office terms is pretty unimportant. Just as Stalin enquired how many divisions the Pope had, so could any Home Secretary enquire how many votes the Channel Islands had and know that he would get the same answer, as reassuring in political terms as the first had been in military. And so I'm afraid the outlook on that score in no way gives cause for optimism. Indeed, I would go so far as to say, Podger, that there is nothing that could effectively be done to frustrate

Twite in any proposal he might make. One must just hope that reasoned argument will prevail. If that fails then I fear that the island authorities will be powerless.'

Podger stroked his moustache with great firmness and gave an authoritative 'Harrumph!' before addressing Arthur with some solemnity. 'Partially right, Arthur, but only partially, I fancy. Remember your aim, which was essentially to maintain the political and financial status quo. If that can't be done by reasoned argument or by petitioning the Privy Council, you need to see if there's some other way of doing it, don't you?'

'Well, theoretically yes, Podger, but in this case it doesn't work as there isn't any other way.'

'Poppycock!' said Podger firmly. 'Poppycock and piffle, Arthur! You've overlooked the fact that Twite is vulnerable. You yourself told me, you may remember, that he has a weakness for the ladies and for the bottle. Our obvious best course of action is to exploit those weaknesses, and to compromise him.'

The protuberant blue eyes had taken on a steely glint and Arthur stirred uneasily at the realisation that his easy-going friend could be a bad person to have as an enemy.

'But Podger,' he protested, 'the local authorities can't go around compromising under-secretaries. It's simply just not within the realm of possibility.'

'Quite so, Arthur, quite so. That's precisely why I said you were partially right. You were totally right to conclude that the island authorities would be powerless, but you overlooked what we might call the private sector. Nothing to stop well motivated private citizens from doing something that officials couldn't afford to be mixed up in, is there now? Eh?'

Arthur regarded him with a dropped jaw and a glassy look in his eyes. He spluttered feebly. 'But, but, Podger, what you're proposing is nothing short of a conspiracy!'

'Just so, Arthur. Just so. Conspiracy's a good word. Yes, the right word I think. Fits the bill perfectly.'

'But private citizens simply can't go around conspiring to compromise under-secretaries.' Arthur's voice quavered with something approaching outrage at the very thought.

'Why not, Arthur? Why not? Just give me one good reason. Just one!'

'Well. Er. I mean, you simply can't. The very idea is simply preposterous.'

'Nonsense, Arthur! Absolute nonsense! It's just your thinking that's too rigid and blinkered. Why on earth shouldn't private citizens so arrange things that an under-secretary could be tempted to do something foolish? He's a free agent. He doesn't have to do whatever it might be but, if he does, he's brought it on himself. Self-inflicted wound, you might say. What? Nothing illegal in that old man, nothing illegal at all.'

'Nothing illegal, Podger? You're quite sure of that?' asked Arthur, doubt beginning to form in his mind as to whether his first instinctive reaction might have been too hasty. 'Nothing illegal, you say, Podger, nothing illegal. No question of blackmail then?'

'No, no Arthur, of course not,' said Podger reassuringly. Then, breaking into a quick barking chuckle, 'Ha! Ha! Blackmail you say, Arthur, blackmail, eh? Good thinking, good thinking, Arthur, Ha! Ha! What? That's rich, Arthur, that's what it is, rich.'

Arthur began to feel that Podger's solution, sounding so drastic when first propounded, might have something to commend it, perhaps even quite a lot to commend it. After all, by its very nature compromise must be largely if not entirely the fault of the person compromised. In the event such extreme measures, would not be needed. Just a contingency plan, never likely to be put into operation and, if the worst came to the worst and it had to be used, it would be non-attributable as no officials would be involved and would genuinely not know what was afoot. Podger had been quite clear about that, but Arthur felt it to be a point of such cardinal importance that he would be justified in asking for that reassurance to be repeated.

'No officials involved, Podger. You're sure of that?'

'Totally old man, totally. It's a matter for you, of course, but I would have thought it only fair to inform the Bailiff in very general terms that, in the perhaps unlikely event of having to use extreme measures, there is good reason to hope that Twite can be successfully encouraged to put his foot in it up to the knee and that a small body of right thinking private citizens are at this very moment bending their brains to that end. You could say that this information is, of course, in the strictest confidence and is no more than contingency planning for what might be done if all efforts through official channels looked like being of no avail. Just to make sure that he doesn't haul the flag down or throw the towel in, or any of that rot,' Podger concluded, staring as if absentmindedly at his empty glass.

Arthur observed the look and acted upon it. He could feel his excitement mounting as he poured the whisky.

'You know, Podger,' he said, 'I'm coming round to thinking you're right and that I shouldn't put in my note but something on the lines of your outline appreciation instead.'

His brow clouded momentarily as he thought of the sacrifice and waste of his so lovingly composed minute. 'But there may be a bit of a snag,' he went on. 'I couldn't very well do that without acknowledging that the thinking behind it was yours, and then you'd be involved whether you wanted to be or not.'

'No, Arthur. No. Far better that my name's not mentioned, so that the Bailiff has no idea of who's working on this problem. I don't want any acknowledgment, and in any case the words will be yours.'

Arthur thought for a moment. 'Well,' he said slowly, 'it certainly could be managed like that if you've really no objection.'

'Absolutely none, I assure you. Go to it, Arthur, and set out the general scheme of things in your polished and persuasive prose.'

'If you really mean it, Podger, then I think I will.' Arthur's eyes gleamed momentarily at the prospect of compiling a report that was crisp and definite. Perhaps, on reflection, not too crisp and certainly not too definite; nonetheless, a report or analysis which would go some long way down that dangerous and unfamiliar path. An analysis which, though strewn with escape clauses, would effectively parallel Podger's appreciation.

'But who are the people who will be working on this?' Arthur enquired. 'In fact you said, didn't you, are already working on it.'

'Figure of speech Arthur, figure of speech. What I meant was, they will be by the time your paper reaches the Bailiff. As to who they are, I haven't recruited them yet so I can't tell you. And far better if you don't know anyway, as the Bailiff has in a sense made you an official by asking your advice.'

'Yes, I think that's probably right,' said Arthur. Then, looking at Podger's empty glass, 'will you have another?'

'Perhaps just one for the road, or Satu ampat jalan, as we used to say in Malaya,' Podger replied. 'Then we must both set to on our different tasks.'

Arthur reflected, as he poured the farewell drinks, that Podger's 'What whatting' rate had been remarkably low throughout their conversation, and he felt his confidence growing as a result. I always suspected that it was all a front to hide a keen brain, and now I'm sure of it, he thought.

Aloud he said, 'Well, good luck, Podger, in your enterprise.' He raised his glass. 'Damnation to Ernest Twite.'

Podger regarded him approvingly. 'A good toast, Arthur, a good toast. Damnation to Ernest Twite it is. May we get his knickers well and truly twisted.'

CHAPTER TEN

When the Bailiff showed Sir Arthur Crabbe's analysis to the Lieutenant-Governor, Sir Humphrey was impressed, if not astounded.

'Well, I'll be damned, Fred,' he said. 'I'd never have thought the little fellow had it in him. It reads just like an appreciation. In fact it is an appreciation. No civil servant could have written this. You can actually understand it. Jolly rum, Fred. Jolly rum. I think he's got someone behind him, Fred. Arthur Crabbe couldn't lay out such a crisp note, that I'm certain of. Anyway, doesn't matter. It's certainly persuasive reasoning there's no doubt about it. Nice to know, or of course officially not to know, that there's a body of properly motivated citizens already preparing Twite's downfall if he is so stupid as to invite retaliation.'

'I'm not at all sure you're right, Humphrey, about Arthur Crabbe having someone behind him. I think highly of him, as you know. He's shrewd, very experienced in the ways of Whitehall and, I think, has a good brain, perhaps not quite first class but not far off it. As for it being in the style of an appreciation, surely he could have picked that up in the ministry. If he didn't and you're right in thinking that he's got someone with a military background behind him, it could only be that chap Brigadier Simpson because I know for a fact that Richard Fox never had any staff training. He told me so himself. The mere thought of it being Simpson is laughable. I don't know how well you know him, but the man's an ass.'

'Well, Fred, I don't know him at all well but one certainly wouldn't take him for an intellectual, I'll grant you that. More suitable as the subject of an H.M. Bateman cartoon I'd say. So I suppose you must be right, in which case I've underestimated Arthur Crabbe badly. Amazing to find a civil servant who's prepared to commit himself as far as Crabbe has done. Admittedly there are a few saving clauses here and there, that's of course the habit of a lifetime and one could hardly expect otherwise, but basically it's a clear, unambiguous note.

'But beyond that, which amazes me in itself, what amazes me far more is that, reading between the lines, he's actually acted on his own authority and initiative to get together a body of people, almost a partisan group, one might say, who are probably at this very moment plotting various ways of bringing about Twite's undoing. I find it quite astounding in someone of Crabbe's background, but I suppose it only goes to show how wrong one can be.' Sir Humphrey paused, a slight frown adding emphasis to his perplexity.

'Yes. That bit worries me, I'm afraid,' the Bailiff said. 'I just hope to heavens it doesn't get to the stage of them actually doing anything. As a matter of fact, I think we may all even be surprised by the moderation of Twite's proposals. These Labour chaps are great at rhetoric when in opposition but they become more responsible when in office.'

'That's certainly been the case in the past,' Sir Humphrey agreed, 'but I rather fancy you may be faced with a totally new situation with this lot. The next few days or perhaps weeks will show.'

'Let's hope not, although I must admit in my heart of hearts I'm very much afraid you may be right. Then, if Twite gets carried away and makes some quite unacceptable proposal, and he's backed by the Home Secretary, we're liable to have a semi lynch law situation with this group of Arthur Crabbe's going into action. I only hope to God they keep within the Law. Do you think I should put a stop to it, Humphrey?'

'The Governor considered. 'No, I don't, Fred,' he said after a few seconds' thought. 'For one thing, there may be nothing to put a stop to as these are just contingency plans at this stage. For another, you don't know who the people are, other than Crabbe, and you don't know whether they'd listen to him and of course, if they won't, you haven't the power to stop it anyway. But, more importantly, you might be jolly glad of their help. And remember, you know nothing officially and can in no way be held responsible for or linked with whatever may happen. And neither can I, I'm glad to say,' he added with a smile. 'You know my position, Fred. Officially, of course, I should be strictly neutral, but you know full well where my sympathies would lie in an issue such as we may be faced with. I will certainly do anything I can to help, within the limits of constitutional propriety.'

'Thank you, Humphrey,' Sir Frederick replied. 'I know I can rely on your support, but I've a nasty feeling that events may well move beyond our control.'

'Well, we'll soon know,' said Sir Humphrey philosophically. 'Now that the invitation has gone out, the next move is up to Ernest Twite.'

CHAPTER ELEVEN

The reports which now began to reach Arthur Crabbe from senior ex-colleagues in some of the major ministries were depressingly, indeed alarmingly, of a pattern. He had asked to be given as early an intimation as possible of the major policy objectives of certain ministers so that he might make an assessment of the general thrust of the new Government.

He had, in confidence, explained to his highly placed friends why he needed this information, much of which would merely be confirmation of what had been in the Labour manifesto while the remainder would become public soon enough.

Because of these two facts, his friends felt able to comply without straining their consciences. Indeed their willingness to help was strengthened by a shrewd suspicion that one of the priority objectives of the new administration would be to reduce the power and influence that they themselves traditionally exerted.

How this was to be done was not yet clear, but the rumour was that political appointees were to be introduced into each permanent under secretary's office. These individuals would have access to all departmental papers and would report to ministers in parallel with the PUS. It would also naturally be incumbent on them to inform their minister if, in their view, the PUS or any other senior official was being obstructive or seeking to delay the preparation of legislation.

The first real indication that the manifesto might have understated and indeed concealed the real intentions of the Government came in the report from the Ministry of Defence. The two major points of the manifesto had been unilateral nuclear disarmament and the immediate dismantling of American bases in the United Kingdom with, of course, the withdrawal of all American forces. In parallel with this had been a pledge, which may have given some reassurance to patriotic Labour supporters, that Britain would continue to contribute conventional forces to NATO. What now transpired, so Arthur read with alarm, was that those forces were to be halved. Further to this, trade union membership was to become mandatory for all non-commissioned ranks within the three Services. For serving officers it would remain voluntary, at least for the time being, but was to be compulsory on first commissioning in the future.

Arthur knew these decisions could not have been better calculated to destroy the morale and reduce the fighting efficiency of the Armed Forces if they had been inspired by Moscow as indeed, he reflected, might well have been the case. Once the proposals became known the Chiefs of Staff would, of course, resign in a body and many of the better senior officers would follow their example but, as Arthur knew only too well, their place would be taken by others of lesser ability and integrity who would not find it difficult to persuade themselves that it was their duty to do so.

The report from the Home Office was just as worrying in its own field and again showed that the manifesto had not fully disclosed the Government's intentions. Play had been made with the emphasis to be placed on community policing, but what had not been said was that it was proposed to abolish the post of Chief Constable and to place all local police forces directly under the local police authority, which would be enlarged to have a full time executive body. Care would be taken to ensure that all local police authorities were made up of progressive elements that would fully reflect the Government's views and wishes. These were known to include the abolition of the riot squads and the replacement of the special constabulary by what was referred to as a more democratically motivated force.

The proposals for the prison service were not yet known, so Arthur's informant had written, but Arthur had no doubt that they would also be progressive and enlightened and would constitute a criminal's charter of unique benevolence and understanding, thus further increasing the already unacceptably high risk to the lives and property of law abiding citizens.

The projected financial legislation, so far as the individual was concerned, was nothing short of horrific. In outline it was proposed to institute several measures which, taken together, would effectively and almost immediately ensure the disappearance of what the Government regarded as the privileged classes.

Currency exchange controls were to be established which would effectively impose a near total prohibition on the movement of private funds from the United Kingdom. Emigration would immediately become impossible for anyone who could not be guaranteed a job in the country to which he wished to emigrate and those citizens already living abroad on monies drawn from the United Kingdom would have to pay UK tax as well as that of their country of domicile as all double taxation agreements were to be abrogated.

A wealth tax would be imposed, as forecast in the manifesto but it would not (as had been implied, though admittedly not stated), be a once and for all imposition, but an annual tax. As a concession it would be reassessable on application to take account of investments, property, jewellery, works of art and any other valuables which it had been necessary to dispose of during the preceding twelve months.

Next, and this had been popular with a large number of Labour supporters, the upper limit of taxation was to be set at 100 per cent so that no one would be permitted an income above a certain level, yet to be decided.

The final measure, which had not been disclosed in the manifesto as it would just as surely have lost votes among all but the most active and dedicated supporters of the Labour party was that at the death of a single person, or on the second death in the case of a married couple, the State should be the sole beneficiary. 'Only by measures such as these,' Arthur read, 'together with the immediate abolition of the House of Lords and of all private education to be followed, in the latter case, by the tight control and direction of state education so as to make the youth of the nation more socially aware, can the class system be broken and a people's democracy at last be brought into being.'

Arthur Crabbe considered the evidence and concluded, with little difficulty, that he should advise the Bailiff to be prepared for proposals from Ernest Twite which the Bailiwick would almost certainly consider anti-pathetic if not downright unacceptable. What the specific proposals were, Arthur's Home Office informant had been unable to discover, as they had not been disclosed to officials but had been prepared by Ernest Twite personally with the assistance only of his private secretary and a confidential shorthand typist.

This private secretary, so Arthur had been told by the same informant, had been hand-picked by Ernest Twite. He was a young man named Cyril Smallpeice who was well known within the Civil Service for his left wing views, and who was also a known homosexual. He had first come to Twite's notice during the period that Twite and Stote had worked together within the Inner London Education Authority. In the course of their duty they had visited a Gay

110

Liberation club of which Cyril Smallpeice was a member, having just, as he so originally put it, come out of the closet. Ernest Twite, though certainly not of that persuasion himself, nevertheless took an enlightened view of gays, whether genuine or just viscious experimenters, and had been much taken with Cyril's undoubted intelligence and his left wing sympathies.

While writing his note to the Bailiff, Arthur felt that there was only one crumb of comfort he could offer. His enquiries had revealed that there was, certainly for the immediate and mid-term future, no intention of attacking or even attempting to weaken the position of the Monarchy. Those influential in party affairs were shrewd enough to sense that any such attempt might well bring about the downfall of the Government, while a continuation of the status quo would lend a certain respectability to the more extreme measures in the legislative programme. Should the Government succeed in gaining a second term, then the position might well be different.

But for the moment at least the Privy Council would remain in being. It followed from that, so Arthur felt able to assure Sir Frederick, that there was no apparent threat to the constitutional relationship.

Having completed his note he wrote on similar lines to Podger to warn him of the need for his irregulars to be prepared, and for plans for the possible compromising of Ernest Twite to be completed as soon as possible.

When the Bailiff received Arthur Crabbe's note he immediately asked whether Sir Humphrey was free and able to receive him. The answer to both questions being 'Yes', Sir Frederick lost no time in arriving at Government House. He showed Sir Humphrey the note without comment.

When the Lieutenant-Governor had finished reading it he grunted and then looked quizzically at his visitor. 'Well Fred, what happens now?' he asked. 'What does A do?'

111

'I don't think A, or I in this case, can do a great deal, but at least we're warned that Twite's visit will almost certainly be more difficult and his proposals even less welcome than we had expected.'

'Yes' the other mused. 'I suppose Crabbe will have warned his irregulars?'

'Yes, I feel sure he will have done,' the Bailiff said. 'And in any event I don't feel that I can ask him. In a very real sense the less I know the better. Whatever befalls Twite, if it comes to that, must be seen to come as a complete surprise to me. The only guarantee of that is that it should be a genuine surprise. But tell me, Humphrey, when do you think we can expect firm dates for the visit?'

'Just came in less than an hour ago, Fred. Confirmed that he will arrive p.m. next Thursday, spend Friday with us, Saturday to Monday p.m. with Guernsey, Monday night with us and leave Tuesday morning. In a parallel signal to Guernsey he's apparently said that he doesn't want to be bothered with visiting Alderney or Sark, which has irritated all concerned quite a bit. You may also like to know that he's got off on the wrong foot with me.' Sir Humphrey's tone became grim. 'Do you know, Fred, that private secretary of his had the gall to send my staff a signal, obviously with Twite's knowledge if not on his instructions, to say that his master did not want to be received with a Guard of Honour, as he did not hold with military pomp and ceremony and that it would be quite acceptable if he was met at the airport by the Lieutenant-Governor and the Bailiff. This was the answer he got back.' The Lieutenant-Governor tossed a flimsy across the desk. It read as follows:

'From: Office of the Lieutenant-Governor, Jersey.

To: Home Office.

Personal for Smallpeice from Point. Your ET1/J refers. Dates and times agreed. For your information there is no longer a garrison in Jersey and Mr Twite would not in any event be entitled to a guard. His Excellency, as Her Majesty's representative, does not meet politicians of Mr Twite's standing. Neither does the Bailiff. Please inform Mr Twite that he will be met by myself and by the Bailiff's secretary.'

Sir Frederick blanched slightly. 'Good God, Humphrey,' he said, 'that isn't going to help much, it's practically a declaration of war, before the man's even arrived.'

The General's face reddened and his jaw set obstinately. 'It's war anyway, Fred, and you might as well face up to it. Even if it wasn't I wouldn't dream of letting a little nobody like Twite get away with an insolent signal like that!' It was clear that Sir Humphrey's blood pressure had suffered a sharp rise and his eyes popped menacingly.

'Yes, of course, Humphrey, I take your point,' the Bailiff said in an effort to restore calm. 'But nobody though he may be, he's unfortunately got a good deal of power so far as the islands are concerned.'

'That doesn't excuse ignorance, arrogance and bad manners,' the Governor snapped.

'Has he upset Guernsey in the same way?' the Bailiff asked.

'Yes indeed he has, if anything even more so. James Havelock was on the 'phone just now and he's spitting blood, not only about receiving the same sort of signal that I did, but also at Twite having the effrontery and rudeness to ignore James' advice and to say that he did not consider either Alderney or Sark to be of sufficient importance to warrant a visit. He'd also just got the news that the private secretary fellah is a homo and he hit the ceiling in one.'

Sir Humphrey smiled reflectively, cheered by the memory of the admiral's voice on the telephone. 'He's refusing to put up either Twite or Smallpeice and is arranging for them to be put into an hotel. His exact words, as I recall them,' said the General approvingly, 'were "No bum boy will cross the threshold of Government House so long as I'm here, nor will anyone else who openly condones such behaviour, and that includes bloody Twite." So you see, Fred, that my signal must have been positively welcoming in comparison to whatever James sent.' Sir Humphrey chuckled, his good humour quite restored. 'You know, Fred,' he said, rubbing his hands, 'I'm quite looking forward to watching this encounter from the sidelines. Should be most entertaining, even exciting!'

'I'm sure you are, Humphrey,' said Sir Frederick. The unbiased observer could not have failed to note that he looked depressed and apprehensive and that his tone was bleak.

CHAPTER TWELVE

Before the reports had begun to reach Arthur, Podger had called together those whom he knew he could rely on for the planning and execution of Operation Twite and had asked them to do some preliminary thinking on possible ways of embarrassing, harassing and finally compromising Ernest Twite, should any of these actions prove necessary.

On receipt of Arthur's note he called them together again. With Richard's agreement they met at the Hall as that would be the main scene of action and also because most of those with a role to play would be living there. Almost all of those not living there would be dining at the Hall on the Thursday and the Monday nights.

They sat or stood around in an eager and expectant circle. Scratcher hovered in the background, as no doubt his co-operation would be needed and it was in any event necessary for him to be privy to what was afoot. Besides, Podger thought to himself, he would not be surprised if Scratcher came up with a bright idea or two. Of Scratcher's political reliability there could be no shadow of doubt; he stood as far to the right as did Ernest Twite to the left.

Podger began by telling them what Arthur had learned. 'So you see,' he concluded, 'there seems a very high probability that we shall have to go to the ultimate level and compromise him and, while we're at it, we might as well consider compromising that nasty piece of work Smallpeice as well. Eh? What? In broad outline I suggest we keep at a fairly low level of conflict to start with, that's to

say on the Thursday concentrate perhaps on embarrassment so as to wrong-foot him from the start and put him off
his stroke for the visit as a whole. Then, if we have to as it
seems we will, we can go all out for compromise on the
Monday. How does that strike everyone? Does it fit the bill
or has anyone got a different idea? What? Eh?'

Richard was the first to speak. 'I'm a bit unhappy about
this idea of embarrassing him from the start, though I see
the reasoning behind it. Makes it jolly awkward for Pussy
and me, you know, and I can't see how we can square it
with the normal obligations of a host to a guest.'

'Take your point, Richard. Take your point,' Podger
said. 'I had actually thought of it myself, and to keep your
hands clean, and Pussy's too, of course, we'll have to keep
you out of the front line as it were. It depends what sort of
embarrassment we decide on, but in general I think we
should keep it as non-attributable as possible.'

'What? Make it look like an act of God, or successive acts
of God, do you mean?' asked Connie.

'Absolutely so, old dear,' answered Podger. 'Got it in
one.'

Connie's already ample bosom inflated still further as
she drew a deep breath to calm herself in the face of this
mode of address. There was however a barely detectable
hint of frostiness in her tone when she said 'It's a pity poor
dear Arthur isn't here. I'm sure he'd have the most
marvellous ideas. He is so clever, you know.'

She looked around at those in her audience who had so
far been deprived by a cruel fate of an opportunity of
bathing in Arthur's brilliance.

Pranger was one such. 'Brainy cove is he? Fond of fish, I
suppose, and carrots for night vision, I shouldn't wonder! I
imagine he's at cockpit readiness so why don't we give him
the wire? Arthur, Arthur, scramble, scramble, scramble.
Steer 142 degrees angels zero, join wing formation at the
Hall, or words to that effect. Phone's over there, I fancy.

Why not let's press on regardless, Richard, eh? Summon this Arthur chappie, I say. Sounds as though he might have a wheeze or two up his jumper.'

Connie looked just as Britannia might have looked if she had suddenly discovered a particularly revolting shish kebab on the prongs of her trident. She swelled even further and her resemblance to an overdeveloped pouter pigeon was most marked until, after a second or two, there was a rending noise under her left armpit as a tormented seam gave way in protest.

Before she or Richard could speak, Podger saved the situation by an unusual if not unique display of tact. 'Absolutely, couldn't agree more. Arthur's brain is phenomenal. Should be in the Guinness Book of Records. He's just the chap we want. I mean to say, it would be a pushover if we had his advice.'

'Piece of cake, what?' interjected Pranger with enthusiasm. 'Pukka gen merchant, eh?'

'Bull's eye,' agreed Podger. 'Once those grey corpuscles started to churn in earnest Twite simply won't have a chance.'

Connie looked as Britannia might have done had she discovered on closer inspection that what she had mistaken for a shish kebab was in fact a particularly succulent piece of underdone fillet steak.

'But,' Podger continued, 'unfortunately it's not on. Because Arthur is advising the Bailiff, he genuinely mustn't know our plans, so that both he and Fred can be seen to be above reproach, like some character whose name escapes me. Rather fancy it was an Eyetie female of some sort. Couldn't have been Lucretia Borgia, could it? No, of course not. Silly of me. What?' Podger's brow furrowed in an effort to remember.

There was a quiet cough in the background. 'I rather fancy, Sir, that you have Caesar's wife in mind,' intoned Scratcher.

117

'By Jove, you're right, Scratcher!' Podger's brow cleared as he turned and smiled at his informant. 'Jolly old Caesar's wife it was, though I'm not sure which one. Anyway, What? I mean to say that's why we can't have Arthur. Jolly sad, but nothing to be done about it, I'm afraid. Absolutely nothing, you know, eh? Mean to say, absolutely nothing, what?' he said, apparently confident that repetition would add clarity to his point.

'Jolly bad do,' said Pranger. 'Mission aborted on take-off. What a waste of all those grey cells in the bomb bay!' He sighed sadly and sank back, a spent force for the time being.

Podger once more took control. 'Well now,' he said. 'Has anyone come up with any bright ideas?'

There was a hush, such as might be heard in any lecture hall when questions have been invited from the student body.

Charlie broke the silence. She had been christened Carlotta, after a rich Italian godmother but, as what at the time Pranger and Pansy fervently hoped would be the last of their brood, she had been nicknamed Tail End Charlie, and the Charlie part had stuck. Her intervention was typical of her wicked mind. 'How would it be,' she said tentatively,' if I hovered behind Mr Twite's chair while one of you got him to raise a hand by some means or other. Then I would leap from behind, pop my skirt over it and say "Oh, Mr Twite!!" while someone took a photograph. How about that?' she concluded, smiling demurely, like a milkmaid with ideas.

'Good thinking,' said Podger. 'Exploits surprise. One of the principles of war. Yes, definitely a possible runner, but Phase 3, I fancy. Don't you know, what?'

'It would be even better,' chipped in Urse, 'if you could get him to raise both hands at the same time so that I could get my skirt over the other one.'

'Bang on!' said Pranger. 'Co-ordinated quarter attacks. Just the ticket!'

118

Podger was equally enthusiastic at this proposed escalation. 'By Jove, Yes! What? Pincer movement. Enfilade fire. Perfect ambush! Definitely a possible for Phase 3, but has anyone got anything for Phase 1, the embarrassment phase. Eh?'

'It's jolly difficult, isn't it?' said Pussy. 'I mean, it goes against the grain a bit but I suppose we could get him in the wrong clothes with Scratcher's help. You know, make it black tie if he thinks it's lounge suit, or vice versa. I could also organise a few complicated things to eat so that he'll have to wait and watch before he knows how to tackle them and what implements to use, if any. But it's all pretty minor stuff and if he's thick skinned it won't make much impression on him.'

'Well, it's better than nothing,' said Podger. 'Not a winner, but sound stuff. Don't suppose he ever wears a dinner jacket, in fact don't suppose he owns one, so it would be safe to dress for dinner both nights. If we could think of a way of getting him to drink the water in his finger bowl that might unsettle him,' Podger mused.

'What about a whoopee cushion?' suggested Pansy. 'I know it's a ploy that can only be used once, but it might have some effect in unsettling him. We'd have to blame it on Johnnie for having left it lying around, but you wouldn't mind that, Urse, would you?'

'No, of course not,' said Ursula, 'but do you know that's just reminded me that there's a much better thing on the market now. One of Johnnie's friends had one and I think it's in all the joke shops. It was invented by a Chinaman called Ah Pong and was originally marketed under the trade name of WHO? ME? I think it still sells under that label though it's also packaged and sold with a plain PONG label. Don't ask me how it works because I haven't the faintest, but I expect Johnnie knows. Anyway, it's like a ventriloquist's machine except that whoever is operating it can project a most foul smell instead of a voice. Everyone's

119

in on the joke, except the victim, of course, and looks at him in a pretty meaning manner while he, poor devil, at the apparent seat of this appalling smell, attempts to protest his innocence. But I gather it's so effective in operation that even the victim comes to have doubts. Hence, of course, the original label of WHO? ME?'

Everyone approved in their different way and it was clear that a very definite thumbs up had been accorded this particular idea. There had been a chorus of 'Oh, what fun!', 'Simply unbelievable', 'Good Heavens, what next?', 'Pretty wrinkly, but not bad!', 'Crumbly, but worth a throw', 'I think Arthur might have approved', 'Spot on!' and 'I say, what! Dashed good, what? Yes, dashed good, by Jove.'

Podger brought them back to reality. 'Good show, Urse, yes, good show, by Jove, we'll certainly use that one, by Jove yes! What's next then? Anyone got any more ideas?' His blue eyes, only slightly bloodshot, regarded them fixedly.

Then, when there was no reply, he addressed his host. 'It could be, Richard, it just could be that people might think more clearly, might indeed even be inspired, if you were to, as it were, broach the old cask, what? Mean to say, don't want to seem out of order, or pushy, or trying to give grandmother good advice or anything of that sort but, there's no doubt about it, ideas come more easily once the cork is out.'

Richard was appalled. 'Good God!' he said. 'I've been so carried away by our common problem that I've totally overlooked the first duties of a host. Scratcher! Please see to it that everyone has whatever they would like as soon as you can.'

'Yes, of course, Mr Richard,' said Scratcher, moving into action apparently slowly, but with deceptive efficiency. In no time at all everyone was furnished with the drink of their choice.

'If we review our assets,' Podger, said 'there's no doubt that we've an unusually large dog and an unusually large number of cats at our disposal. Is there any way in which we can exploit either or both of these?'

'Well now, let's see.' Richard was thinking aloud. 'Dolly's a pretty good crotch nudger, but usually only to her favoured friends and I can't see that she's likely to take to Twite in that sense, and still less to Smallpeice. A pity. It tends to unsettle even old friends and might have quite an effect if only we could get her interested, but I don't see how we can.'

There was a deferential clearing of the throat from outside the circle. 'If I might suggest, Mr Richard,' said Scratcher, 'the answer may lie in aniseed. There was a time in my early days when in my professional work I was frequently brought into contact with dogs who might well have been, and indeed often were, relied upon to be hostile. I found that aniseed worked wonders and that it was a veritable panacea, or perhaps I should say laissez-passer. Once they got a good whiff of it the snarls disappeared, the canine eyes twinkled, the tails wagged and it was clear that, in their affections, I ranked close behind Mr Cruft, Mr Spiller and Mr Spratt. It is, I think Sir, not too fanciful to suppose that had I been somewhat older, had blue eyes and been able to sing I would have been acclaimed as a sort of doggie Frank Sinatra. But I digress. To come back to the point, I am sure you will find that aniseed will serve your purpose.'

There was a murmur of respectful acclaim and it was left to Pussy to strike the only questioning note. 'That sounds marvellous, Scratcher.' She looked at him with wide admiring eyes as she spoke. 'But how can it be administered?'

'Not too difficult, I think, Ma'am,' Scratcher replied. 'When I take both gentlemen's clothes for pressing I shall have ample opportunity.'

121

'Roger,' said Pranger, 'Roger, Red Leader. I read you strength niner. Stuff a load of aniseed up the crotch what? Whacko! Great stuff indeed!'

'Precisely, sir,' said Scratcher. 'A little judicious application of aniseed to the seams in that particular part of the garments concerned will meet the bill adequately, I think you will find.'

Pussy let out a long sigh. 'Scratcher, you're marvellous,' she said. 'I've always known it.'

Scratcher acknowledged her praise with a modest and courtly inclination of the head and then proceeded to dispense more drink to those who stood in need. In the van of that body stood Podger, and he reacted to the refilling of his glass as might a flower, drooping in the heat, react to the sound of clear gurgling liquid.

He was once more the man in charge. 'Well, then, that's fixed, eh? What? Aniseed in the strategic spot, and Dolly into action as soon as Scratcher can fix the necessary.' Podger looked at Pussy. 'Better see that she abstains from crotch nudging from now on. That's it. A crotch denial policy. Make her all the keener when she's let loose on Twite and Smallpeice. Can't wait to see her at the charge!' He gave one of his barking, hyena-like laughs.

'Now, what about the cats?' he went on. 'Surely we can use them somehow?'

His hostess looked at him approvingly with her big melting eyes. 'Of course we can, Podger. There must be a way in which they can help. The pussy persons would hate to be left out, I know.'

'Yes,' he said. 'Er, quite. Must be a way. Yes. Definitely. Has to be a way. What? Eh?'

Connie provided the information that put them on the right track. 'You won't have seen it yet, Podger, but Arthur is building up dossiers on Twite and Smallpeice for the Bailiff and also, of course, for us. They're totally nondiscriminatory and are just a collection of known facts, most of which will probably have no bearing at all on Twite's visit. I've had a look at what Arthur's written so far and, as you can imagine, it makes pretty nasty and, in the case of Smallpeice, sordid reading. However, two bits of information that I recall clearly are, firstly, that Twite can't abide cats and, secondly, that Smallpeice adores them. I don't know if that gives us anything to work on?'

Everyone looked at Pussy as the authority on cats. 'Yes,' she said. 'It does, but it's difficult to know what to expect, or what one can do to get the result we want, which is presumably for the cats to mob Twite and put Smallpeice in Coventry. Much as I love them,' she went on, 'I must admit that pussy-people can be quite tiresome at times. They'll often make up to someone who hates cats, and ignore the cat lover totally. So, you see we might get the result we want without doing anything, but you can't be sure. Cats are great teasers and I'm almost certain they've a sense of humour. But it's difficult to say, as pussy-persons don't smile very often and have perfect poker faces.'

'If I might be permitted, Ma'am.' Once more it was Scratcher who had the ready solution. 'I think there is little difference between this problem and the last. It is essentially a matter of assessing the animal's psychology. For dogs, aniseed; for cats, fish. So, for Mr Twite we need something fish-based which will have the effect of making him seem immensely attractive to our feline friends.'

Here Scratcher gave a false and forced smile. 'The dear little things must find him irresistible if our object is to be achieved. The susbstance which will do that is based on Trassie, which is a dried shrimp paste much favoured by the Indonesians, so I understand. Its disadvantage in the natural state is its immensely strong smell, although cooked, so I am informed, it is delicious. It has been marketed in Europe with some tasteless chlorophyll additive which has killed the smell without affecting the flavour. Killed the smell, that is,' Scratcher paused for effect, 'for human beings, but not for animals.'

'You mean it's still got the original niff for them?' asked Pranger. 'Nothing to stop the main force bombing bang on target. By Jove, that's cunning, I must say. Rather like one of those dog whistles that only dogs can hear, eh?'

'Precisely, Sir,' said Scratcher.

'No difficulty about applying it, Scratcher?' asked Richard.

'No. None, Mr Richard. It comes in powdered form and can be covertly applied to whichever bit of clothing may be desired.'

'Sounds as though that'll settle Twite's hash, all right. Submerged in a sea of meowing feline approval. It'll drive him mad,' said Podger happily. 'Now, Scratcher,' he asked, and it said much for Scratcher's standing and magnetism that he should be singled out in this way, 'your track record is absolutely first class so far. Can you cap it all, do the hat-trick, call it what you will, by telling us how to keep the cats away from Mr Smallpeice?'

'As it so happens, Brigadier, Sir, I think I can.' Scratcher would have been less than human if he had not basked in their approbation and sought to prolong the denouement. 'It is not an easy task, as you will appreciate, Sir,' he said. 'Cats are naturally attracted by anything unusual in human beings. They love artists, eccentrics and anyone sympathetic and out of the main stream. They might even, and probably would, be attracted by,' and here Scratcher's lip curled, 'the unusual personality, if I understand it aright, of Mr Smallpeice. But I think we can satisfactorily settle his hash, if I may put it like that.'

Scratcher allowed the tension to rise and the interest in his audience to approach fever pitch. 'Yes,' he continued. 'As I say, I think I can. There's a new substance, just come on the market, which will meet the requirement exactly. It seems as though the manufacturers might originally have been seeking a formula to keep tom cats away at certain periods and overdid things a little. In fact, Sir, not to labour the point unduly, they were so far wide of the mark that they have produced a substance which has so much overkill and so little discrimination that it will keep any cat away from anything, regardless of sex or specie. It is known,' and Scratcher's tone became sepulchral as though to deny the possibility of humour, conscious or otherwise, 'it is known,' he repeated, 'as PUSS OFF. A very reliable product, I believe, and one virtually certain to have the effect which you ladies and gentlemen are seeking.'

Pranger exploded with enthusiasm. 'Puss Off did you say? Great! Right on target! Left. Left. Steady. Bombs gone! Bandits three o'clock high, Red Section. Puss off. Puss off. Go! I like it. Cracking stuff! Just the job.'

His daughter regarded him with a mixture of tolerance and pity. 'Yes, Daddy,' she said, 'I think we all agree.'

'By Jove, yes!' said Podger, once more taking control. 'Frightfully good show, Scratcher, frightfully good. We're really getting somewhere now. So that deals in general with Dolly and the cats. Is there anything else we can think of?'

There was a silence as they considered his words. It was broken by Constance. 'I was wondering,' she said, 'and of course if it was possible it would, I suppose, be harassment and wouldn't be any good so far as embarrassment went.' Her voice tailed away with a hint of despondency. 'And in any event I can't believe that anyone could seriously consider it as harassment, more like an accolade really. Although I don't really know.'

'What,' asked Podger, not unreasonably in the circumstances, 'are you getting at, Connie, my dear?'

'The poltergeist,' she said. 'If we could call that lively spirit to our aid it might prove a powerful ally indeed. But how to do it? We know from Maeve O'Cork that its motivation is the prevention of the sale of the Hall and, as Mr Twite will not be in the market, there will be nothing to

125

alert and activate it. Unless', and here she stopped and looked slowly around the circle of attentive faces, 'unless you, Richard, were to invite Maeve O'Cork to come and stay, in which case the visit of such a one, a psychic persona of great and proven power, might have the desired effect of animating the poltergeist.'

'Yes. Well. It certainly did last time she came.' Richard thought about it. 'There wouldn't be any difficulty in putting her up, would there, Pussy?' Receiving an affirmative shake of the head, he went on. 'No, I thought not. But can we be sure that poltergeist activity would be to our advantage?' He looked around. 'I mean, perhaps Twite might be psychic and regard it as a spirit welcome, right and fitting for one of his standing.'

'I don't think so,' said Constance. 'I shall have to check on it with Arthur but I'm virtually certain that Twite is an atheist and what I believe he calls a rationalist. If so, and I'm sure I'm right, he will be totally dismissive of ghosts and any spirit activity and is liable to be severely frightened if the poltergeist goes into action.'

'Well now,' said Richard, 'this needs a bit of thought. The west wing is spooked to high heaven with recognised residential phantoms. Fully paid up union members, as it were, who may feel that their approach or reaction to Twite and Smallpeice should not be influenced or directed by management. Might object to the mobilisation, enlistment and deployment of the poltergeist, in fact.'

'Spirit world about to tear itself apart?' observed Pranger with enthusiasm. 'Polter-Scabs and Blackleg-Geists. Get the old phantom pickets on the job, what?'

'It's really not a matter for merriment, still less for ribaldry. Indeed, such a display may well have served to forfeit the goodwill of the spirit of whose aid we stand in need,' said Constance, looking at Pranger with something akin to distaste. 'You are quite obviously unaware of the fact that our dear spirit friends have immense sensitivity – in contrast,

126

if I may say so, to some in this room.'

Queen Mary, finding something nasty in her salad, and suffering from indigestion at the same time, might conceivably have looked more disapproving, but Constance would have run her a very close second.

Richard moved in before the breach could widen. 'I think the idea could have a lot in it, but what if they got frightened and decided to move to an hotel? Then we'd be poorly placed for any action in Phase 3, wouldn't we?'

'That's true enough, darling,' said Pussy. 'But surely Government House would ensure that, shall we say, all hotels were fully booked?' She smiled innocently and disarmingly.

'Good thinking,' said Pranger with enthusiasm. 'All diversionary airfields closed, what?'

'That's it,' chimed in Podger. 'Enemy force encircled. All possible lines of retreat blocked and covered. But do you think you can do it, Richard?'

'Yes, I think so,' Richard answered slowly. 'It would certainly be unusual, but this is after all a pretty unusual set of circumstances. I'm sure the Governor's office would agree, and the hotel management would certainly do what they were asked. They might be curious about the reason but they could be relied upon to be discreet.'

'Right. Well, let's fix it up that way, then,' said Podger decisively. 'After all, it's only a precaution against what is not much more than a remote possibility. It presupposes three facts. One, that Maeve O'Cork will accept your invitation, Pussy. Two, that her presence in the Hall will activate the poltergeist, and three that any such activity will put a severe wind up Twite and Smallpeice, sufficient in fact to cause them to move.'

'Or not to move, as the case may be,' corrected Pranger with every semblance of glee. 'Main runway closed, remember? Conditions below minimum for safe take-off and no alternates available. Waste of time even to start engines, let alone taxi.'

'Yes, of course, that's right. Being sure that they're under this roof, come what may, must make it easier to plan for Phase 3.' Richard spoke absently, deep in thought. Then he seemed to take a grip of himself. 'Very well, then, Podger. We'll try and get Maeve O'Cork to come, and I'll set things up with Government House. And I think that's probably about as far as we can go for the moment, isn't it?'

Forestalling any possible disagreement he moved swiftly to reinforce his assumption of authority. 'Some more drinks, please, Scratcher.' He looked round benevolently, his mastiff-like features communicating a somewhat creased and wrinkled goodwill. Pussy was entranced.

'Oh, how lovely,' she said. 'Now I'm really beginning to believe that we'll get that horrid Twite by the . . . . . . what is it? I've forgotten the word.'

'Short and curlies?' suggested Pranger helpfully.

'That's it exactly, Pranger, darling.' She smiled her thanks. 'Short and curlies it is.'

CHAPTER THIRTEEN

Ernest Twite was not in the sunniest of moods as he prepared to leave for Jersey. He was outraged by the telegrams that Smallpeice had received from the secretaries to the two Lieutenant-Governors, and this sense of outrage was fuelled still further by the blunt refusal by the Ministry of Defence of his request for an RAF executive jet to be placed at his disposal. The communication, which was not sent to his office but which was from the permanent under secretary at MOD to the PUS at the Home Office, thus humiliating him, Twite, still further, had read: 'Please inform Mr Twite that save in the case of emergency, and then only when authorised by the appropriate secretary of state, passage on Service aircraft will not be agreed for members of Government below cabinet rank.'

He seethed with fury, and the worst part about it was that it was impotent fury. In each of the three instances there was little, if anything, that he could do about it.

In the case of Jersey, he had already vented his anger on a contrite and wilting Smallpeice for not having known that there was no garrison in the island. That had been a bad mistake. As for his arrival, there was nothing that he could do other than treat the two secretaries in such a way that the press and television, who were certain to be there, might get the message that this was not how he, Twite, was accustomed to being received.

The Guernsey telegram had merely informed him that His Excellency the Lieutenant Governor regretted that it would not be convenient for him to receive Mr Twite and Mr Smallpeice at Government House during Mr Twite's forthcoming visit. No reason had been advanced, and Twite's immediate reaction had been that he should demand an explanation for this perceived but unexplained insult. Then, after second thoughts along the lines that the Governor's wife might be desperately ill, he decided to wait and to gather the reason at first hand when he visited Guernsey.

The refusal from the Ministry of Defence had infuriated him most of all, not because of the refusal itself but because of the phrase 'Member of Government'. He had, as he saw it, been deliberately denied the courtesy title of Minister in a communication from a civil servant of the first rank to a colleague of the same standing. The knowledge that it could be argued that this was technically correct and that the formal title of Minister began at Minister of State level did nothing to improve his temper.

The aggregate effect of these slights and insults had induced a savagery in Ernest Twite which far transcended his normal level of vindictive spite. This savagery of mood had been instrumental in his decision to override the advice, and even warnings, of his departmental staff that what he had in mind to do would, when he eventually disclosed it to them in the strictest confidence, be unacceptable to Cabinet, unacceptable to the House and could even result in a constitutional crisis.

Ernest Twite knew better. He knew he could count on the backing of the Home Secretary and was equally confident that the Chancellor would be short-sighted enough to view his proposals with favour. With those two key figures in agreement, it was most unlikely that a majority of the cabinet would oppose them, whatever their officials might say.

In the House there would be no defection from Labour ranks, so a majority could be forecast with virtual certainty.

130

True, there would be howls of outrage and anguish from the opposition benches, but the certainty that that would be so only served to strengthen Twite's conviction that what he was about to do was long overdue, and that his name would go down in history as the man who had had the courage to end a 900-year-old anachronism, an anachronism which was an insult to the working class and which had no place in the classless society which Labour had promised in their manifesto.

It would also ensure, Twite reflected with malicious pleasure, that the Channel Islands would cease to be so-called tax havens. That this, by driving away foreign banks and crippling the finance sector, would in the short rather than the long term prove disadvantageous to the United Kingdom, bothered Twite not one whit. He was concerned solely with the class struggle. He wished only to see the islanders, made up in his imagination almost exclusively of rich tax evaders, taxed at U.K. rates and, most rewarding thought of all, to see the post of Lieutenant-Governor abolished in both Bailiwicks.

Indeed the Bailiwicks themselves would cease to exist, at least under that title, as Ernest Twite was determined on nothing less than an end to the independence of the Channel Islands. Henceforth they would form part of the County of Hampshire and the inhabitants would pay tax at United Kingdom rates. There would be no more nonsense about Lieutenant-Governors and Bailiffs. The Islands' interests would be represented by one, or just conceivably two, members of Parliament, while the existing States of Deliberation would be remodelled as councils at rural district level, substantive business being handled by Hampshire County Council.

That, Twite reflected with grim satisfaction, would put a full stop to privilege and snobbery, and would be welcomed by the working classes in the islands who did not as yet have the benefit of a strong union organisation, let

131

alone a closed shop. As for the warnings of constitutional crisis, he simply did not believe them. They were no more than the imagined fears of over cautious and nervous officials who had grown resistant to change or reform.

He summoned Smallpeice. 'When do we need to leave, Cyril?' he enquired.

'In about half an hour, dear. I do hope we've got over our nasty grumps.'

Cyril Smallpeice, like many of his unusual persuasion, was intelligent, but this was not immediately apparent as his manner was that of a classic music hall poof. Like Twite, for whom he had a great admiration, he had what he thought of as a social conscience.

It was perhaps to be expected, if not indeed inevitable, that his conscience should be particularly aroused by what he regarded as discrimination against gays, lesbians and ethnic minorities. The blacker those in that latter category were, the more his conscience was pricked. It was quite wrong, he felt, and indeed totally indefensible, that recruitment to the Civil Service should be closed to homosexual negroes, and it was equally a matter for regret and shame that their chances of being elected to Parliament were remote if not actually non-existent. Cyril's ideal under-secretary would have been a gay negro. He sighed as he realised that the forces of reaction and prejudice were such that the realisation of this dream was a long way off.

Meanwhile, he would have to be content with Ernest Twite. And Ernest Twite, apart from his sexual tastes and the colour of his skin was, as Cyril realised, far from being an unsatisfactory substitute. He was sympathetic to gays and lesbians and was indeed helping to swell their numbers by supporting those in education, mostly militant feminists, who were busy confusing young children by teaching little boys to sew and cook and little girls to be mechanics and carpenters.

Above all, Cyril recognised, Ernest Twite had qualities

which he himself could never aspire to but which, nonetheless, he greatly admired. He was ruthless, unforgiving and a bully. For all his small frame and at times waspish and querulous manner, Ernest Twite was butch, and he had Cyril's devotion as well as his admiration.

'Come along now, dear,' he said, when he got no answer to his query. 'You really must cheer up, or poor Cyril will be quite upset. You know we're going to have a simply lovely time in Jersey and Guernsey, and you're going to have your way with all those silly Bailiffs and Lieutenant-Governors. They'll be simply shattered, and Cyril will be so proud of his clever Minister!'

Not for the first time, Ernest Twite congratulated himself on his choice of private secretary. He indulged Cyril Smallpeice when they were in private, whether his chosen role was commentator, rapporteur, jester or, as in this instance, fussy nanny. Whatever the circumstances, Cyril seldom failed to improve his mood.

'You're right, Cyril,' he said. 'We're certainly going to give those stuffed shirts the biggest shock they've ever had!' His mood lightened perceptibly.

'Oh, goodie!' said Cyril.

'You're quite sure the department hasn't leaked, and that my announcement will come as a complete surprise?'

'I've been totally exhausted trying to ensure just that, Minister, and I'm reasonably confident that my efforts haven't been wholly wasted.'

Now that their departure was imminent and they would soon once again assume their public relationship, Cyril slipped back into more formal speech.

'The details might get there ahead of us, but I very much doubt it. Just a general warning that you're not exactly bearing glad tidings from the islands' point of view is all I would expect to have been received at the other end.'

'Good. Apprehension may be no bad thing, so long as they have misjudged the situation. Then, the reality will be

133

likely to strike them with even greater force. I can just see them, can't you? Flabbergasted and destroyed in a few short moments! Think of it, Cyril. Nine hundred years of cobwebs, of stuffy outdated protocol and humbug, swept away on the instant. And swept away, Cyril, by you and by me, for I won't forget that you have had a major part to play in drawing up the new arrangements.'

'Yes, it will be a great moment indeed. But we shall surely not witness their reaction at first hand, shall we? I thought it was your intention, Minister, to make the announcement direct to the press and television immediately on arrival. That is so, isn't it? You will make your major statement – reveal all, in fact – on first arrival?'

'Yes, indeed I will, Cyril. Hit them with everything before they know what's happening.' Ernest Twite's mood was becoming positively buoyant as he tasted his triumph in advance. 'So stupid of them to give me a totally free run with the media like that. Once I've had the microphone for even a few minutes without interruption they'll never recover. I'll have the initiative and I'll make sure I keep it. That's all I want on the aircraft, Cyril, just that page of notes to cover my speech on arrival.'

Twite's humour was quite restored.

CHAPTER FOURTEEN

In the VIP Lounge at Jersey Airport Commander Point and the Bailiff's secretary awaited the arrival of the Air UK Flight. If it arrived at the time now forecast it would be 40 minutes late, due to technical trouble, the artificially cheerful but at the same time disinterested and disembodied female voice informed them. Geoffrey Point regarded the Bailiff's secretary, Roger Taitt, with some solemnity and with a certain tension in his manner.

'Well, Roger, we'll soon know the worst, and I have a feeling it will be pretty bad. But I'm quite sure we were right to persuade our respective old gentlemen, not that they needed much persuading, that a full blown press conference, properly organised, of course, was the right answer, and that Twite should not be pestered on arrival.'

The fact that Geoffrey was only six months younger than the Governor made no difference to the style of address. They both thought of their respective masters with respect and with affection. Because of this, 'old gentlemen' had always seemed a suitable title.

Roger Taitt smiled his agreement. He was a good twenty years younger than Geoffrey, but the two had much in common and seldom saw things differently.

'Yes. "Not be pestered" is a good phrase. He'll be mad as hell!' Geoffrey smiled frostily as he acknowledged the likely accuracy of that forecast.

'I hope you're right. The madder, the better, in fact, though I can't say I'm altogether looking forward to being

135

on the receiving end of his reaction. I just hope he keeps his temper, that's all, and remembers that he's on our ground rather than his own.' His blue eyes took on a cold and distant look.

On board the aircraft, a Fokker Friendship, things were not going well. Twite, having been advised by a colleague, had laid claim to two of the four seats that had more leg room than any other. His bid had not been successful. In the seats he had coveted sat a young man, whose face was familiar, and a girl with a green and orange cockscomb of hair. Twite looked at Cyril and came as close as is possible to hissing in non-sibilants. 'Who's that awful young oaf?' he enquired.

'Ernest, dear,' Cyril answered,' you really must get your act together, you know, get contemporary, if you're going to continue to con all those lovely voters. That's none other than Sylvester Foreskin, the leader of the new rave hit group Circumcision. I don't know who the girl is, but she's probably only one of many like her.'

Ernest Twite considered the matter. To be more accurate, he considered two aspects of the matter. The first was to what degree Sylvester Foreskin might be considered a competition for television coverage. The second was whether there should not be a ceiling on earnings imposed on such as Foreskin. That he could behave in this flashy and ostentatious manner and be so effectively pushy that he could keep a minister out of the best seats might prove many things, but it proved one thing beyond argument. Foreskin was undertaxed, and rather than fiddle around with a structure which, Ernest knew, would be evaded or circumvented, the only answer was an income ceiling. Ernest felt that this was a long overdue reform and that, for private citizens, the top limit should be set somewhere just below the salary which he was currently enjoying. He emerged from his happy vindictive dream.

'Ah yes, Sylvester Foreskin. I knew the face was familiar.

But what about the girl. Isn't she a bit old fashioned with all that cockscomb stuff?'

'Madly, my dear. Madly! No doubt she represents a chapter or period in his career which he wants to preserve, to keep unchanged. So frustrating and embarrassing for the poor girl.'

'What about television, Cyril? You're sure he's no threat, and that Jersey are properly alerted to the importance of my visit and what I shall say on arrival?'

'Well, Ernest dear, I couldn't go quite so far as that. Briefing of the media is in the hands of the local authorities you know, but I've no reason to think that it won't be satisfactory.'

Twite was grumpily reassured. 'I hope you're right. You usually are. But what about these infernal seats? I can't move my legs!'

'They are a trifle tight, aren't they, dear,' answered Cyril. 'But you know, they will have met the criteria laid down by your colleague at the Ministry of Civil Aviation, or is it Transport now? I get so confused by all these changes. Anyway, the lovely man I have in mind is Terence Quiver, one of us at ministerial rank at last or perhaps I should say, more accurately, one of us recognised as being of ministerial rank. Such a lovely man,' he concluded. 'But I do agree, Ernest dear, that he has been the teeniest weeniest bit mean on this matter of leg room.'

'Well,' Ernest snapped peevishly, 'the least we could have expected, apart from the best seats, would have been special attention and complimentary drinks. We haven't had either! What do you have to say to that, Cyril?'

'Oh, Ernest dear. Please don't get so cross. I'm sure it's all a mistake and that that lovely big Amazon of a hostess will kiss it better straightaway.'

The Amazon hove alongside. 'Last orders, gentlemen,' she said. 'We'll be asking you to put your trays in the upright position soon after we begin the descent into Jersey

Airport.'

'Last orders!' Ernest Twite's voice came out as a sort of baffled explosion. 'Last orders, did you say? We haven't had first orders yet!'

'I'm sorry you should have been disappointed', she said. 'But you see, we've had some very important people on board,' she smiled, glancing coyly over her shoulder. 'Sylvester Foreskin, you know. It's not every day that we have someone like him travelling with us. I'm afraid that when that happens the standard of service for ordinary passengers inevitably suffers, however much we may regret it.' She smiled a Junoesque smile. 'But I'm sure any inconvenience you may have suffered has been more than made up for by travelling in such exciting and distinguished company.' Not waiting for an answer, she terminated the exchange with a well worn 'We hope you have enjoyed your flight with us today and look forward to welcoming you aboard in the future.' She passed on, her front teeth bared in a formidable smile and her constrained and massive buttocks demanding passage.

Ernest Twite's fulminations and Cyril Smallpeice's attempts to calm him down were alike interrupted by the crackle of the Intercom

'Ladies and gentlemen, we shall shortly be landing at Jersey Airport. Please remain seated until both engines are stopped and the door is open ready for disembarkation. And please, ladies and gentlemen, on this occasion keep your seats long enough to allow our distinguished passenger, Sylvester Foreskin, to leave the aircraft first, as the media will be waiting. We hope you have enjoyed your flight with us and look forward to having you aboard again in the future. Thank you.'

There was a click as the intercom was switched off, and the captain's words no longer competed with the deeply held views of Ernest Twite, views which he was putting steadily and with a certain measured vehemence to Cyril

138

Smallpeice and anyone else who happened accidentally to be within receiving range.

From time to time the flow of words ceased and nothing but a choking sound emerged. There could be no doubt about it, put even in the most matter-of-fact terms: the Minister was anything but pleased or satisfied with the turn of events. He was, as Cyril would have said, 'Ever so upset, and in a terrible bate.'

He turned on his subordinate. 'Cyril,' he managed to force the words out haltingly, almost choking in his anger and sense of outrage, 'Cyril,' he panted, 'tell that great goon of a girl who I am. Tell her I'm a minister and that I demand to be allowed to leave the aircraft ahead of a—' his voice faltered and choked 'ahead of a—' again he struggled for coherence; 'ahead of a moron like that!'

'Ooh, Ernest dear, don't take on so, please,' said Cyril. 'Think of the votes you might lose if you're reported as being nasty to Sylvester! It simply isn't worth it.'

But Ernest Twite was beyond such psephological calculations. 'Votes or no votes, Cyril, I shall leave the aeroplane before Foreskin! See to it!'

Cyril managed to attract the Amazon's attention, something desperate in his eye communicating the fact that he had need of her assistance. She hove to with a mixture of reluctance and slightly puzzled hauteur.

'Is something wrong, sir?' Disinterestedness gave way to discipline, bolstered by a dawning curiosity. What could it be that the insignificant, ratty-looking little man and his poof of a companion wanted? Vivienne de Jong, born Maud Bolton, wondered. She towered above them and, in an automatic gesture, bared her front teeth. What was left of her plucked eyebrows rose.

It seemed to her that the ratty one was past speech and might need medical attention as soon as they landed. Her professional poise momentarily deserted her. 'Ooh!' she said, addressing Cyril. ''E does look something awful!

Shall I see if we've got a doctor on board? If not we can radio for one to come to the airport.'

Struck by remorse she added, 'I'm sorry, luv, that I didn't notice 'e'd been taken bad before, or I'd 'ave done something sooner.'

Her elocution lessons and her deportment training deserted her and she was, for those few moments at least, plain Maud Bolton, full of concern for what she took to be an unfortunate in need of her help and comfort; vulnerable and off guard, full of human concern.

This glimpse of the real person behind the professional exterior did not last long. As she listened to the words of Cyril Smallpeice the transmogrification from Maud Bolton to Vivienne de Jong proceeded apace, and it was an unadulterated Vivienne de Jong, seemingly even taller and more formidable, who listened to his closing plea.

'So you see dear, don't you,' Cyril finished; 'Mr Twite, as a Government minister, is far more important than a pop star, and you really must let him off first. You will, won't you?' he ended with an engaging smile.

Vivienne de Jong considered the matter. They were already taxi-ing in, and her ample flanks denied all passage.

'No,' she said. 'I won't. The captain has absolute authority on this aircraft and he has already decided that Sylvester Foreskin, who is a guest of the airline, should leave first. Even if I wanted to do as you say, and I don't, I couldn't without seeking his authority, and it's far too late for that.'

As though in justification and illustration of her words the aircraft turned to starboard, the gentle pressure of the brakes being applied communicated itself to those sitting within the fuselage and the engine note died as they came to a stop and, simultaneously, there was the clatter of the steps being wheeled up to the rear door.

Ernest Twite struggled to his feet, spluttering. 'I am a minister of the Government, and I demand to be let off this aircraft first, before anyone else, before that pop star!'

Vivienne de Jong looked down on him without apparent sympathy. Her face remained devoid of emotion and there was no warmth in it. Had it been a 1930s movie she would undoubtedly have said 'Is that so?' As it was she said nothing, but allowed her attitude and her sheer physical bulk to speak for her. Then she resumed her professional smile, though her eyes remained cold. 'I always vote Conservative myself, she informed the near gibbering Twite.

Turning her back on him she took a bright farewell of Sylvester Foreskin and continued to block the aisle as he posed, smiling and waving, at the top of the steps for the benefit of the cameramen. As he descended the steps the cameras and newsmen closed in to interview him and she stood aside to allow the other passengers to disembark.

First among these, by dint of unashamed pushing, was Twite. As he passed Vivienne he gave her a malevolent look. In a choked voice he said 'Your chairman shall hear of this,never fear!'

As he emerged from the aircraft door, closely followed by Cyril, he attempted to reassemble his features into something approaching normality for the benefit of the waiting cameras, and rehearsed, for the hundredth time, the startling phrases with which he proposed to catch the headlines and signal the end of an era to this island nest of rich idlers and tax evaders.

But where were the cameras, and where were the interviewers and jostling newpaper men?

Slowly it dawned on him that something was wrong. There were cameras and reporters in abundance but they were all clustered around Sylvester Foreskin. But what of his own arrival? Was the visit of a minister of lesser importance and news value than that of a pop star? The shattering and unbelievable suspicion that it might have been judged to be so by the media began momentarily to form in his mind.

141

Then, suddenly, he knew where the blame lay. It would not be the Media. They would not have ignored and insulted him in this fashion unless there had been direction or persuasion on the part of the island authorities. Scarcely crediting the conclusions that he himself had been forced to draw by the evidence of his own eyes, he turned pale, and his fury was such that his legs began an uncontrollable trembling and his breathing became so rapid that it interfered with the operation of his vocal chords.

He was about to attempt to make Cyril privy to the cauldron of emotion which was seething within him when Geoffrey Point and Roger Taitt came forward.

'Mr Twite?' Geoffrey said in a matter-of-fact tone. 'I'm Geoffrey Point, His Excellency's secretary, and this is Roger Taitt, the Bailiff's secretary. You, I imagine,' his level and expressionless gaze shifted to Cyril, 'must be Mr Smallpeice. If it is convenient,' he addressed Twite once more, 'I shall now conduct you to the Hall to meet your host and hostess, Group Captain and Mrs Fox. His Excellency has made his official car available and we can leave immediately if you are ready. Immigration formalities have been waived, and a Government House car will bring your luggage on later. Shall we go?'

While Geoffrey had been talking, some colour had returned to Ernest Twite's cheeks and his breathing had become a little easier and less rapid. But his legs still trembled and his voice, when he spoke, had a marked quaver.

'But this is a disgrace! Why is there no press and television? Why have not proper arrangements been made for me to be interviewed on arrival? Is the visit of a minister such an everyday and minor occurrence that it is to be ignored? Who is responsible for this, this', his voice rose to a querulous crescendo and he shook, as if with an ague, 'this insult to the Crown? I demand to know!'

Geoffrey regarded him thoughtfully. 'I think perhaps, Mr Twite, we would do well to pursue this matter elsewhere.

142

This is after all a public place. However, I will say this. It is not customary, nor would it be seemly, for important visitors to the island to give press or television interviews before they have called on the Lieutenant-Governor and the Bailiff. The arrangements that have been made, which include a full dress press interview tomorrow, have been made with the approval of both those gentlemen. So far as an insult to the Crown, as you term it, the matter simply does not arise.'

'What do you mean, "does not arise"?' Twite demanded furiously. 'I am a minister and, as such, I represent the Crown! I have been insulted and so, therefore, has the Crown! Let us at least be clear on that point, Commander!'

Geoffrey regarded him stolidly, and with little apparent favour. 'Mr Twite,' he said flatly but with measured emphasis, 'I am afraid you are suffering from a misapprehension. No one does, or can, represent the Crown in this island except His Excellency the Lieutenant-Governor, who is Her Majesty's personal representative.' For the first time his eyes glittered and his expression hardened. 'And now, Sir, it is I think time to leave. I shall lead the way.'

Geoffrey turned abruptly and strode towards the big black Daimler that stood waiting, its uniformed chauffeur ready at the door. Twite and Smallpeice followed, Cyril doing his best to calm his minister down.

Roger Taitt, his duty done, moved towards his own car and considered the account which he would shortly have to give to Sir Frederick of the dramatic start to the minister's visit. Roger was a trifle worried. It was one thing to try and get Twite off balance. It was quite another, and could turn out to be counterproductive, to have put him into such a blinding rage. They had not calculated on Sylvester Foreskin and the frustrations which, Roger guessed, must have taken place on the aircraft. Again, of course, Geoffrey was hardly the man to turn away the wrath of a man like Twite, whom he would instinctively despise. All his training made for directness of speech and action. He would remain polite so long as Twite's behaviour stayed within bounds, but that was all.

Ernest Twite settled himself into the back seat of the Daimler and continued to glower. Geoffrey climbed in beside him, leaving Cyril to take one of the two occasional seats that could be pulled out when required. The Daimler drew smoothly away, its engine note the merest whisper. The noise, or lack of it, was the catalyst for speech.

Twite could no longer contain his thoughts, thoughts made more vehement by the vicarious pleasure which, in spite of himself, he could not help feeling at riding in this luxurious motor car.

'Ridiculous extravagance!' When Geoffrey made no reply he added, 'Even the Prime Minister uses a Rover, and cabinet ministers use Ford Granadas.' Twite forebore to add that junior ministers like himself had to make do with whatever car the Government car pool sent them. But the thought rankled.

Geoffrey still did not speak, but his jaw took on a more than usually obstinate set.

'I suppose it's all down to the taxpayer as usual!' continued Twite and then, recollecting that the citizens of Jersey were in his view absurdly lightly taxed, he added, 'the English taxpayer I mean. No doubt you've got some fiddle going to make sure that that's so!'

Geoffrey's tone was icy as he turned towards Twite. 'To take your points seriatim, Mr Twite. You will find that a Daimler or a Rolls Royce is the standard official vehicle for those appointed as Her Majesty's official representative, be they a Governor-General, a Governor, a Lieutenant-Governor, a High Commissioner or an Ambassador. The Prime Minister, and still less more junior ministers,' here Geoffrey permitted himself the luxury of a sniff, 'do not fall within that category. However, you know full well, or at least should know full well, that the Prime Minister does use a

Daimler whenever it is appropriate to do so.

'On your second point,' and here Geoffrey's eyes, which already resembled blue ice, took on an even sharper glitter, 'the upkeep of His Excellency's establishment, including this motor car, is paid for out of crown dues, revenue surrendered to the island some years back. Not a penny of taxpayers' money is involved!'

Ernest Twite made a strangled noise but no recognisable word passed his lips. Cyril Smallpeice had winced as Geoffrey made his points, and now sat nervously and surreptitiously wringing his hands.

Nothing more was said until the Daimler slowed and drove through the main gates of the Hall, themselves an impressive introduction to what was to come. As they continued down the long drive Geoffrey said, somewhat unnecessarily, 'This is the Hall. No doubt your host and hostess will be waiting to receive you.'

CHAPTER FIFTEEN

Scratcher approached the side door of the Hall just as the Daimler turned in through the gates. He knew, from telephoning the airport, that the flight had been 40 minutes late, and he knew to a hairsbreadth how long the road journey would take at that time of day. He moved with an unhurried and measured tread. He was in an expansive and anticipatory mood.

Always, when there were guests staying at the Hall or whenever there was formal entertainment of any kind, there was a truce between himself and Mrs Jones, a truce they both realised was essential if the Hall was to give of its best, which, as a result of their joint efforts, it never failed to do. But a truce on major confrontations, which both depended on for their adrenalin flow, did not mean that point scoring was put totally into abeyance during those periods when, by mutual agreement, grosser insults were withheld.

Scratcher reckoned that, by any criterion, he had come off best in that morning's skirmish, and it had certainly been no more than that. Mrs Jones' deafness could be a formidable weapon on her side when she chose to fall back behind its ramparts or to advance it as a major piece of artillery in a formal and major engagement. But when she was relaxed and off guard, as in this current truce period, it made her vulnerable to verbal feint and double feint, should anyone be so unkind as to seek to take advantage of it.

Scratcher had no scruples on those grounds. He was uncomfortably aware that, over the years, Mrs Jones had got the better of their major exchanges and therefore, so he reasoned, it was all the more important for him to redress the balance by expert sniping whenever opportunity offered.

Today Mrs Jones had played into his hands. He had merely penetrated the outer perimeter of the kitchen defences to confide to Mrs Jones the information that the visitors were about to arrive soon.

She struggled into wakefulness from her afternoon nap. 'He's not a coon, Mr Itch! He's as white as you are, even if he does come from Birmingham. We haven't all got your prejudices, you know!' Slowly it dawned on Mrs Jones, from Scratcher's hurt expression, that she had got things wrong and had misunderstood his message. She hastened to make amends. 'You know, Mr Itch, the last thing I want is a row.'

Scratcher matched smile for smile. 'Yes, I know, Mrs Jones,' he replied. 'You are an old sow.'

She nodded amicably, and resumed her nap.

Scratcher hugged himself in silent victory. Now, standing by the door, flexing his fingers in preparation for the opening of hostilities, he checked that the right amount of aniseed was ready for him to administer, with feather touch, as unwelcome and unworthy guests passed through the door. Aniseed, he felt, would be enough to start with. The cats could be brought into play later. All that was necessary now was to tip Mr Twite and his secretary just slightly off balance before Mr Twite made his call on the Lieutenant-Governor and on the Bailiff.

The journey from the front gates to the Hall itself had not been without its effect on Ernest Twite. The spaciousness, the rare shrubs and noble trees, dominated by a giant cedar, made a perfect setting for the Hall, which was itself a most imposing building. Twite's feelings were in part those which might have animated his grandfather, or even his father, those of a would-be servant without references who sought a position in the great house. But transcending those feelings natural to his bloodline and his deserved place in society were those that the tolerance of the present century had allowed him to exploit. By criminal deceit which, outside of politics, might well have been actionable, he had contrived to appear all things to all men while remaining an embittered and implacable enemy of what he loosely termed 'The Establishment'.

The need to woo voters was past, and he could now show his true colours. The Hall was without question an Establishment house, and his political self told him that he should react accordingly. On the other hand, so the spirit of his grandfather urged, and would not be entirely denied, there were other considerations. The Foxes might be bloated plutocrats he, Ernest Twite, was dedicated to taxing out of the Hall into a suburban semi. On the other hand, they were undoubtedly of what his grandfather would have called 'The Quality' and were offering their hospitality to him, Twite, who before 1946 could only have gained admittance to the Hall through the tradesmen's entrance.

For a few moments the dichotomy unmanned him and it seemed possible that a new Ernest Twite, someone less embittered and less full of bile, might struggle to the surface. But only for a few moments. By the time the Daimler drew to a halt, Ernest Twite was once more back in full command, all incipient weakness suppressed and all senses alerted for expected slight or insult.

The door was opened by a grave and dignified figure whom Twite correctly took to be the butler. He inclined his head and enquired 'May I take your hat, Sir?'

'Can't you see I haven't got one?' came the peevish reply. Scratcher pursed his lips in what could have been interpreted, and indeed was by Ernest Twite, as a disapproving gesture. 'Ah. Quite so, Sir,' he intoned. 'Good afternoon, Commander,' he said, looking at Geoffrey over the top of Cyril's head.

'Good afternoon, William,' replied Geoffrey, aware that this was an occasion when Scratcher's formal mode of address should be employed.

'And now, gentlemen,' Scratcher continued, taking notice, if only verbal, of Cyril for the first time. 'If you will please follow me. The Group Captain and Mrs Fox are expecting you.'

As he turned, his eyes fixed on Twite's trousers. 'Excuse me, Sir,' he said, and bent down to remove a large white thread before resuming a stately advance. Arrived at the sitting room door, Scratcher stood to one side and announced the visitors in tones which would have earned him honours in any toast masters' competition

'Mr Twite, Mr Smallpeice and Commander Point, Ma'am.'

Ernest Twite just had time to be aware of a very pretty dark woman and a large man with a creased and worried expression, both with polite welcoming smiles on their faces, before becoming fully taken up by the effusion of his canine welcome. Pranger's crotch denial policy had certainly had an effect on Dolly. She took off for Twite's crotch like an overweight greyhound which had just sighted its first hare for months.

And what a delicious crotch this new found friend of the family had! Its peculiar smell acted on Dolly like an elixir, and she nudged and tossed and wagged her massive tail in a fever of enthusiasm.

In the few seconds that it took Richard to disentangle Dolly from the assaulted guest, Ernest Twite had been effectively put off balance and his confusion was only equalled by the pretended embarrassment of Richard and Pussy. Apologies were extended and concern expressed.

In the comparative calm which succeeded the brief period of canine action, Geoffrey managed to effect the introductions. He finished by reminding everyone that the

Minister and Mr Smallpeice would soon have to leave for the Minister's calls on the Lieutenant-Governor and the Bailiff.

Pussy was the attentive hostess. 'Of course, Geoffrey. But I think there's time for a cup of tea or a drink first, isn't there?' Not waiting for an answer she prattled on, smiling at Twite and Smallpeice. 'But I'm sure you'd like to see your rooms first. Let me lead the way, and then you can come back for a drink before you go. I'm sure you must have had tea on the aircraft,' she added, thereby unconsciously twisting a knife in Ernest Twite's smarting wound.

She led off accompanied, by four of the most supercilious looking cats that Twite ever remembered seeing. Had he known the customs of the Hall he would have taken uneasy note of the fact that the normal complement of cats-in-waiting had been increased. As it was, he felt nothing more than the vague aversion which was always brought on by the sight of cats and still more, as in this instance, by feline company. Cyril Smallpeice was not so affected. In fact, he was entranced by the elegance of the escort, led on this important occasion by Emma.

'Oooh! What darling pussycats. Cyril thinks you're just the most adorable furry bundles!'

The evident sincerity of his view was not without its effect on his hostess. She made no remark but no one, she reasoned, could be all bad who was such an obviously sincere cat lover. Her admittedly low opinion of Cyril rose a point or two and momentarily she felt a twinge of guilt at the sad fate that awaited him once Puss Off had been applied to his clothing.

At the entrance to the west wing the cats halted and settled down to await their mistress' return. If Dolly had been with them she would have put her tail between her legs and started to whimper. The cats, being rational and pragmatic animals, made no such foolish demonstration. They simply recognised that the west wing was haunted and declined to cross its portals. The entrance to the west wing was marked not by a door but by thick velvet curtains which could be drawn to minimise the draught in the long corridor that stretched ahead of them. The curtains also served as a landmark, as Pussy proceeded to explain.

'All these doors look just the same, so the best way of knowing which is your room is to remember how many doors it is past the curtains. Your's is three beyond, Mr Twite, which is here.' She opened the door. 'And yours, Mr Smallpeice, is the next one, four beyond. I've put you in adjoining rooms as I'm sure you'll have work to do from time to time. There's a telephone in your room, Mr Smallpeice, in case you have need of it. I think you'll find you have everything you need, so we'll see you downstairs in a few minutes.' She flashed them a quick smile and left them.

Their departure from the Hall followed soon afterwards without further incident. Left to himself, Twite would have elected to call only on the Bailiff. His business was strictly political and it was, in Twite's view, no concern of the Lieutenant-Governor, even though his post would be swept away. But Twite was not left to himself. He was steered by Geoffrey Point, and Geoffrey steered him first to Government House.

The interview was stiff and formal. The surroundings brought out the worst in Twite and his manner was even ruder and more arrogant than usual. He deliberately avoided the correct form of address of 'Your Excellency', or even the courtesy of 'Sir' due to a distinguished soldier and a much older man. His chosen opening was 'Hullo'. The General's manner was frosty, and once it was clear that Twite did not propose to make any substantive disclosure, he terminated the call with a stiff 'I have work to do Mr Twite. I will not detain you further.'

Geoffrey hustled Twite and Smallpeice from the room before the former realised that he had been dismissed. He was out of the room and on his way to the Daimler before he fully took in what had happened.

'I trust, Commander,' he spluttered, 'that the Governor is not so rude to all his visitors!'

'The matter has not been put to the test, Mr Twite. He has never before received a visitor so uncivil as yourself. And now, if you will be so good as to get into the car, we have some ten minutes to waste before Sir Frederick will be ready to receive you.'

The call on the Bailiff was almost equally brief. There were only four people in the room, the fourth being Sir Arthur Crabbe in his role of honorary political adviser to the Bailiff. Twite said bluntly what he intended should happen and enjoyed the electrifying effect that his words had on his audience. A shocked and white-faced Sir Frederick looked at Twite with something close to disbelief.

'I find it hard to give credence to your proposals, Mr Twite. They will certainly not be acceptable to the people of Jersey.'

'They are not proposals, Sir Frederick. On the contrary they are decisions which need only the ratification of Parliament, and that is assured. The people of Jersey will have no option but to accept them.'

'I warn you that we shall appeal to the Privy Council, Mr Twite.'

Twite smiled, his expression a mixture of arrogance, venom and superciliousness. 'You do just that!' he said.

The Bailiff looked at him with distaste.

'And you propose to disclose your plans in full at tomorrow's press conference?' he enquired.

'Certainly.'

'Then I must warn you again that you will be roughly handled by the media.'

'I'm quite used to that. The lackey press is always on the side of reaction and automatically opposes democratic progress. And I need no warnings or advice from you, Mr Bailiff, thank you all the same,' he ended impertinently.

This was too much even for Sir Frederick, who was essentially a man of peace.

'In that case, Mr Twite, we may consider this interview terminated.' He rang the bell for Roger who, correctly interpreting the look on the Bailiff's face, shepherded Twite and Smallpeice from the office without waiting for instructions.

Twite left with a sneering smile on his face. Cyril Smallpeice was also smiling, full of admiration for his master's butch performance. He had, Cyril reflected, really laid it on and no doubt he would perform just as toughly at the press Conference. Geoffrey, who had been waiting in Roger's office, took charge of them for the journey back to the Hall.

Left to themselves, the Bailiff and Arthur Crabbe gazed at one another in mute despair. Arthur was the first to break the silence.

'I blame myself, Sir Frederick, for not having foreseen this possibility. But, really, it goes so far beyond the bounds of what anyone might have considered reasonable that such a thought never crossed my mind.'

'Don't blame yourself, Arthur. No one could have foreseen this. I shall fight that awful little man, of course, but I'm very much afraid that he's worked it out pretty carefully and that we've little chance of success by using normal means.' Here he regarded Arthur quizzically.

'So, Sir Arthur, deeply grateful though I am to you for your advice, I feel that matters have now progressed to the point where you might now more usefully exercise your talents in what we may perhaps term a less orthodox field. A field of which I have no knowledge, but some hope!' The Bailiff permitted himself a slight smile, which Arthur returned.

When Arthur Crabbe had gone, Sir Frederick telephoned first Sir Humphrey and then the Bailiff of

Guernsey. Sir Humphrey took the news calmly, merely remarking 'Really doesn't surprise me, Fred. He's such an awful little rat that he's obviously capable of anything and totally closed to any reasoned argument. You'd like me to tell Havelock, I take it?'

'Yes, please, Humphrey. I'm just about to ring Bill Dumaresq,' came the reply. 'We'll talk tomorrow.'

The reaction of Sir William Dumaresq was much less calm. He had not had as good information as Arthur Crabbe had managed to obtain, and the shock was therefore all the greater.

'Good God. The frightful little shit. I simply can't credit it. You're sure you've got it right, Fred? Yes, of course you have, it's just that I can't believe it. Well, he'll get a pretty warm reception here, that I assure you! I thought Havelock was being a bit high-handed in refusing to receive the pair of them, but it looks as though he was absolutely right.'

That and more like it. The two Bailiffs commiserated with one another, and rehearsed the action that it was constitutionally open to them to take. Finally they agreed various contingency and clandestine measures which it might be prudent to take on a non-attributable basis. When they replaced their telephones neither man could be said to be confident, or even optimistic, but they were at least agreed.

Sir Frederick rang the bell for Roger and told him what he wanted done. He could be relied upon to convey the impression that what he would say had in no way derived from Sir Frederick himself but was merely his, Roger's, reading of what Sir Frederick would have wished to see done, had it been possible to consult him on so delicate a matter.

His instructions were threefold. To get straight on to the boss men of the press and television to alert them to what Twite would say tomorrow, so that their most waspish interrogators would have time to be prepared. To sound out the trade union leader, who was as well aware as the next man of the undesirability of disturbing existing arrangements, on the possibility of mounting pickets and spontaneous demonstrations at short notice; and finally and most delicately, to convey to the chief of police the thought that some slight delay in rescuing Twite and Smallpeice from a rough handling might not be altogether unwelcome and could be attributed to a shortage of constables caused by the need to police the trade union pickets.

Sir Frederick felt he could do no more. The measures which he had just initiated would have an effect, but salvation could only come, if salvation was possible, through the efforts of Crabbe's irregulars.

CHAPTER SIXTEEN

The news that the Twite gauntlet had been thrown down reached the Hall very quickly. Arthur lost no time in informing Podger, who passed the vital intelligence on to Richard with a request for maximum harrassment. But even before this word had been passed the opening shots of the campaign had been fired. Literally. Because the poltergist had awoken.

As Scratcher admitted Twite and Smallpeice to the Hall, their ears were beset by a cacophany of banging trays and falling pictures.

'What's that, William?' asked Twite, startled.

'I'm sure I couldn't say, Sir,' replied Scratcher. 'Unless, of course, you mean the poltergeist,' he added in a matter of fact tone.

Just at that moment the vulturine form of a scrawny female with red hair, flying beads and bobbing Adam's apple hove into view and regarded them with staring eyes, her great beak of a nose thrust forward like a game dog at the point.

'Have no fear,' she said. 'Our spirit friends have merely detected some change in aura. Can it be that either one of you two gentlemen has it in mind to purchase the Hall?'

Their staring uncomprehending expressions gave her her answer.

'No? Well, then, it can only be my own presence which has excited them,' she said somewhat complacently.

'That, of course, is the penalty that one is liable to pay for

156

being a psychic personality when one visits haunts such as this.' She raised her right arm.

'Be calm, restless spirit. Relax and seek peace!'

There was an immediate diminution of sound, but it was obvious that not all troops under command had received the cease fire. Trays continued to impact and pictures to fall, though in decreasing numbers. Maeve O'Cork turned to the goggling Twite and Smallpeice and, arranging her features in what might have passed for a shy and fetching smile in a get-together of bald headed eagles, said 'I trust you will not be offended if I revert to American usage. I have often found it most effective when the dear spirit world gets a shade over excited.' Facing the source of noise she drew herself to her full height and thundered –

'Now hear this! This is Maeve O'Cork speaking. Pipe down on pain of immediate loss of privileges!'

There was a crescendo of noise as though in recognition of and applause at the firm smack of authority and then, abruptly, there was dead silence.

She smirked at her incredulous audience. 'You see' It is quite simple. Even the most unruly spirits will obey. Though, of course,' and here she contrived to resemble a young and shy vulture who was nothing if not self-effacing. 'Though of course,' she repeated, 'I cannot deny that my fame as a medium makes it that much easier. The name of Maeve O'Cork is a byword in the spirit world.'

Twite and Smallpeice looked at her with varying degrees of alarm. Neither was quite sure whether he was dealing with some elderly and deranged female who had merely taken advantage of the noise made by some workmen in the next room, or whether they were looking at a famous medium and had been witness to a poltergeist haunting. Both felt uneasy in the extreme.

Cyril could come up with no more than a long quavering 'Oooh!' indicative of his nervous state. Twite, though made of sterner stuff, was conscious of no longer being in control of the situation.

The butler had melted away. There was no trace of either the Group Captain or Mrs Fox and, although he knew there were other guests staying at the Hall, he had not yet met them and, for all he knew, they might be no more stable than this Maeve O'Cork who had so animated the last few moments. He clung to one impression. Unless he was completely wrong, Maeve O'Cork had been quite positive on one point. And that was that the Hall was haunted. He pursued this one fact.

'Am I to understand, Madam, from what you say that this house is haunted?' he enquired in a somewhat unsteady voice.

'But of course!' Maeve O'Cork answered. 'This is one of the great classic houses of Great Britain so far as spirit activity is concerned. The west wing alone has a classic pattern of haunting which has intrigued many authorities.'

'The west wing, did you say? Oh, no!' Cyril all but wailed. 'I simply can't bear it! That's where our rooms are.'

'You need not feel that you have cause for alarm. Indeed, you should feel privileged at being about to undergo an experience that many would deeply envy. I do not think that either of you is likely to be visited.' She regarded them with her vulture's head cocked to one side. 'No, I feel sure you will not be visited, as you do not emit the right vibrations and your aureole is all but non-existent, but you will certainly know of their presence by the chanting and by the organ music.'

Ernest Twite felt there was no answer that could usefully be made and, smiling somewhat uncertainly, he moved towards the west wing, a plaintive Cyril at his heels.

'It's too, too awful. I know I simply shan't sleep a wink!'

'Well, we're stuck with it for tonight,' said Ernest, 'and we leave for Guernsey tomorrow and won't be back here until Monday. If we find that we're in any way disturbed tonight, then we can book into an hotel for Monday night.'

Cyril had to rest content with that.

Pussy's informal party had gone by the board. There were now nine staying at the Hall with the addition of Maeve O'Cork. Ernest of the Three Widows had been invited as her dinner partner, so making ten. But Pussy had felt she simply had to invite Constance and Arthur because of Constance's relationship with Maeve O'Cork which, though Connie would have maintained she was no more than a simple acolyte, seemed fast to be approaching that of owner-manager. And that made twelve, which was a bad number for seating, so Podger and Prue had been called to the colours to make up a table of fourteen. Scratcher had confirmed that neither Twite nor Smallpeice had dinner jackets with them, so word had gone out that the dress was black tie.

The timing of the dinner was 7.30 for 8, but the activists met a good hour earlier in Richard's study, where they would not be disturbed. Scratcher was again present as an observer.

Arthur set the scene with a report of Twite's insolent performance in the Bailiff's office. Because it was a first-hand report, and because he was Arthur Crabbe who was nothing if not meticulously accurate, they had to believe what he told them. Even so they had difficulty in accepting the enormity of what Twite was hell bent on doing.

Only Pranger was bold or stupid enough to voice his incredulity. 'You sure, Arthur, old man? Sure it's the pukka word and that you're not handing out duff gen?' A freezing look and a silence you could cut answered his question.

When Arthur had finished they sat for a few moments in a silence broken only by snorts and mutterings as their disbelief gave way gradually to a collective fury. As they looked at one another it was clear to each of them that they were of one mind. Twite had forfeited any claim to sympathy and there was no reason, indeed the reverse, for them not to mete out the worst treatment that they could

159

jointly devise. Smallpeice, as an accessory, shared his master's guilt and would receive much the same handling.

Podger broke the silence. 'Well now, Arthur. That's a great help. Thanks very much. Puts us in the picture nicely.' He ruminated briefly. 'You know, in some ways his having come out in the open and having adopted such an extreme position, if you know what I mean, what? makes it easier for us. We don't have to consider whether we should do this or that, but just go ahead and give him the full treatment.'

'Give him the gears, eh?' said Pranger with enthusiasm. 'Full throttle and pile the Gs on so that he'll black out if he tries to stay with us. Wizard show!'

'Yes, something like that,' agreed Podger, 'though I don't think we want to depart from the framework of our original plan. Maximum harassment is the cry for the moment, and we should keep the compromise phase until Monday night, by which time they'll both be a bit groggy.' They murmured their agreement.

'I think things aren't going too badly,' said Richard. 'It was a marvellous idea of yours, Connie, to enlist Maeve O'Cork as an unconscious addition to our ranks. I understand from Scratcher that the poltergeist came in absolutely on cue and put the wind up the two of them when they came back a little while ago. Isn't that so, Scratcher?'

'The two gentlemen did appear somewhat animated, Sir, but their apprehension seemed to relate more to the west wing than to the poltergeist.'

'Yes, well, we're just going to have to hope for the best so far as the west wing is concerned,' said Richard. 'Just have to hope that the phantom organist is on form and that the chanting is up to scratch. Nothing we can do about it if they're in a temperamental mood and decline to perform — unless, that is,' and he looked suddenly at Connie, 'unless you think Maeve O'Cork could stir them up into giving a rousing performance once Twite and Smallpeice have turned in?'

'I'm sure she could,' said Connie, 'I've every faith in the ability of that wonderful woman.' Her eyes shone.

Scratcher coughed deferentially. 'I cannot speak for the chanting, Sir,' he said, addressing Richard, 'but we are what I believe is known as "solid" on the matter of the organ music. I took the liberty of hiring a small organ this afternoon from the music shop and it is currently secreted in the west wing. I shall be happy to give a rendition if the phantom organist fails to oblige by, should we say, 3 a.m.?'

'Scratcher darling, you really are a genius!' cried Pussy, clapping her hands in her enthusiasm, an enthusiasm which was reflected by the whole group. Though somewhat embarrassed by the involuntarily excessive warmth of Pussy's mode of address, Scratcher was nonetheless well pleased with their reception of his initiative.

'Right then,' said Podger. 'Battle stations, what? Everyone knows the general line and the one or two set piece effects. Remember that everything has to look natural.' Habit nearly made him finish with the routine 'Any questions?' but he checked himself just in time.

'Roger,' said Pranger. 'Message received and understood. Everyone on the top line with fingers out ready to give the old "two six" when required, what?'

'Ah, yes, yes indeed,' said Arthur, 'though I must confess to a certain ignorance, perhaps it would not be unduly exaggerating the case to say near total ignorance, of what you intend.'

'Jolly good thing that that should be so, Arthur, old man. That way your reactions will be totally natural and will give a bit of cover to some of us who'll be having to put on a show of surprise.'

The word 'cover' jerked Pranger's head out of his large whisky glass. 'Cover! That's it, Arthur, top cover! Make sure you're not making contrails and remember to come at them out of the sun! Tallyho!'

'Er. Quite so, quite so, er, Pranger.' This was Arthur's first acquaintance with Pranger Phipps and he had had some difficulty in believing his ears. Compared to Pranger, Richard, the paucity of whose vocabulary Arthur deplored, was a veritable master of the spoken word. Here was a man using the slang and the jargon of his youth. Surely this was not normal? Arthur reflected and, as he did so, the truth dawned on him that it was, in fact, a common fault of which he, Arthur, was not entirely free. Many of his mannerisms, expressions, quotations and affectations dated from his undergraduate days. But, he told himself in reassurance, these were civilised habits, not really to be compared with the brash, vulgar though undoubtedly colourful and picturesque speech of more than forty years ago now issuing, as though from a forgotten past, from the lips of this curious individual.

Richard, as the host, now took control. 'I think, as Podger said, it's time we all moved in. Ernest could arrive at any minute and Maeve and the other two will be down soon. Are we all set? Are the cats fully mustered and Dolly on hand? Urse, is your machine ready to go? Is the cushion in place? Puss Off and the Trassie derivative applied, Scratcher?'

Those responsible assured him that all was in readiness.

'One thing,' added Podger. 'If everyone agrees, I think Dolly and the cats should not operate at the same time. We'll get far more effect if we separate them, with Dolly leading, I suggest, as they've already seen her in action. Charlie, you're going to slip out to launch the cats, aren't you? So hold them back until Dolly's done her worst – or best, perhaps I should say.'

They nodded agreement and there was a general movement towards the sitting room as Scratcher, addressing Richard, enquired 'Might I ask, Mr Richard, if you intend to propose the Loyal Toast?'

162

'No, Scratcher, I hadn't thought of doing so. Why do you ask? Because it would have happened if they'd been staying at Government House?'

'No, Sir, not entirely, though no doubt that would have been the case. I ask because it occurred to me that it might be a further means of embarrassing the two gentlemen as I doubt whether they are familiar with the procedure.'

'Sounds like good thinking,' said Richard, looking around. They were clearly all in favour.

'Very well, Scratcher. The Loyal Toast it is!'

CHAPTER SEVENTEEN

Looking sleek and well fed, Ernest arrived before the others had come down stairs. His beard had been freshly trimmed and, if there were a few more lines around his eyes and if the seams on his tanned face had deepened in the last few months, it seemed if anything to have made him more personable. Charlie, always susceptible to older men, confided to Urse that she thought him a 'doll'.

'Bad luck,' answered Urse. 'He's sitting next to me at dinner!'

After he had greeted his host and hostess and been introduced to the Phipps, whom he had not met before, and was armed with a large pink gin, Ernest uttered, getting his priorities right,

'Capital pink gin, Richard, so few people stock Plymouth these days! Tell me, what's your verdict on Twite and his writer. Is it keel hauling first or should they be run up to the yardarm straight away? Alternatively, they could be flogged round the fleet, you know, having made sure there were enough ships present to be certain that it would be terminal. Those were the days, you know. Must have been great days! "Hands aft to witness punishment", has a nice ring to it, don't you think? Wish we could apply it to those two!'

After this uncharacteristically long speech Ernest took a restorative pull at his drink and regarded his host expectantly.

'It's every bit as bad as we thought it might be, if not

164

worse. They'll be getting rather a discomfiting time tonight, but I can assure you that you needn't feel sorry for them. Your surprise and that of Maeve O'Cork, who knows nothing of all this, will be invaluable in lulling any suspicions they might otherwise entertain.'

With what seemed impeccable timing, Maeve O'Cork entered the room closely followed by Twite and Smallpeice. She had certainly dressed to the occasion. A voluminous and filmy gown of pale rose coloured chiffon, such as Miss Havisham might have worn had she ever been sufficiently in spirits, seemed to give a somewhat softer line to her angular figure, but she had been unable to do anything about her scrawny neck other than swathe it with a superfluity of bizarre and striking beads, through which her Adam's apple seemed to peer and nod in agreement with her words.

Her cadaverous face was so heavily made up that, apart from the eyes, it seemed incapable of expression, but her eyes glittered as imperiously as ever. She had added to her inches by means of a tall and imposing ostrich feather held to the purple velvet band which encircled her red hair by an equally imposing diamond clip.

Her entrance was marked by the sound of brass trays impacting outside in the hall. Podger did not count the number accurately but he fancied it was the equivalent of 17 guns. The fact that the sudden noise was followed by absolute silence made it apparent to everyone that it had, in fact, been intended as a salute. It certainly seemed that the poltergeist or poltergeists, for even Maeve O'Cork had found herself unable to be quite definite on that point, recognised that she was a person of authority and, possibly under the misapprehension that she was an American, had been rendering their version of 'Hail to the Chief'.

Twite and Smallpeice exchanged apprehensive glances, Cyril in particular looking pale.

Maeve O'Cork, noticing their worried looks, hastened to reassure them. 'Have no fear, my friends, for these are not malevolent spirits. Playful perhaps, but no more!'

Such good as this might have wrought was immediately undone by Ernest of the Three Widows.

'That's as maybe, but I wouldn't count on it in the west wing,' he boomed. 'To go there, let alone stay there, is what we call "Standing Into Danger".'

Cyril Smallpeice's 'Oooh!' of horrified alarm changed abruptly to a muffled 'Ouch!' as Dolly took him enthusiastically between the legs and heaved ecstatically with her powerful neck muscles. Another newcomer with the same delicious scent! She could hardly believe her luck, after that barren period when all crotches had mysteriously become closed and forbidden territory.

She set to with a will to make up for lost time, encouraged by Cyril's gasps and cries and, by the time Richard dragged her clear, felt happily that she had made her affection clear. The expected apologies were made and the embarrassing incident covered by the necessary introductions. Under cover of the small talk which then broke out, Charlie slipped from the room.

But Twite was not entirely satisfied. 'That's a very powerful and strange dog you have there, Group Captain. Does she always behave this way with newcomers?'

'No. I'm at a loss to understand it,' Richard lied. 'Perhaps it's because you're party politicians, something she's never met before,' he went on in a feeble attempt to give the incident an element of humour.

Ernest of the Three Widows, who had been listening to the exchange, chimed in cheerfully in a voice tuned and modulated to carry a Force 9 with ease.

'Well, if that's so, that's the only welcome either of you will get in this island on that score. If you have thoughts to the contrary you're on the wrong tack!'

Ernest Twite looked daggers. 'I suppose we're all entitled to an opinion, Captain. Even those of us who don't know what we're talking about!' and turning quickly back to Richard before a return broadside could be fired, he pursued the same theme. 'I notice, Group Captain, that with the exception of the Bailiff's lackey,' and here he indicated Arthur with a half-sneer, half- laugh which, if put to it, he could maintain indicated intended humour and no ill-will, 'with that one exception, every other man here is ex-Service. Did you not think, Mr Fox, that local politicians might like to meet me, or even the other way round, that I might like to meet them, and hear at first hand what motivates this medieval charade and pretence of democracy and why they, as good party members, don't seek to do something about it?'

Richard regarded him steadily, his expression that of a mastiff that is not exactly enthralled by proceedings and is deciding, slowly but with little in the way of goodwill, precisely what its next move should be. He did not actually growl, but his aspect suggested that he might well have done so.

'Mr Twite,' he said at length, in a voice made unnaturally flat and expressionless by his efforts at control, 'I would feel it unfortunate in the extreme if I were forced to remind you that you are a guest in this house. As to the substance of your question, there are no party politicians in this island because there are no political parties. The elected representatives of the people in Jersey, the politicians, if one must use what I confess to finding a sadly degraded term, vote on the merits of any proposal placed before them and not on a perception of party interest. I doubt if any but a handful would wish to meet you anyway, and that handful would not be welcome in this house.'

This crisis in relationship as between host and principal guest was swept away on the instant. Charlie had released the cats. Emma and the Ranee, by virtue of seniority, had been given pride of place on the starting grid. They rushed across the room like two feline Exocets and in an instant were perched, one on each of Twite's shoulders, purring their admiration and devotion into his unreceptive ears.

He got no further than a startled 'What! Get off!' and the beginning of a move to unseat his furry suitors when the main body of the cavalry, which had charged shoulder to shoulder, swarmed up his legs and arms in an attempt to pay fitting homage to this wonderful fish smelling being. Some of them did not make the summit. Picasso, true to form, sought to go no further than the upper thigh and hung, ecstatically if a trife uncomfortably, from Twite's fly. Arthur Marshall did not seek to rise above the stomach and Aneurin Bevan, for whom rats were more important than fish, remained on the alert and settled for such fishy whiffs as were obtainable at ankle height.

Cyril advanced ahead of anyone else to relieve his beleagured minister, impelled by love of cats as much as by concern for his master. Privately he felt that Ernest was soppy to be carrying on so with all those lovely pussies being so nice to him. He, Cyril, would have gladly changed places with him. All those lovely, cuddly, furry bundles were just gorgeous. He simply couldn't understand why Ernest was making such a fuss.

Confident, from years of experience, that he had an affinity with cats, Cyril reached out to remove Emma, who was obviously in command, from Ernest's shoulder. As soon as she got scent of him Emma became a spitting, dangerous creature, her fur standing up and her tail stiff and quivering. Almost at the same time the other cats, starting with the Ranee but virtually simultaneously, found themselves breathing unfiltered Puss Off and acted accordingly.

Cyril was subjected to a full cacophony of feline displeasure and was left in no doubt that he was anything but highly regarded by the cats of this particular establishment. He felt gravely affronted and his cry of 'Naughty, naughty pussies' was deeply felt.

The cats, reluctant but no longer aggressive when handled by non-Puss Off persons, were plucked from Ernest

168

Twite by several hands and, before anyone could remark on the singularity of the incident, Scratcher informed Pussy that dinner was served.

The half hour since Twite and Smallpeice had come downstairs had been so full of action that neither of them had had time to be embarrassed by the fact that they were not properly dressed but, as they entered the dining room and saw the long gleaming mahogany table, the Hepplewhite chairs, the silver cutlery gleaming in the candlelight, the numerous female staff all identically dressed and William, resplendent in a white tie and tail coat, even Twite recognised that they were at a subtle but very real disadvantage caused by what he liked to think of as his socialist principles.

He realised, with bitterness, that he had scored an own goal and that not only the toffee nosed company, but also the servants, were looking down on him and Smallpeice. His typical reaction was to become rude and aggressive. He turned to his hostess, 'I thought all this snobbery of dressing for dinner had been swept away years ago. And servants!' he glared about him.

Pussy smiled at him sweetly. 'Yes, aren't the staff sweet. And so loyal, too. As for dressing for dinner, I really don't know. We always do, but then we always have, and of course it's a matter of what one's accustomed to, isn't it? I imagine you don't dress for high tea, Mr Twite?'

Smiling a gentle smile that did not quite conceal the satisfaction which she felt, Pussy turned to Arthur on her left, denying Twite the right of reply. Arthur was in a state of wonderment. Prue, to whom he was devoted, was on Twite's right so unfortunately he could not see her to weigh her charms once more against those of Pussy, to whom he felt increasingly he was even more devoted, if such a thing were possible. And here was Pussy, very much in the flesh, melting his heart with those bewitching eyes which told him, as clearly as though she had spoken, that he stood

169

high in her favour. And yet Arthur had not ascended to that seventh heaven which the scenario would have seemed to indicate because he was in a state of wonderment and, let it be added, of bewilderment.

And the cause of the wonderment was Pansy Phipps, sitting at his left hand. The bewilderment was caused by the fact that, with Pussy there beside him, his ideal goddess as his immediate neighbour, as it were, he could still find his emotions running wild, and in a totally different direction.

No one had told him the half of it. No one had even hinted that the world could number among its many millions of inhabitants a being quite so perfect as Pansy Phipps. She was a diminutive dream, a small sweet flower that cried out to be cherished.

Arthur was in a state of what might perhaps be termed anxious bliss. Very heaven that it was to be sitting next to this new found angel, he was mindful of the fact that his behaviour should not offend Pussy, of whom he remained inordinately fond in spite of this new turn of events. He was also very much aware of Constance, just across the table on Richard's left.

Richard was talking to Maeve O'Cork on his other side and Constance, momentarily disengaged, was regarding Arthur with a thoughtful look. It would never do, Arthur reminded himself, to upset Connie. He would need to proceed with caution and circumspection. But how, he asked himself silently whilst replying automatically to something Pussy had just said, how on earth could this divine being have married that caricature of a retarded pilot officer called, what was it? yes, that was it, Pranger. Such a ridiculous name, and so much beneath what she deserved.

She needed someone with a dignified name like, yes, well, Arthur would do. Someone with a command of the English language who could flatter and cajole her with a well turned phrase, someone like, yes, well, indeed, someone like himself. And what had she got? A moronic

170

hobbledehoy whose vocabulary, limited to a few hundred words at most, had ossified in 1945, or even earlier. The fact that she seemed quite content Arthur felt was inexplicable and in any event an irrelevance.

At that very moment Pranger's high braying voice carried to him from the far end of the table. He was addressing Ernest of the Three Widows but had, in the way that sometimes happens when conversation suddenly falls away, in fact a much larger audience.

'Well, now you come to ask it, I don't know how it was that we didn't recognise people as "aces" in the last war like they did in 1914-1918. Fact is, I suppose that we did, everyone knew who the top scorers were, but the word "ace" had passed into the language in a different sense. "Ace" was used, you know, just like wizard, bang on, jolly dee. I mean, this wine, for example, would have been considered "ace",' and Pranger imbibed a largish draught by way of illustration.

'As a matter of fact,' and he gave a hyena like laugh, strangely reminiscent of Podger but with a higher and more sustained note, 'as a matter of fact, I suppose you could say that in the original sense I was an ace myself.' He held the pause long enough for interest to mount but not so long that disapproval of apparent boastfulness could begin to show. 'Yes. Destruction of five aircraft used to be the definition in the Royal Flying Corps and Royal Naval Air Service, and still was the criterion used by the Luftwaffe in the last war. Yes, no doubt I'm an ace all right but, unfortunately, a German ace! Pranged five of our own aircraft, no problem! Not entirely my fault, badly shot up and so on you know, but I'm still a German ace! Haw! Haw! Haw!' Pranger revelled in this new found and, to him, hilarious thought.

Twite took advantage of the momentary quiet which followed Pranger's outburst of merriment.

'And you find that funny, Mr Phipps?' he enquired in an acid tone. 'That you should have thrown away and wantonly

171

destroyed five aircraft,' he paused, and then repeated in a magisterial tone 'five aircraft which the taxpayer had paid for and which the workers in conditions of poverty and oppression had toiled so selflessly to build. You find that funny? I am amazed, though perhaps on reflection not altogether surprised, which is a different thing, that that should be so.'

There was dead silence, the silence of embarrassment and outrage. Twite seemed oblivious of the enormity of his offence or, perhaps, just did not care what the assembled company thought of him.

Pranger's geniality deserted him and he shed his assumed air of an affable period piece on the instant. He looked at Twite with a cold gleam in his eye. 'Sorry, Pussy,' he said, shifting his gaze momentarily to his hostess, 'I'm afraid I can't let that pass entirely unanswered.'

Then, back to Twite in a cold measured tone which bore no resemblance to his normal inconsequential and vacuous chatter. 'Mr Twite. As you were not born at the time you may perhaps be excused your ignorance but I, for one, do not excuse your prejudice. I would be the last to imply that the workers who were building aircraft at that time did not work hard. They did, and they were patriotic. But to talk about poverty and oppression is straight nonsense. It may interest you to know, Mr Twite, that my pay on first commissioning as a pilot officer in the Air Force on the outbreak of war was four pounds a week, when few if any of your factory workers were getting less than ten. So much then for the selflessness. As for my having, as you so charmingly phrased it, wantonly destroyed five aircraft, I would only say that the cumulative incidents resulted in my being awarded, and you may think this inexplicable if not laughable, Mr Twite, the Distinguished Flying Cross and the Distinguished Service Order.

'Finally, Mr Twite, and I hope I do not labour the point, I am not Mr Phipps but Wing Commander Phipps. Mister is

172

technically correct for pilot officers and flying officers but in practice is used almost exclusively in addressing warrant officers. And, of course, civilians like yourself,' he added as though as an afterthought.

Everyone started to talk at once in an attempt to smother any reply which Twite might feel inclined to make and to steer the occasion back into calmer and more convivial waters. In fact, Twite had begun some form of strangled answer but Prue, sitting between him and Pranger, managed to cut him off and keep at least the semblance of peace.

Pranger turned to talk to Urse, who was sitting between him and Ernest and hanging on the latter's every word in a successful attempt at teasing Charlie, who was at the other end of the table between Cyril and Podger and out of conversational range.

The various attempts to keep the dinner party somewhere near normal continued. Maeve O'Cork, who was only very vaguely aware that something, which she did not in the least understand, was amiss, was talking anyway regardless of the requirement to keep the conversation going. She and Connie were engaged in a most animated discussion across the front of a somewhat dazed Richard. Animated, that is, principally on Maeve O'Cork's side. She was convinced, so she was telling Connie, that the cats' most peculiar behaviour could only have a psychic explanation.

'The difference in reaction was quite extraordinary. How they were all clearly attracted by Mr Twite and equally clearly repelled by Mr Smallpeice. The explanation can only lie in the occult!'

It pained Connie, who knew precisely where the explanation lay, not to be able to tell the famous medium that for once she was wide of the mark.

'It must be,' Maeve O'Cork continued. 'It can surely only be, that Mr Twite is a white witch and that Mr Smallpeice is

173

a servant of Satan and a practitioner of black magic. Nothing else fits the facts, though I confess neither of them seems particularly well cast in those roles. The vibrations tell that it must be so, and yet I am uneasy, it does not seem all of one piece.'

'Jolly confusing, what?' offered Richard, not perhaps the most brilliant of contributions but the best he could think of at the time.

Trying hard to break out of the cat impasse, Connie suddenly remembered that they needed to enlist Maeve O'Cork's aid to ensure that the regular paid up members of the west wing company of spirits made a competent showing that night. She did not put it in those words, nor indeed did she herself think of it in those terms, but Maeve O'Cork received the intended message and agreed enthusiastically that every effort should be made to ensure that the guests did not miss the stimulating experience of which the west wing was capable. She herself would be happy to encourage the resident spirits to give a bravura performance.

Elsewhere at the table, talk was going on in groups and everyone was taking part except for four who sat silent.

Arthur, who could perhaps be said to be playing a passive role, sat between the two goddesses, who talked cheerfully across him. Their words made little impression on him though he nodded and smiled politely from time to time, taking a chance that they were not discussing the sudden demise of a mutual friend. His thoughts were elsewhere and mainly concerned with the positive aspects of polygamy. In certain circumstances there could be a good deal to be said for it, he concluded. Some equable arrangement whereby, if you had four wives, it was understood and accepted that you would spend three months with each in turn, would fit the bill nicely. But it would certainly have to be well understood, and indeed customary, if Constance were not to be needlessly put out.

174

Considering the scenario in his mind's eye, he concluded that it had few faults. Perhaps, on reconsideration, a week less than three months might serve the case better. After all, he reflected, everyone is the better for a month's break with routine each year.

Cyril also was alone with his thoughts, as was Charlie, his left-hand neighbour. To his right, Pussy was engaged. Though neither could have guessed what was in the other's mind, and why they were so preoccupied and sighed gently from time to time, the fact was that Charlie and Cyril, each in his or her different way, was obsessed with the same subject.

And that subject was Captain Ernest Bathurst, late Royal Navy, more generally known to his familiars as Ernest of the Three Widows. And yet, their way was perhaps not so different after all.

Both were thrilled to their very being by the masculine vigour of Ernest's beard. Both were entranced by his sunbitten, seamed and wrinkled face. Both felt weak whenever they happened to catch his deepset eyes that seemed to tell of the sea, of salt spray and of limitless horizons. Their assessment of his charms differed, though of course they did not know it, in two particulars only.

Charlie felt that just a trifle more hair on Ernest's rather bald head would be an improvement, if indeed it were possible to improve a near perfect being. Cyril felt simply, and with conviction, that he would look even lovelier if he wore an earring.

The fourth person who was neither speaking nor being spoken to was Ernest Twite. Pussy, on his left, was deeply involved, and Prue was talking animatedly to Urse, of whom she was immensely fond and whom she hadn't seen for quite some time. The flow of gossip, of news about mutual friends, of reminiscence, of in-jokes and allusions seemed to Twite, as he listened to it with half a disinterested ear, likely to be endless.

Gradually, boredom gave way to affront and affront, for Twite, was never far from the borders of outrage. Here he was, the guest of honour, one of Her Majesty's ministers, who had been slighted by the lack of suitable company at dinner. Where, he asked himself, were the Lieutenant-Governor, the Bailiff and such apologies for politicians as the island possessed? And not only that. The lack of proper news coverage of his arrival had been unforgivable, he had been made to look ridiculous by some foul canine sex-hound, and mercilessly assaulted by cats. To add to his discomfiture and fury he was, by his own error, indubitably dressed in the wrong clothes.

As he thought these disagreeable thoughts, Ernest Twite's mood was further darkened by memory of the way he had been put down by that man Phipps earlier in the meal. He was, and he knew it, in an inferior position and he must do something to gain the ascendency, not only to satisfy his ego, but also to cut a figure in front of the staff who, so he told himself, would naturally turn to Labour once Jersey was granted the benefit of party politics.

Once he had determined that he would seize centre stage he had only to decide what rod to beat them with. He considered for a moment. With the exception of that retired civil servant, Crabbe, they were undoubtedly a dull lot intellectually. True, that rude fellow Phipps had managed to string a few effective words together, but probably for the first and last time in his life. His host was too much of a gentleman to give trouble, and Bathurst's brain was probably salt encrusted, while Brigadier Simpson, who had not so far uttered, may once have been a modern day Flash-man but, if so, he was long since burnt out and by the look of him, more at home with whisky than with words.

Twite judged that he had nothing to fear and that he would come off best in a debate on any subject. But what should it be? It was no good seeking to get these fools discussing the real issues facing the country which would need to be resolved before the class struggle could be relaxed. They would simply fail to recognise them because, Twite realised, they would be beyond their spectrum of cognisance and, if the slightest hint of his real meaning was to reach their consciousness they would instantly shut it out, unwilling to give credence to his words.

Then, confident that he could worst them whatever the subject, he resolved to engage them on the broad front of Government policy and was about to try and gather the attention of the company when he was conscious of William removing his glass and napkin and, together with other members of staff, clearing the table of all but the candlesticks, silver ornaments and flowers. How could the time have gone so quickly? He recalled with less pleasure than they merited the various courses which, in his irritation, he had eaten automatically and without appreciation.

Now port glasses were on the table and a decanter was placed in front of his host and another in front of his hostess. In a casual unison they removed the stoppers and the port began to circulate. This was a ritual of which Twite had no knowledge and, watching the decanter move away from him to the left he realised, almost with disbelief, that the port would reach him from his host's decanter and that in spite of being the guest of honour his glass would be the last to be filled.

Furious at this imagined slight he pulled a packet of cigarettes from his pocket and lit one with an ostentatious flourish. He was briefly conscious of a general impression of table-wide scandalised disbelief and then William was bending over him and breathing into his ear.

'Not before the Loyal Toast, Sir, if you please. Here is an ashtray.' Twite realised that he had blundered, and obeyed with bad grace, unaware that everyone else was studiously looking elsewhere. William removed the prematurely used ashtray and Twite added worry to his embarrassment as he suddenly realised that he was not sure of what was to happen next.

For reasons totally unconnected with this train of thought he did indeed have good reason to worry but he was mercifully ignorant of the fact.

The decanters came to rest; Richard caught Pussy's eye to ensure that she was ready. Talk around the table suddenly ceased and Richard rose to his feet. Everyone else rose and Twite followed suit. With everyone standing Richard said 'Ladies and Gentlemen, The Queen!' and all those at table, except Twite and Smallpeice, neither of whom knew the drill, responded with varying degrees of fervour. 'The Queen!' carried round the table like a ragged volley of musketry accompanied by a vocal mime from Smallpeice and a non-commital and unintelligible noise from Twite.

This latter noise took on a frenzied disbelieving note just as everyone had their glass to their lips and had taken, or were taking, the first ritual sip of port.

Twite's first intimation that anything was wrong came as he raised his right arm. He was accustomed to wearing braces and he missed the pressure which should have increased slightly on his right shoulder. Before he could analyse the reason for this lack of pressure and take the necessary remedial action which, in justice to Twite, would have needed the split second reaction of a professional boxer, he found that his trousers were around his knees and only prevented from being around his ankles by the closeness of his chair.

The reactions around the table were variously scandalised, enthralled or, in the case of the younger members, one of hilarity heightened by the revelation that Ernest Twite was wearing pink Y fronts embroidered with the initials ET. As an embarrassed Ernest Twite hauled up his trousers and everyone resumed their seats, William approached the back of Twite's chair holding a long red shapeless object in his hand.

178

'It would seem that you have somehow mislaid your braces, Sir,' he said.

Ernest Twite, with a bewilderment that was quite obviously genuine said, or rather spluttered, 'But . . . but . . . but . . . I had them on! I know I had them on! How can they possibly have come off?' He stared around him wildly.

It was Maeve O'Cork who supplied the answer, or the only answer that Twite was going to get.

'I think, Mr Twite,' her ostrich feather swayed and dipped as, regarding him with heavily hooded eyes, she nodded her great vulture-like head as though to emphasise her words, 'I think there can be no doubt that you are the victim of a poltergeist prank. The spirit who could, of course, see through your trousers' – there was an involuntary 'Ooh! Really?' from Cyril that the medium disregarded – 'who could, as I say, see through your trousers, was aware that the initials ET were displayed beneath and wished to lay them bare in order to draw attention to their presence.'

Twite, for whom the evening was taking on the form of nightmare, found that his reasoning powers were running well below full efficiency. He felt stunned, and had no idea what the spooky old biddy with the beads was talking about.

His lack of comprehension communicated itself to Maeve O'Cork and she continued to explain, as though to a backward child.

'Yes, Mr Twite, don't you see? ET, Extra Terrestrial! You will always be a target for the pranksters of the spirit world so long as you carry those letters on your underclothing!'

This diagnosis, which was received with respectful attention by the majority of her audience, was greeted by Twite with what some poet or other once called a 'wild surmise'. That couldn't be true, he felt. It had to be rubbish. And yet, he had undoubtedly had his braces on and securely fastened to six buttons, which were still intact, when he sat

179

down to dinner. His tired brain felt incapable of finding the more rational explanation which, instinctively, he felt must exist.

Pussy, who remembered that the Loyal Toast had been Scratcher's idea, looked across to where he stood behind Richard's chair. He met her very slightly interrogatory glance with a guileless smile. She switched her gaze to Richard who met it with the slightest raise of one eyebrow and the smallest twitch of the lips.

Some few moments later the ladies withdrew, Pussy having decided that in the circumstances it would be better if they took their coffee separately. Twite struggled to his feet, taking grim hold of his trousers, as everyone rose to mark their departure. As soon as they had left the room, and without excusing himself or seeking his host's permission, he performed the manoeuvres necessary to refasten his braces. When that was done and he had his jacket back on again he resumed his seat with an air of sulky bemusement.

In the ten minutes that had elapsed since the downfall of Twite's trousers, Arthur, Podger and Pranger had arrived at the same conclusion as Richard and Pussy and they eyed Scratcher covertly with even greater respect than usual.

As though in collusion, though no word or even look had passed between them, they set to to lend a much needed plausibility to Maeve O'Corks unlikely explanation. They vied with one another to give her 'references' of which she herself would not have felt she stood in need. Words and expressions such as 'International reputation', 'Extraordinary psychic perception', and 'Recognised interpreter for the other side' came in a steady stream from Arthur, supported by Richard, while a powerful covering fire of 'Never got her beads in a twist yet', 'Uncanny the way she always gets in right', 'Pulls more Gs than all the other mediums in the country put together' and like remarks came from Podger and Pranger.

Realising that there was a limit to this sort of thing beyond which praise, however richly deserved and felicitously phrased, would rightly be seen as so much overkill, Richard sought at least a partial change of subject by enlarging on the charms of the west wing.

'If you are lucky,' he informed Twite and a mesmerised Smallpeice, 'you will hear the chanting. You are not likely to see anything if you keep to your rooms but I am sure you will not be disappointed by the organist. Hardly a night passes that he does not play and I am sure you will both be much impressed.'

Cyril's expression made it clear that it promised to be an experience that he, for one, would rather be without and he squirmed apprehensively in his chair. Twite had less concern for what might lie ahead in the west wing. Any misgivings that he would otherwise have felt had long since given way to anger, a slow burning anger caused by frustration and by the ridicule to which, apparently quite by chance, he had been subjected.

He tried unsuccessfully to calm himself with counterbalancing thoughts, and he mentally listed his rout of the Bailiff, the triumph that awaited him at the press conference tomorrow, and the one overwhelming and deciding fact that it was he, Twite, who had the power. He could, and would humble the snobbish tax dodgers perhaps fairly represented, he told himself as he glanced round the table, by those here tonight.

But this promise, even certainty, of triumph to come did nothing to assuage his present hurt. Ernest Twite felt humiliated, and his reaction was to strike out. He recalled his intention, just before the fiasco of the Loyal Toast, of taking these people down a peg or two by rubbing their collective noses in the socialist future. He began to feel better.

'All you people,' he looked around, 'not you, of course, Sir Arthur, though no doubt you feel much the same, all you people, with your military backgrounds must be worried at the prospect of truly democratic government.'

He looked around, challenging them, and was somewhat disconcerted to find himself surrounded by uniform expressions of boredom and unsuccessfully disguised distaste. No one spoke. He tried again, determined to goad them and make them pay for his discomfiture.

'Perhaps you haven't yet realised it, but the old fashioned militarism that you represent will soon be a thing of the past. No more blind obedience from the ranks or from the lower deck. Debate and consent will be the operative words; full unionisation will see to that.'

Podger looked at him coldly, as he might have looked at a particularly scruffy, bolshie and incompetent conscript in the days of National Service.

'You'll find soon enough that the men will laugh in your face. They want no part of your unions and won't join unless compelled to do so. And if that happens they will still thwart you by turning your own weapons against you. They will "work to rule" in union matters which, I'm sure I need hardly tell you, Minister,' and Podger's pronunciation of the title turned a courtesy into a subtle insult, 'means that you will get nowhere. But, it seems from such parts of your so-called manifesto as I found comprehensible, that you will not have to rely on such attempted undermining of the Forces' morale to render the country virtually defenceless. But then, he added reflectively, 'you'd only be putting the finishing touches to the undermining you people began in the sixties.'

'What on earth do you mean?' demanded Twite furiously.

'I'll tell you precisely what I mean.' The Podger who spoke bore little resemblance to the caricature of a retired senior officer which was his chosen camouflage. He spoke with the clipped tones of a brigadier in full command of his subject.

'I mean precisely what I say. It was your Labour Government of that time that insisted on our withdrawal from East of Suez in spite of frenzied appeals to the contrary from Lee Kuan Yew in Singapore and the rulers of the Gulf States. The latter felt so strongly that they even offered to pay the cost of keeping our forces there, to ensure stability in the area. But you wouldn't have it, would you? Oh no! The Minister of Defence even coined a phrase, the rudeness of which has made it memorable. He said, in words perhaps meant to be proud but which linger on as merely arrogant, "British soldiers are not mercenaries", or something very similar'.

'And the result, Minister?' Ernest Bathurst suddenly joined the attack. 'The first Russian cruiser to enter the Indian Ocean passed through the Straits of Malacca within two weeks of your Government's announcement that we were to withdraw from East of Suez. And what is Aden, now, that other centre of great, if not commanding, strategic importance? It is a Russian naval base, is it not? And the fine Royal Air Force base at Khormaksar is a major Soviet airfield.'

'And,' Podger followed up, 'do you believe that the sad events of the late seventies in Iran, although I realise you may not think of them as sad, I of course refer to the betrayal of the Shah of Iran, would or even could have taken place had our forces still been in the Gulf? America, who was admittedly supine, had no base in the area and no Middle Eastern expertise. We could still have had both but for your Government's policy of cut and run.'

'But this is quite monstrous,' protested Twite. 'It is totally unrealistic and out of touch. Those bases were imperialistic and relics of the past and it was long past time for them to be swept away. What ever their rulers may have said, the common people wanted us gone.'

'I doubt, Mr Twite,' Podger again managed to introduce insult into the title, 'I doubt if you are old enough to know

183

anything of this other than by hearsay, and I am certain you were not in Singapore at the time, as I was. The common people were dismayed, even stunned, and many of the older ones were in tears. The only people who wanted us gone were the Communists or other extremist activists. Luckily Lee Kuan Yew saw to it that they ended up in Changhi jail in double quick time.'

Twite swallowed. He recognised that he had greatly underrated the opposition. There were at least two fairly agile and certainly well-informed brains ranged against him, and a further two could still come into action. He would have to be careful and concede a point here or there if the general thrust of his argument was to go his way.

'Oh, very well,' he said pettishly. 'I'm sure you're right, and that there were isolated pockets that behaved in the way you describe. But I was talking in the broad historical sense. The bases were an anachronism and had to go and the common people, even if some of them were confused at the time, have since come to realise that fact.' He continued quickly before anyone had time to disagree. 'But, be all that as it may, the Government would have been forced to give up the bases for financial reasons alone.'

'There you may indeed have a point,' Podger answered. 'As I recall it, that administration was so financially inept that inflation got quite out of hand and it was only the International Monetary Fund that saved us from becoming the equivalent of a banana republic. Or was that your next Labour Government? Every Labour Government since 1964 has been such a financial and social disaster that I find it hard to differentiate.'

Recognising that this was not ground on which he would choose to stand and fight, Twite attempted to brush the point away as being of no real consequence.

'That is, of course, a gross travesty of the facts.' he asserted. 'But we were talking of things military, and surely

184

you cannot have forgotten that it was a Labour Government that introduced the inestimable benefit of the military salary?'

Podger's expression grew even sterner.

'No. Certainly none of us will ever forget that, though inestimable benefit are not quite the words I would have used to describe it. That and the measures that accompanied its introduction, such as the cessation of virtually all allowances and the charging of so-called realistic rates for married quarters was the beginning of the end, which I may say was not long in coming, of traditional Service life so far as the Army and Air Force were concerned. The Navy was not so affected as its pattern of living was different anyway. Whereas before, everyone, officers and men alike, lived in married quarters from choice because of the cheap rents, now you have over 10,000 married quarters standing empty. Army camps and RAF Stations are like ghost towns outside working hours.

'That is the handiwork of your Party, Mr Twite. The destruction of the close ties, friendships and loyalties that bound servicemen together, their close involvement with the intangibles represented by the regiment or the station that distinguished them from civilians, all that has been, or is being, swept away. Soon perhaps you hope you will have what I take it you wanted all along, Services composed of civilians in uniform, living among the community with set hours of work, overtime payment at exorbitant rates, even perhaps the right to question orders in certain circumstances. But it won't happen, Mr Twite. I agree with you that it should, indeed it could not have been bettered by Moscow had the intention been to undermine the British Forces. But of course, that wasn't the intention, was it? The intention was to democratize them, turn the old professional Army into a citizens' Army, more likely to identify with the working class and vote Labour. Well, it hasn't worked, Mr Twite, and it won't. The British serviceman will have none of it.'

185

During Podger's long homily delivered with authority and conviction Twite had had difficulty in containing himself. He had become white and red by turns and had several times tried to intervene, but without success.

As Podger finished, Twite's tongue darted in and out in an attempt to clear the corners of his mouth of the froth that had gathered there. The pressure of his indignation was such that he had difficulty in finding his voice.

I . . . I . . . I . . . I utterly refute everything you have said! There is not a vestige of truth in that . . . that gross distortion of events that you have just related. It is a slur on the Labour Party, a gross insult to distiguished past ministers! To hear you talk, anyone would think that my colleagues and I set greater store by the approbation of Moscow than by the wellbeing of our constituents!'

'If the cap fits, wear it!' growled Ernest Bathurst.

Before Twite could draw sufficient breath to start again, Richard intervened. He had never known such naked antagonism to surface over the port. Plain speaking, perhaps, but this was in another league and something which he felt strongly had gone far enough. Their aim had been to unsettle Twite, to wrong-foot him and to harrass him, but in the last few minutes it had got beyond that and, as host, it was he felt incumbent on him to put a stop to it.

'Well now, gentlemen,' he said, rising, 'I'm sure the ladies are waiting for us. So, shall we move? Mr Twite, shall we lead the way?'

As the men began to enter the room, Pussy was quick to note Richard's anxious look and Twite's set expression. She rose to the occasion quickly.

'Ah, Mr Twite, here you are then! Do come and sit here between Lady Crabbe and Miss O'Cork. You've not had the opportunity to talk to either of them yet.' Twite sank into the seat indicated and attempted to arrrange his face to accord with at least the minimum social criterion.

Cyril, meanwhile, had been led by Ursula to a chair next

to the one Pussy had temporarily vacated. 'You've not had a chance to talk to my mother, I know. Or to me, for that matter! She flashed him a pert smile which, totally false though it was, so closely resembled the genuine article that Cyril smiled happily back and Arthur Crabbe, a second witness to Urse's smile, set to wondering whether he had not been wrong to judge her so harshly. She was, after all, a damned pretty woman, roguish, provocative, most amusing if kept out of reach of shoe laces. Yes! Perhaps he had been a little hasty in his judgement.

Urse sank into her chair and gestured to Cyril to do the same. As he did so a most frightful farting noise resulted. It was as far removed from the old fashioned whoopee cushion as a Covent Garden performance of the Flying Dutchman was in its turn removed from an impromptu rendering of Knees Up Mother Brown in an Old Kent Road pub. The only thing they would have had in common would have been the volume of sound. The manufacturers of this particular device might indeed even have had Wagner lovers in mind. The fearsome noise continued, with realistic trills and crescendos occasionally seeming to challenge the authority of the woodwinds and the cello.

All eyes were on Cyril Smallpeice as the noise was too sudden and dramatic to allow of polite dissimulation. He gulped, as might some startled inhabitant of an aquarium.

'Oooooh!' he said. 'I never!'

But public opinion was not to be so easily put to one side. The majority of those present, who knew that Cyril was an innocent victim, managed a convincing barrage of outraged stares. Only those not in the know showed any humanity.

'Bad luck, Smallpeice,' grunted Ernest Bathurst. 'Port does that to you sometimes, particularly in a quartering sea, and there's not a damned thing you can do about it.'

Maeve O'Cork was all solicitude. 'Poor Mr Smallpeice,' she said. 'Are you sure you are in proper health? If not, I would be happy to administer an enema later tonight.'

'An enema!' squeaked Cyril. 'Ooooh! I say! But no, I'm quite all right, thank you.'

'Well, so,' Maeve O'Cork's eyes lit up as though with reluctant admiration, 'so it has to be those naughty, naughty spirits at play once more!'

Speculation on her verdict and interest in Smallpeice were alike cut short by a new circumstance. A most frightful smell had suddenly filled the room, its volume and power clearly both too great to have been generated by anyone so puny as Smallpeice.

For the few moments that it took Charlie to familiarise herself with the controls and centre the smell on Twite, neighbour looked at neighbour in wide-eyed disbelief. Then, slowly, all eyes became fixed on Twite.

No one could possibly have accused the manufacturers of Who? Me? of not having delivered the goods. Any case brought under the Trade Descriptions Act would not have stood a chance. The smell was authentic and, in terms of volume, the manufacturers had been generous to a fault. They had also imbued their product with a lingering quality that added significantly to the discomfiture of the chosen victim.

Twite's nostrils, like those of everyone else in the room, had picked up the smell initially as being extremely potent but uncertain as to its point of origin. Slowly, as the unmistakable and socially unacceptable odour seemed to grow in strength, Twite became aware that everyone in the room was looking at him with expressions of disbelief. 'How,' their covert glances seemed to say 'could one person possibly be the source and sole author of this socially most unfortunate incident?'

Twite glanced about him desperately and became conscious of his isolation. Constance and Maeve O'Cork, in addition to drawing away from him, had also given a meaningful twitch to their skirts. With increasing discomfiture it began to dawn on Ernest Twite that the origin of the smell was indeed seated on or around his person. Could it possibly be? he thought wildly. No, of course not! But in spite of this reassurance he shifted uneasily in his seat. The smell was unmistakable, and it was certainly centred on him. He had overheard Bathurst's remark to Cyril. Could it possibly be that the effects of port could be as strong as this, even without the benefit of a quartering sea?

Ernest Twite's eyes looked as though they were getting ready to roll as he sought desperately for a way out. Unless the spooky old Irish bean was going to come out and claim that the spirits were being playful once again, and there was no sign of that, he was on his own.

Suddenly the aggressive Twite, the rude, arrogant, and even insolent Twite had had enough. All he sought was escape from this nightmare scene and the privacy of his bedroom. Gathering up Cyril with a glance he excused himself to Pussy and Richard and, with perfunctory 'Good nights' around the room, he stumbled out blindly, with Cyril at his heels.

As he left, Charlie turned a knob and the smell died.

CHAPTER EIGHTEEN

Twite and Smallpeice had elected to have breakfast in their rooms and the hour of the press conference was approaching before they appeared, Cyril once more in attendance on his minister. Both looked haggard.

Richard greeted them cheerfully. 'Lovely day. I hope you slept well?' Twite regarded him without evident goodwill.

'If you have ever slept in that wing, Group Captain, you no doubt know the answer, which is "not well" and "very little". Distant organ music and chanting for the first two or three hours and then, just when one had dropped off, a veritable recital which lasted for two hours. It was very loud and quite exhausting.

'And what time was this, pray?' enquired Maeve O'Cork eagerly.

'I looked at my watch so I can tell you pretty accurately Miss O'Cork. Near enough from 3 a.m. to 5 a.m.'

'Just as I thought!' she replied enthusiastically. 'Just as I would have expected! Those are of course the hours when human resistance is at its lowest and when, by contrast, the power of the spirit world is at its most potent!' Her beads jangled prettily as though in cheerful corroboration.

Richard hastened to change the conversation. Holding a local paper out to Twite he said jocularly: 'Got your picture on Page One, I see, in spite of the distinguished company you flew in with!'

Twite looked at the proffered paper which had as banner

headlines 'SYLVESTER FORESKIN PREPARED TO TAKE ISLAND BY STORM'.

Underneath were numerous pictures of the great star and a long interview which included his views on marriage, ecology, education, proportional representation, the future of the Falkland Islands and the trades union movement. To all these questions his answers were strikingly similar and couched in simple words which his fans would understand. 'Yer, werl, know wot I mean?' jostled for pride of place with 'Yer, werl, I mean, that's it, innit?' and the authoritative 'you'd better believe it, Mister!'

Tucked away at the bottom of the page was a small picture of Twite looking like an infuriated gnome, with the caption 'Another arrival was Mr Ernest Twite, Junior Home Office Minister, who is here for talks with the Bailiff, Sir Frederick Marais'.

Twite threw the paper on a table with an expression of disgust, 'They'll be singing a very different tune in their next edition,' he said grimly. 'Just you wait and see!'

Further conversation was prevented by the arrival of Geoffrey, come to collect Twite and Smallpeice for the press conference which was to be held in Government House.

The arrangements, which had been mutually agreed, allowed for an opening statement by Twite of 15 or 20 minutes' duration, to be recorded by radio and by television. This would be followed by up to 30 minutes of question and answer, again to be recorded, followed in turn by one-to-one interviews with the chosen interviewers of press, radio and television.

When all was ready, Twite rose and looked about him with the challenging and arrogant air of confidence which he customarily affected in the House of Commons. He had prepared his statement well and he wasted few words as he told them what Parliament would ordain following the few short months needed for the preparation of the necessary legislation.

191

He was puzzled by the reaction, or rather lack of reaction, from his audience. He would have expected starts of dismay, expressions of disbelief, anxious whispering, a turmoil of fidgeting and the rustle of unease. In place of this he was met by an almost uncanny stillness. They listened in dead silence, expressionless and motionless. Expressionless, that is, apart from the eyes. And their eyes carried a uniform message of hostility and contempt.

He suddenly realized that what he was saying to them did not come as a surprise. They had been warned in advance of at least the outline of his statement. The Bailiff's Office, there could be no other source, had clearly tipped them off. He was furious with himself for not having put an embargo on his message and for having allowed himself to be outflanked in this way.

The silence continued even after Twite had finished his statement and, resuming his seat, looked around expectantly for questions, being careful to keep his best side to the television cameras.

'Come, gentlemen,' he said, as the silence persisted. 'I am at your disposal, and I am sure there must be many points of detail on which you, or your readers, viewers or listeners will be anxious for clarification.'

The silence was broken by Channel Television's equivalent of Robin Day. Angus Smert-Fert, of mixed German and Scottish ancestry, had been brought to Jersey as a small child by his mother when his father died. She had relatives in the island and he, remembering little if any of his earlier childhood, felt and thought as though he was Jersey born and bred. He was a tall, thin, overconfident young man who wore horn rimmed glasses and a bow tie in honour of his hero.

Being younger and more brash or, as he would think of it, more contemporary and with it than his unknowing mentor, he did not feel the same need for courtesy and a measure of decorum when interviewing a difficult if not actively hostile subject. For Angus Smert-Fert the world had moved on from the classic demolition interviews of the 1950s and 1960s. Mortal thrusts need no longer be courteously delivered and he saw no need to waste good money on velvet gloves. Smert-Fert, though not disdaining the subtler means of verbally reducing and confusing an opponent, relied primarily on shock tactics. He did not mind how rude he was and neither, so long as his viewer rating remained high, did his employers.

'I have one question, Minister.' His voice seemed guileless, even friendly. Twite responded in like vein. Perhaps this was going to be easier than he had thought and the media had accepted the inevitable.

'Yes, please, Mr Smert-Fert. I will do my best to answer.' He began to smile ingratiatingly, but the incipient symbol of goodwill froze and then vanished as Smert-Fert asked his question.

'Have you seen a good psychiatrist recently, Mr Twite?'

The words came not as a whiplash, which would have been one alternative, nor as slow, drawn out, lingering venom, which would have been another, but as a plain matter-of-fact question.

To viewers it would seem that Smert-Fert was filled with concern for the minister who, on the strength of his statement, might well be, indeed probably was, mentally disturbed.

Twite blustered into a hasty response.

'I fail to see the relevance of that absurd and insulting remark. I cannot dignify it with the title of question.'

'The relevance, Minister,' and now Smert-Fert's manner had changed from seeming concern to cold disdain, 'the relevance is that there must be doubt about the mental health of any responsible person who makes a statement such as you have just made.'

Twite managed the semblance of a sickly smile and attempted the role of an elder statesman who had suffered

193

these headstrong young men before.

'I fear, Mr Smert-Fert, that you are in danger of making a fool of yourself.'

'If I do, Minister, I feel sure that in present company I shall do no more than take second prize.'

The room thrilled to that verbal punch, delivered with speed and aplomb, and a reporter took up the baton from Smert-Fert.

'Surely, Minister, you must realise that the people of Jersey won't stand for this for one moment?'

Before Twite could answer, other voices joined in:

'The island's loyalty is to the Crown, not to Parliament, can't you see that?'

'What gives you and your Government the right to overthrow the constitutional relationship?'

'The people here no more want to be subject to England, as represented by the House of Commons, that the Falkland Islanders do to the Argentine. Haven't you even realised that?'

Twite struggled to speak above the growing hubbub.

'Please! Please! It is no good shouting at me. These are matters of Government policy and have been decided. And that is an end to it!'

Smert-Fert started to speak, and the other voices died away in anticipation.

'Have the island authorities been consulted in this matter?'

Twite looked at some papers and made as though to ignore the question until a growl of 'Answer! Answer!' forced him into speech.

'There was no need. The matter is, as I have said, decided.'

'"Decided", you say, Minister. "Decided". That I find very odd.' Smert-Fert appeared to weigh the word. 'You and your party claim to stand for democracy and for the right of ordinary people to speak on their own behalf. But what

194

you are proposing to do here is a travesty of the democratic process. You are attempting to apply a totalitarian or dictatorial solution, to insist that the people of Jersey should be answerable to Westminster whether they would or no.

'Tell me, Mr Twite, and these other gentlemen here and, through them, the people of Jersey, what makes you think that you and your Government have the right to force this change on people, and I can guarantee you this, Mr Twite, on people who want no part of it? And I tell you this,' Smert-Fert continued before Twite could attempt a reply, 'I cannot accept the substance of what you say.'

There was a sudden silence and questioning looks were exchanged. There was clearly a feeling that Smert-Fert was building up to something.

'You say these matters have been decided. But what I must insist on calling your 'proposals' have not even been laid before Parliament, let alone agreed by that body. So they have been decided by some individual, is that not so, Mr Twite? My question to you, therefore, is "Is that individual the Secretary of State for Home Affairs"?'

Twite tried to lose the substance of his answer in words.

'What you say is, of course, theoretically and, in this instance, also factually correct, but you must accept, Mr Smert-Fert, and as an experienced commentator and interviewer I am sure you do, that the substance of any given matter is often, as it were, more substantial than the sum of its component parts. And so it follows that the answer you seek must also be multifaceted. It will mean one thing to one person and something different to another according to the nuance of interpretation that may be applied.'

'The answer I require, Mr Twite, is neither multi-faceted nor open to any nuance of interpretation. It can be given in one word. Either "Yes" or "No". And the question, if I may remind you, is whether what you call "decisions" and I call "proposals" have the approval and endorsement of the Secretary of State for Home Affairs?'

Twite attempted to bluster.

'There has as yet been no need for my Right Honourable friend to become involved. He and I are of one mind and . . .'

'So!' Smert-Fert interrupted. 'So, Mr Twite, is it a fact, and are we to understand, that these proposals that you parade before us in the guise of Government decisions have no real substance and are generated solely by the ambition and personal spite of a junior minister, namely yourself?'

'But! But I have already told you that there is no doubt . . .'

'Thank you, Mr Twite. I have no further questions.'

Twite attempted to recover. Smiling uneasily he addressed the company.

'Perhaps if we proceed to the individual interviews which have I believe been arranged, we might be able to arrive at a more sensible and balanced presentation of the facts for the benefit of the public.'

No one responded, and the unmistakable bustle of busy men preparing to move elsewhere filled the room. Twite could hardly credit his senses. He turned to Geoffrey.

'What about the interviews that you arranged, Commander?' he snapped.

'I think, if I read things aright, that you can forget about them, Mr Twite.' The clatter of the media leaving with their heavy equipment and without so such as a backward glance reinforced his words. 'Their minds are clearly made up and they see no point in talking to you further.'

'But, but . . . this is quite monstrous! This is an insult to me personally and to the Government! I demand that you do something!'

'Interested as I am in your priorities, Mr Twite, I am not at all clear what it is that you have in mind. Surely you are not suggesting that I should in any way attempt to influence the media, let alone seek to dictate to them as to what they should or should not say or do?'

'No, no, of course not!' spluttered Twite, beside himself with irritation. 'But there must be something! Surely ministers are not to be insulted with impunity in this way? Are you going to stand by and let it happen, Commander?'

'Perhaps I may point out that "it" has already happened. Had you asked me early enough for your question to have relevance, my answer would have been "yes". It is no part of my responsibility, Mr Twite, to protect you from the consequences of your own words. And now, we have some 40 minutes or so before your next engagement which, if your remember, is to address local trade union representatives. Perhaps you would like to return briefly to the Hall in the interval?'

Twite assented with bad grace.

Thirty-five minutes later the Daimler approached the Assembly Room where the meeting was to be held. Twite was delighted to see that there was what looked like a picket line outside and that he was to be greeted by a forest of placards. Whether the placards would solely be ones of welcome, whether they would chronicle the grievances of the local trade unionists or be a mixture of the two was, he felt, or minor importance. The main point was that the workers were solid and had learnt the importance of organised protest. Even in this medieval backwater the high water mark of oppression and exploitation had perhaps been reached, and the class war had taken hold.

He was excited by these encouraging signs that the working class would welcome his blueprint for their future, as he had felt sure all along they were bound to do.

Ernest Twite was smiling with satisfacton as the Daimler began to move slowly through the massed ranks of placard carriers. In seconds the smile changed, by way of an uncertain and uncomprehending leer to a stony look of stunned and angry disbelief. For the placards did not accord with his imaginings.

On the contrary, if he was to believe his eyes, they carried a common message, couched in various forms, to the effect that he, Twite, and his proposals, were alike unwelcome in the island of Jersey.

The captions varied, ranging from the jocular 'Bad luck Twite, we won't bite,' standing next to 'Tough titty, Twitey, not tonighty', moving through the run of the mill 'Hands Off Jersey', 'Leave us alone', 'We like things as they are', 'Go home Twite', to the acrimonious 'No party politics here', 'Stop meddling in our affairs', 'No Marxism here' and 'Go back to Moscow'.

Twite was still struggling with his disbelief when the car drew to a halt and he was formally welcomed, or at any rate met, by the local trade union boss, Smedley Armpit. Smedley, whose father had been a devoted grower of peas, was a big man, slow of speech and of movement. He customarily wore a singlet but, today, he was more formally attired, and moving awkwardly. As he led Twite into the packed but silent hall it gradually became apparent that his formal dark suit owed less to the image of a welcoming civic dignitary than to the formal garb of the undertaker.

Arrived on the platform, he motioned Twite to sit and then addressed his fellow Trade Unionists.

'Fellow Jerseymen', he said, 'I won't call you brothers, still less comrades, has might be more familiar to our visitor. We hall know that Mr Twite hintends, if he can, to make Jersey part of Hampshire. I know that you, like me, would hoppose that with every bit of power and hinfluence that our movement could bring to bear bot,' and here he paused and looked slowly around his assembled members, 'bot I am sure you will hagree with me that it would be hundemocratic not to let Mr Twite put his case, if case 'e has.'

A majority of those present accepted what he said but it was by no means unanimous. There were hostile shouts from one corner of the hall, of which 'Come off it, Smedley, throw the bugger out' was perhaps the most polite.

Smedley raised his voice. 'Come on lads, quieten down now. Mr Twite has the floor.'

Twite rose uneasily. This was by no means the reception, or the audience, that he had been expecting.

'Fellow workers,' he began, remembering that he had been warned off comrades or brothers. But it did him no good. 'Garn, tell us another! You're no worker!' came the first heckle followed by a shushing noise from the older element who were curious to hear what Twite had to say.

He spoke briefly, judging it best to do so, but he spoke with conviction, outlining the strengths and benefits of English trade unionism which they would, of course, enjoy, once Jersey was part of Hampshire.

When he sat down there was no applause and the hostile barracking started again from the back of the room.

Smedley Armpit rose, his great bulk dominating the room and seeming to emphasise the insignificance of the minister.

'Quiet, lads!' The barracking stopped, and he carried on in his accented Jersey English, not so different to the ear from Afrikaans, with the letters O and U almost invariably transposed.

'It mosst be hobvious to you, Mr Twite, that we don't want no English trade union practices hintroduced over yere. But you probly don't honderstand why, so I shall tell you. For the first part it's really op to the Bailiff to hexplain, bot hin a very few words, we've ron our hown affairs for centuries over yere and we hintend to carry on doing so. Hand as for what you say about trade unions, it seems to oss that yore record 'as been disastrous both for England and for your hown menmbers. The record of 'igher wages, lower productivity, restrictive practices, the closed shop and all the rest of yore tarry diddle 'as priced England out

199

of the market in hindustry after hindustry and 'as increasingly priced your members out of their jobs.

'Over yere it's true that we 'ave lower wages, but we 'ave lower taxes too, and the cost of living, it's lower as well. True, we 'ave a branch of the TGWU over yere, bot we hoperate it differently.

'Something you could find 'ard to honderstand, Mr Twite is that we 'ave no hadversary politics in Jersey, no feeling of "Them" and "Hoss" or "Class stroggle" as I suppose you'd call it. As hoften as not the foreman and even the boss were at the same school as we were. They play fair with oss and we play fair with them. And the result, Mr Twite, is that strikes are very very seldom resorted to, hunemployment is all but non-existent and both Jersey and our union members are flourishing and prosperous.

'Well, I think that's about it, Mr Twite. I suppose, out of politeness, I should thank you for coming but I can't do it. We just want you to stop meddling and leave hoss alone. Now that you've seen that the workers over yere want no part of your politics and all that you represents, I 'ope, Mr Twite, that you'll think again. You've no call to try and make hoss part of Hampshire against our will and I 'ope you realise we'll have non of it.'

Throughout the time that Armpit had been speaking, Twite had been struggling for control and at the same time trying to calculate to what degree, if at all, he should consider modifying his plan. He had been prepared for outright hostility from the Bailiff and the wealthy immigrants but he had been sure that he would be welcomed by the local working class. From the moment that he had found this was not to be, his emotions had been on an ascending scale.

First had come shocked disbelief, then incredulity and bewilderment, giving way in their turn to disappointment which had itself led to anger, a raging anger that now possessed Ernest Twite. These fools of peasants, half-French in influence and some of them in blood, were telling him, Ernest Twite, to stop meddling! He'd give them 'meddling' before he was finished! The fools didn't realise, or even begin to realise, how much power he had over their future.

Red in the face and having difficulty with his breathing, he glared at them and spoke briefly.

'You, brothers,' and he laid heavy and unfriendly emphasis on the word, 'will regret this day's work when you are a small and insignificant part of Hampshire! For part of Hampshire you will become, and don't you think otherwise!'

Twite realised that his words were ill-judged, and began to regret them even before he had finished speaking. The resentment and animosity in the hall became almost tangible, something that could not be overlooked and would not be ignored. The noise level with its overtone of hostility rose sharply.

Suddenly Armpit, heavy and judicial in his unaccustomed black, had two thickset, low-browed and unfriendly looking brothers at his side. For the first time he raised his voice.

'Quiet, lads!' he shouted. 'We don't want Mr Twite to think we're bad mannered nor rude. No, we don't want that. Hand heverywons entitled to won warning, aren't they, lads?' His pleasant and reasonable tone suddenly hardened as he turned to Twite.

'Hand you've 'ad yore warning, Mr Twite! Any more like that and you'll end op in the 'Arbour! Bert and Harry yere will be only too 'appy to oblige.'

The muscle-bound brothers nodded their assent and flexed their fingers in a disturbing manner. Their faces were expressionless but they gazed at Twite reflectively, perhaps assessing just how far they could jointly throw him, and whether that distance could constitute a record.

'But, but . . .' blustered Twite. 'You couldn't do that! That would constitute a serious assault, perhaps

201

"aggravated" or even "with intent to cause grievous bodily harm"!' His confidence rose. 'I'd have the law on you, Mr Armpit!'

'You wouldn't get too far, Mr Twite. Bert and 'Arry 'ave very, very short memories, hand all the lads yere would have seen you trip op hand fall in, wouldn't you, lads?'

There was a cheerful roar of assent and renewed cat-calling. Geoffrey moved to Twite's elbow.

'I suggest that we leave, Minister. You have just about the right amount of time to get ready for the States luncheon being given in your honour.'

Twite allowed himself to be led from the room, his eyes not fully in focus and his expression one of stunned disbelief.

CHAPTER NINETEEN

Later that day Ernest Twite arrived in Guernsey. Before his arrival Sir William Dumaresq had received another telephone call from Sir Frederick Marais and both had spoken, separately and at length, to the Permanent Under Secretary at the Home Office, Sir Doubtful Chimes. It was thought by those who knew him that Sir Doubtful's father had had the Civil Service in mind when he had the infant christened.

Whether or not there was anything in this theory, there was no doubt that Sir Doubtful did nothing to disprove it. Beside him, Arthur Crabbe's haverings would have passed as decisiveness and his verbosity as a model of concise presentation.

Sir Doubtful had reached his position at one of the pinnacles of the Civil Service, recognised as a mandarin, a Knight Grand Cross of the Bath, by the simple expedient of delaying his advice on the matter in hand until it was clear that he was odds on. Sometimes it failed when some 66–1 idea came from nowhere to sweep the board, but by and large it was a device that put him, as a civil servant, in much the same category as Gordon Richards had enjoyed as a jockey.

His department, to be fair, was perhaps more than any other, at risk, but it had an unequalled record of own goals. Not many countries had Queens to be sure, but certain it was that no other country had security so lax that a deranged individual was able to penetrate to the Queen's bedroom. The responsible ministry? The Home Office. The responsible official? The PUS. The same questions and the same answers when the Queen's bodyguard was found to be a homo, caught out looking for a bit of rough.

Not, to be sure, in Sir Doubtful's time, but the memories lingered on, and in a slightly less ostentatious way the Home Office record had continued to engage more than passing notice.

And indeed it could do little else. Almost anything that happened that was not to the liking of the citizenry at large was held to be the fault of the Home Office and, by extension, of Sir Doubtful.

There was, of course, the convention that the Secretary of State took full responsibility and, indeed, if it was a resigning matter he traditionally did so. But no one among the professionals was fooled for one moment. Final responsibility for regrettable errors – and in the Home Office regrettable errors, known to the staff as cock-ups, were a way of life – lay, short of the Home Secretary, with the PUS. That harassed and overworked official took ritual blame as a matter of course for events almost always beyond his control and often beyond his knowledge. It was in many ways, in spite of the honour of the appointment, a most undesirable and uncomfortable post.

There were only two ways of handling it. One was to stand up like a Hittite mighty in battle and hope to cut your way to promotion, not that there were many posts more senior, and the other was to opt for the permanent defensive, to concern yourself from day to day with damage limitation, with the shuffling off of responsibility on to other departments whenever opportunity offered and, when it did not, with the best possible presentation, short of outright falsification, of unpalatable but inescapable facts.

By temperament, inclination and conviction Sir Doubtful embraced the second way. And so, as a result, he was able

204

to offer little in the way of encouragement or even hope to the two Bailiffs when, full of righteous anger, they rang him separately to protest at the outrageous behaviour and proposals of his junior minister.

He protested his innocence, and indeed his ignorance until just before Twite had left for Jersey, but he could promise nothing. Yes, it was true that Twite and the Home Secretary were birds of a feather. Yes, it was true that the Cabinet would be likely to accept a proposal on the lines now being advanced by Twite. Yes, of course he would ensure that the Secretary of State was appraised of their views ahead of the official letters. No, he could not hold out any hope that those same views would be likely to influence the march of events. No, he could not commit himself on the difficulties which must arise as a result of the constitutional relationship. That was a matter for the Solicitor-General.

Yes, he also wished that Ernest Twite would drop down dead. His sympathy was with them, he would do his best, but he would be less than honest if he were to encourage the expectation that these proposals would be thrown out. The Privy Council was the last Court of Appeal, and Twite's belief that an appeal would be denied coincided with his own view. Diabolical, but there it was. Revolution by the ballot box. Nothing to be done about it. A confidence trick? Criminal deception? They were perhaps dangerous words to use and not ones that he personally could possibly endorse, nor indeed should he really condone their use.

But he recognised them for what they were, an expression of anger and frustration from one old friend to another, given and received in confidence. So sorry he couldn't do more. If there was anything they wanted they had only to ask.

Ernest Twite's visit to Guernsey began badly and got worse as it progressed. Trade union pickets were out in strength at the airport and made a good background for the TV shots of Twite's arrival and hostile reception by representatives of the media.

But that would have rated as a warm welcome when compared to his reception by Sir William Dumaresq. Someone with a less thick skin that Ernest Twite would have been destroyed by the coldness of the older man's expression and tone of voice and by the contempt in his eyes. But Twite held all the cards, and he knew it and was not put off balance by the Bailiff's opening salvo.

'Ah, yes. Mr Twite, isn't it? I gather from Sir Frederick that we have nothing to say to one another, so I suggest we confine our meeting to those occasions of formal entertainment which the States of Guernsey are duty bound to arrange for a member of Her Majesty's Government. You are, as you know, staying in an hotel, as Sir James Havelock has not found it convenient to receive you. It is generally regarded as the best hotel in the island and the management will, I am sure, see to your comfort and to that of Mr ah, er, Smallpeice, is it not? Yes, of course, Smallpeice. Unless there is anything you wish to know I will consider your call as paid. I believe your taxi is waiting and my secretary will escort you.'

Sir William pushed his chair back preparatory to standing and then added as an afterthought: 'As you do not even wish to see the other Islands of this Bailiwick, nor show yourself to the inhabitants, before ending their centuries old independence, you may find your visit here overlong but it is too late to change that now. If time hangs heavy and you wish to leave the hotel at any time, please inform the senior police officer present so that an escort may be provided.'

'Police officer? What do you mean?'

'Yes, I have thought it wise to provide a police presence. You possibly do not realise, Mr Twite, that you are the most unpopular person, I would go so far as to say hated, to set foot in this island since the German Occupation ended in May of 1945. It has not perhaps occurred to you,' the blood rose to Sir William's cheeks and his voice took on the higher tone of tightly controlled fury, 'that if your proposals' he practically spat the word, 'your so-called proposals become law, not only will hundreds of years of tradition and a way of life be swept away on the instant but thousands of people, literally thousands, Mr Twite, will be ruined.'

'Nonsense,' Twite snapped back. 'It's the rich tax dodgers who will pay English tax that they should have been paying all along who'll be the ones to feel the pinch. And high time too!'

'I will not bandy words with you, Mr Twite, but I can assure you that you simply don't know what you're talking about. The rich, who are mostly extremely conscientious and generous in their support of island affairs, will simply move elsewhere. It is the older people, retired on pension, who will not be able to meet your bill, Mr Twite, and will have to sell on a flooded market with few takers and grossly deflated property values. Deflated by you and your precious proposals!'

'I don't accept what you say, Mr Bailiff, but I recognise unreasoning hostility when I see it! Am I to take it that it is for this same reason that the Lieutenant-Governor does not find it convenient, that was the word I think, convenient to receive me?'

'No, that was not the reason.'

'What was it then? I demand to know! I am not prepared to be insulted in this way and denied an explanation.'

'You are in no position to demand, Mr Twite, and His Excellency is under no obligation to furnish you with the reason for his decision, but I have his permission to do so on his behalf should you so press me.'

'I do press you!'

'Very well then. Remember that you did so. The reason that Sir James refuses to receive you is because you condone the, to him, quite unacceptable lifestyle of Mr Smallpeice, here.'

'But he can't do that! Parliament has ruled on the matter. He can't adopt that ludicrous, old fashioned and blinkered attitude in defiance of Parliament's ruling!'

'He not only can, but he does, and that's an end to it!'

'It certainly is not an end to it! The man is quite clearly unfitted to hold his office and I will see to it that he is removed!'

'Sir James holds his appointment at the Queen's pleasure. I do not fancy that Her Majesty would be over-sympathetic to your complaint.'

'That's what you say. I'll find a way to run him out of Office never you fear!'

'Have a care, Mr Twite! The Lieutenant-Governor has the power to deport you as a danger to law and order and if you make threats of that nature he might be tempted to use that power!'

'He wouldn't dare!'

'I wouldn't count on it, Mr Twite. Sir James is a much decorated officer who has dared many things in his time. And what would he have to lose, as under your proposals his office ceases to exist anyway? Think of the publicity, Mr Twite. A minister, albeit very junior, being deported! The Mother of Parliaments might spring to your defence, but I very much doubt it. It's much more likely that the Press would tear you apart and you would become an object of ridicule. I suggest that you think again and keep a closer guard on your tongue than you have seen fit to do in the last fifteen minutes.'

Sir William rose. Twite made as though to speak but apparently thought better of it. The interview was over.

As the Bailiff had said, Twite's visit to Guernsey promised to be overlong. Ignored by press and television, his hotel picketed by hostile trade unionists and under what amounted to police protection, Twite was furious at the rough verbal treatment he had received and frustrated at his inability to do anything effective about it.

The next morning he decided to try to walk off at least something of his ill humour. The hotel was situated in a pleasant part of the island not far, so Twite understood, from some spectacular views.

With Smallpeice at his side and with two local plainclothes men following at a discreet distance, Twite set off. He walked fast, with his head down. He was immersed in thoughts which boded no good for the future of his new found enemies. Sir William and Sir James together with, of course, Sir Humphrey and Sir Frederick, would be satisfactorily swept away as though they and their offices had never been.

But what of creatures such as Geoffrey Point, Angus Smert-Fert, Smedley Armpit and even Vivienne de Jong? Point would go with his master, Armpit would be brushed aside by the militant element that he would arrange to be infiltrated within the next few months. The stewardess he knew he could crush, so that left only Smert-Fert. Him he would need to treat with a certain circumspection, but he felt that ways might be found.

His acrimonious musings were brought to a sudden stop by the realisation that a strange individual, together with two solid-looking but more ordinary men, were collectively blocking his path.

The man, apparently in his early sixties, with a grey beard, short grizzled hair and a leathery skin acquired perhaps at sea, perhaps as a grower, had suddenly gone down on one knee and was declaiming in Guernsey French, a patois that few if any modern Frenchmen would fully understand. Twite's plain clothes escort came running forward and were just in time to hear the key phrases of the Clameur de Haro, for such it was

'Haro! Haro! Haro!
A l'aide mon prince!
On me fait tort!'

Onesimus Gorey, of mixed Jersey and Guernsey parentage, was a lay preacher and had a near-fanatical gaze which, because he was on one knee, wasted much of its power in the general area of Ernest Twite's fly. His complaint, for such it was, having duly been laid in proper form with two witnesses present, Onesimus Gorey rose to his feet and beamed his eyes full on Twite.

Onesimus's eyes, which had been likened to blow torches or twin lasers, capable at a pinch of cutting metal, did nothing to restore Twite's composure. Onesimus Gorey's words had been totally unintelligible to Twite but they had been delivered with such fire and ferocity that he was left with the unsettling impression that he had either been declared anathema or else had been made the subject of a particularly virulent and no doubt potent curse. It therefore came as a relief, but also something of an anti-climax, when Gorey growled 'I'll see you in Court', turned on his heel and strode away accompanied by his two burly companions.

'What on earth was all that? And what did that man mean by "I'll see you in Court"?'

'That, Mr Twite, was the "Clameur de Haro",' replied the senior of the two officers. 'It dates back to Norman times when it constituted an appeal to the Duke of Normandy, the "mon prince" whose aid is sought. It still has the force of law over here. Once a complainant has raised the Clameur, the person complained against must immediately cease the action complained of until the matter is ruled on by the Court. Its one limitation is that it can only be raised in connection with property, I think I'm right in saying.'

'If that's the case, I can't think what that man imagined he was doing. I don't even know his name or where he lives, so how could I possibly have harmed or be harming his property? The whole thing's total medieval rubbish!'

'That would certainly seem to be so, Minister, though no doubt the Procureur or the Bailiff will consider the validity or otherwise of the Clameur and let you know their ruling.'

210

'What do you mean, "their ruling"? And who or rather what is the Procureur?'

'The Procureur is what Jersey, and I think you on the mainland call the Attorney General. It's either him or the Bailiff, I'm not sure which, who has to say whether a Clameur was properly raised.'

'Well, that's all right then, as quite obviously it wasn't in this instance.'

'Yes, so it seems, Minister, though I'm sure Sir William will be in touch with you as he'll know you'll be anxious.'

'Really? I'm not at all anxious. I regard the whole thing as nonsensical!'

'Just as you wish, Mr Twite.'

Twite did not have long to wait.

Within the hour the Bailiff was on the telephone. 'I'm afraid I must ask you to come to my Chambers, Mr Twite. I'm sorry to say we are faced with a most delicate and embarrassing situation arising as a result of a Clameur raised by a certain Mr Gorey, and now registered and duly sworn. Your police escort will arrange transport.'

'But, Mr Bailiff, this is quite ridiculous! Some great deranged creature mouthing gibberish and you tell me it's a delicate matter! You can't be serious!'

'You have to believe me, Minister, when I tell you that the matter is indeed delicate and that we need to discuss what should now be done. I shall expect you in 15 minutes' time.' So saying, Sir William replaced his receiver.

Twite raged impotently and rounded on Smallpeice.

'You should have warned me about this ridiculous Clameur! It's like there being no garrison, all over again, and no proper arrangements with the press. You've simply not put enough work into preparing for this visit, Cyril!'

Cyril wilted. 'Ooooh Ernest, don't! You'll make me ever so upset!'

Twite was still fuming when they met Sir William ten minutes later. The torrent of complaint and protest which he

211

had been rehearsing on the short journey from the hotel was stillborn. One look at the Bailiff's expression told him that this was not a time for bluster.

Sir William's words matched his solemn look.

'A charge against you has been laid in due and proper form by a Mr Gorey and a summons will be issued requiring you to answer to that charge in the Royal Court.'

'What charge, for Heaven's sake? This is utterly preposterous!'

'I wish it was, Mr Twite. Indeed I wish it was, but Mr Gorey's complaint would appear to have a certain substance. The Clameur, the means by which he drew attention to his grievance, relates to property, and Mr Gorey alledges that the legislation which you are seeking to introduce will drastically reduce the sale value of his house and land, and he calls on you, as is normal, to cease such action forthwith. There can be no doubt that, prima facie, Mr Gorey would appear to have an excellent case.'

'But this is just crazy! I am not subject to this archaic Guernsey law!'

'I'm sorry to have to tell you, Mr Twite, that while in this Bailiwick you are subject to its laws just like anyone else, unless you can claim immunity from prosecution.'

'Well! Exactly so! As a minister I can and do claim Crown immunity. So I fail to see that there is any problem!'

'I wish it was as easy as that, Mr Twite, but regrettably it is not. For one thing it could be argued that, for the purposes of the law, you are not in fact a minister.'

'What?!' Had Twite been an older man he might have been judged close to apoplexy.

'I'm afraid so, Mr Twite. I am not aware of the exact position but since you are not a Minister of State it could, I think, and certainly would be argued on Mr Gorey's behalf, that your status entitles you to no more than the courtesy title of Minister and that you cannot therefore claim Crown immunity.'

212

'But this is simply ludicrous! A simple telephone call to the Home Office will give you all the assurance that you need.'

'I would it were so simple. It is not I who require reassurance, Mr Twite, but the Royal Court.'

'But the Court must accept the word of the Home Office!'

'Not necessarily so at all. The Court might well find that although you may rank as a minister in England, the position is different here. It might be held, and would I am sure be argued, that you and your proposals have no standing unless you are acting, and can be seen to be acting, with the authority of the Privy Council and unless it can be shown, in parallel, that your proposals have that body's prior approval. I think, Mr Twite, that it might be somewhat difficult for you to attempt a defence on those lines. If you were to argue that you and your proposals have the backing and authority of Her Majesty's Government, I cannot guarantee that the Court would be overly impressed as the writ of Westminster does not run here, other than in matters of defence and foreign affairs, save with our consent.'

'That is simply not true, Mr Bailiff! The Home Secretary has the right to intervene at any time "In the interests of good government", and well you know it!'

'I am indeed aware of the position, Mr Twite, which is not precisely as you seem to believe. To begin with, the Home Secretary, as such, has no standing in this Bailiwick at all. True, that same individual, acting in his capacity as a Privy Councillor, has the right to intervene, but the Council would only sanction such intervention in the very gravest of circumstances. It is very much a last resort measure and not one that could be invoked lightly or indeed, as you would seem to think, wilfully or irresponsibly.'

'Then what do you suggest?'

'My first reaction on learning the facts was to do nothing, let the summons be served and the law take its course. But that would put us in uncharted waters and, while it might destroy whatever credibility you may have as a politician by making you a national laughing stock, it could at the same time be counter-productive as the island's customs could be represented as archaic and in need of reform. There can be no doubt also that the appearance of a minister, of no matter how junior a status, Mr Twite, in the local Court would be an undignified event from which no one would benefit, and from which only acrimony and dispute could arise.

'So, and not I assure you out of any sympathy for you, I have decided that the only responsible solution is for me to ensure that you leave the island before the summons can be served.'

'You mean that I should cut and run?' Twite's voice shook, partly with indignation but partly also with a dawning realisation that this was no fantasy and that he did indeed stand in danger of humiliation or, even worse, of ridicule if he ignored what Sir William was saying.

'Yes, if you wish to put it in stark terms. But it could be presented differently. It could be said for example that your programme had been changed as you had expressed a wish to visit Sark and Alderney.'

'But I don't want to visit Sark or Alderney and, anyway, they're in your Bailiwick so couldn't the summons be served there?'

'It could be arranged that the summons will be served when you return to Guernsey.'

'But I wouldn't return to Guernsey. I'd fly direct from Alderney to Jersey.'

The Bailiff regarded him impassively.

'Exactly so,' he said.

CHAPTER TWENTY

The boat that had been hired at short notice to take Twite and Smallpeice to Sark was neither large nor comfortable. It was a 36-ft converted fishing boat, largely open to the weather and still, in the bilges, retaining a faint memory of its previous calling. This, together with the smell of diesel fumes, combined to form an aroma which was as unfailingly nauseous to landlubbers as it was irresistibly attractive to small boat men.

Twite and Smallpeice were landlubbers. As the boat passed Herm and Jethou and Sark came into view, they moved into the wind versus tide and heavy overfall conditions of the Great Russel and this became only too apparent. Smallpeice was so much of a hopeless landsman that the first uncontrollable wave of nausea found him facing into wind.

It was two demoralised, exhausted and bedraggled individuals who were landed at Creux Harbour after some forty minutes during which the boat named (perhaps somewhat less than felicitously) Gentle Annie had seemed to them about to sink or capsize at any moment, an event which at times appeared to be a not altogether unacceptable alternative to a continuation of the hellish corkscrew motion to which Gentle Annie seemed addicted.

Their cases were taken and dumped into a flat trailer with cross benches and a rudimentary cover. This contraption, which they were bidden to enter, was towed by tractor and formed the only means of transport, cars being forbidden on the island.

The inhabitants of Sark, some 500 souls, are not by nature garrulous and are at one with the inhabitants of the Western Isles in their liking for strong drink and in the reserve which they show to strangers. By the time that the tractor started to tow them towards the tunnel leading to the steep hill that formed the only road access to the interior no word had been spoken, the only sound uttered being a grunt from the tractor driver whose burly back spoke his contempt for those who, like his miserable passengers, clearly had no stomach for the sea.

In the five to ten minutes that it took the tractor to tow them to the top of the hill, some 300 feet above sea level, Twite had time to reflect on the odd fact that no one had met them at the harbour.

At the top the tractor stopped and the driver, having put their cases down by the roadside, evinced no further interest.

There were three or four horse-drawn carriages, evidently waiting for hire, and after looking in vain for a welcoming delegation, or even a welcoming individual, Twite approached the nearest driver.

He happened to be a little nut brown man called Philip. He was old, so old that the younger generation in Sark were not sure whether he was a de Carteret, as his Christian name made probable, or a Carre, Hamon, Baker, Le Feuvre or Falle. It was possible that his surname was something quite different, but not very likely as those six family names dominated the island and had a near-monopoly of the burial grounds, to one of which Philip, so the impartial observer might conclude, would be committed in the not far distant future.

But that day he was still seemingly unaware that 'man is but grass' was anything more than a catchy saying, and his button eyes twinkled as though his tomorrows had been guaranteed by a particularly prestigious and successful firm

216

of underwriters.

He did not say 'What ho, my hearties!' when faced with Twite and Smallpeice, but his jaunty manner suggested that he had only just succeeded in biting back some such greeting.

Twite recognised that this little berry of a man was a strong character and addressed him civilly. 'Could you please take us to Government House?' he asked.

Philip's English, like that of all Channel Islanders who spoke patois, in his case Sarkese, which is even less intelligible than its Jersey or Guernsey counterparts, was heavily accented with aitches often dropped or added, with Os and Us mixed with fine abandon and with occasional French construction to the English words.

Philip looked at them reflectively with a twinkle in his little curranty eyes. 'No, Hi couldn't. Not honless you know somwey Hi could drive this yer trap hover water. We 'as the Guernsey Guvnor, hos', hand 'e don't 'ave no 'ouse yer. Hits peraps the Seigneurie you want?'

'What's the Seigneurie?'

'Hits wer the Seigneur of Sark is to.'

'You mean where he lives?'

'Yes, that what Hi said, that's wer e's to.'

'Well, could you drive us there, then?'

'Hi could. But it wouldn't do you no good.'

'Why on earth not?'

'Becos the Seigneur 'e's not to the Seigneurie, 'im.'

'But you just said he was.'

'Yes, that's right. 'e his bot 'e hisn't has 'e's habsent de l'Ile.'

Twite controlled his mounting irritation with an effort.

'Well now, could you please tell me where I should go then. I've come to see whoever it is in authority here. My name is Twite and I'm a Home Office minister on a visit.'

The twinkle disappeared from Philip's eyes.

'Oh, so you're that bogger! Hi'm surprised they didn't

drop you in the 'arbour. Would 'ave done hif they'd know 'oo you wer, Hi'm shore. Hits the Seneschal you want. 'E'll give you a yerful! Cor! Not 'alf 'e won't! Get in. Hi'll take you.'

Throwing their gear into the carriage and barely giving them time to get in themselves, he climbed up in front of them and shook the reins. Soon they were moving at a smart clip through the quiet, deserted and unmade lanes of Sark's flat interior, ringed by the high cliffs falling for the most part almost sheer to the deep water just off the rocks below.

It was, and is a paradise, but Twite and Smallpeice had little time in which to appreciate this fact and none in which to enjoy it. Two young men who had been cycling towards them stared hard as they passed, after calling a cheerful greeting to Philip. Twite glanced over his shoulder, made curious by the intensity of their stare, and saw them stop and dismount, looking back at the carriage. After a hurried word together one of them took something from his pocket and after consulting it briefly they turned their bicycles and were soon calling on Philip to stop.

Philip reined in and the carriage came to a halt. The two big and muscular young men addressed him. Being perhaps in their late twenties they were very much of the younger generation with only a nodding acquaintance with Sarkese. As a consequence their English was only faintly accented and suffered few if any curiosities of construction.

'Where are you taking those two, Philip?' asked the taller of the two cyclists.

'To the Seneschal, so Jack can tell this bogger,' and here he indicated Twite, 'what we think of 'is hideas for taking over Sark!'

'I don't know what yarn they've spun you, Philip, but they're drug smugglers wanted by Interpol.' Then, turning to his companion, 'Get round the other side, Hilary, in case they try any funny stuff.'

218

Hilary moved purposefully to his allotted station. Then, addressing Twite, 'And now, Mr De Vries, I am formally arresting you and your companion,' and here he looked at Cyril, 'Mr Van der Secker, is it not? on a charge of smuggling narcotics, and I must ask you to accompany me.'

Twite's bewilderment gave way to fury as his control snapped.

'I don't know who the hell you think you are, you insolent oaf, but by God you'll be sorry before I've finished with you! I'll have you know that my name is Twite and that I am a Home Office minister, and this is my secretary, Mr Smallpeice.' Cyril gave a muted squeak of outraged assent.

The tall young man regarded him levelly.

'All very convincing, Mr De Vries, but I'm afraid it's no good. I have a photograph here of you and your companion, sent to me by the Jersey police. The accompanying letter says that you are both likely to bluster and to claim British nationality, that your accents are perfect, and that you in particular, Mr De Vries, are a consummate con-man. Here, as you can see, is the photograph, so you might as well save your breath.'

He produced the photograph from his pocket and an astonished Twite and Smallpeice gazed at a reproduction of a Police 'Wanted' sheet showing their own likenesses above a line typed in capital letters reading DE VRIES AND VAN DER SECKER.

Twite's jaw dropped as he stared in anger and disbelief.

'But this is some ridiculous joke, except that it's not in the least bit funny! Have I come to a set of islands inhabited by madmen? I demand to be taken to a 'phone so that I can speak to the Home Secretary.'

'You can demand as much as you like, Mr De Vries, but you're not going to be taken anywhere except to Sark prison.'

'But this is crazy, this is some nightmare hoax! Who are you, anyway? And what is your authority? You are not in uniform! You have no warrant. I demand that you stand back and allow me to see the Seneschal.'

'Oh, you'll see the Seneschal, all right Mr De Vries. I'll bring him to see you in prison. He'll be interested, I know, to see the most important prisoner we've had for years. The only important prisoner we've ever had, in fact,' he corrected. 'As for my authority, I am John Carre, senior constable of Sark,and this is Hilary Le Feuvre, the junior constable. This is my badge of office.' He produced a miniature police truncheon, bearing the Sark arms, from his top pocket.

'No more argument! Philip, drive the prisoners to the prison. Hilary and I will escort you.'

The carriage set off escorted by the two young men on bicycles.

Arrived at Sark prison, a sort of granite beehive, reputedly the smallest goal in use in the British Isles, Twite and Smallpeice got out of the carriage.

'That'll be one pound seventy-five,' said Philip.

'One pound seventy-five!' shouted Twite. 'You can subtract it from the damages you're going to have to pay as an accessory to wrongful arrest!' Then, to John Carre, 'I refuse to go a step further until I've laid a complaint with the Seneschal.'

'Don't make things difficult for us all, Mr De Vries. Just move along in, please.'

'I absolutely refuse! Lay a finger on me and you will face a charge of assault as well as wrongful arrest.'

'Very well, Mr De Vries. Have it your way.'

Twite and Smallpeice suddenly found themselves lifted bodily and, their feet scarcely in contact with the ground, propelled inexorably into the cell. Twite shouted abuse and struggled furiously. Cyril enjoyed the rough masculine embrace. The stout door was slammed upon them and the bolts rammed home on the outside.

When John Carre arrived at the Seneschal's house with the news that he and Hilary Le Feuvre had arrested two criminals wanted by Interpol for drug smuggling, Jack Hamon was suitably impressed.

'Cor, that's something, eh?' he said. 'Well, I suppose we'd better tell the Guernsey police so that they can decide what's to be done. I expect they'll pick the boggers up tomorrow. You sure they're safe for the night, John? You remember some drunks managed to break out a few years back, eh?'

'Yeah, they're fine, Jack. We've got a new door since then, and anyway this lot is too puny. But just in case they've got an accomplice, Hilary and I will take turns to watch during the night. He's there now.'

'Well, that's fine then. What's their names?'

'De Vries and Van der Secker.'

'Couple of Dutchies, eh? Just write it for me on this bit of paper, John, so as I'm sure to have it right when I ring Guernsey in a minute. Cor, but you boys did well! Makes up for the bad news I got a little while back from Sir William that that there Home Office bogger Twite had changed his mind and was coming after all, in fact I expect he's here already. Probably booked into one of the hotels and going to call on me tomorrow. That's a call I could do without, I can tell you. The mad bogger wants to make us part of Hampshire, or some such.'

John Carre was looking at him open mouthed.

'What an amazing coincidence! De Vries claimed he was Twite. Oh no, not a coincidence! I see it now. He and Van der Secker must have come over from Guernsey in the same boat. Quick of him though, to think of it. Shows what a smart operator he is.'

'Yes, that's quick thinking all right,' agreed the Seneschal. 'I'll come to the prison at nine tomorrow morning unless Twite decides to call very early, in which case I'll let you know, John. Make sure you keep De Vries and the other fellow safe.'

'I'll do that all right, Jack, don't worry.'

In elated mood, John Carre, went off to share the night's

221

vigil with his junior constable, stopping on the way to pick up some fish and chips and beer, something easy and suitable as a celebratory meal. The prisoners would have watery vegetable soup, stale bread and water. And lucky to get that, many would have said.

No one stayed in Sark prison for more than 48 hours before either being released or transferred to Guernsey, and anyone can go without food for that length of time, and probably be all the better for it. Water was another matter, particularly for the dehydrated drunks who were the occasional and more usual occupants of Twite's and Smallpeice's spartan and Victorian cell.

It was a thoughtful and worried Seneschal who arrived at the prison the next morning to find his constables in cheerful mood, having just had a large breakfast of eggs, sausage, bacon, tomato and fried potato while the prisoners, no doubt tormented by the smells of cooking, had cold lumpy porridge made with water and served without either milk or sugar and stale bread with a scraping of margarine.

'I can't make it out, John, but something's wrong somewhere. The Guernsey police say they can't find any trace of a De Vries or a Van der Secker on the Wanted List.'

'Well, Jack, you know how the Guernsey police are. Not too bright, eh?'

'I'm not so sure about that, John. It used to be like you say but they've got some pretty bright young ones in there now and it would have been them, the juniors, who would have been doing the checking.'

'But for goodness' sake,' John's tone was one of exasperation, 'all they have to do is to get on to Jersey. Here, look! Here's the Jersey wanted list with the pictures of De Vries and Van der Secker. I mean, you could do it yourself, or I could do it. I don't know what's got into that Guernsey lot!'

Jack Hamon was looking at the photographs intently.

'You know, John, it's funny, but I've seen that De Vries somewhere before, or a picture of him perhaps, unless it's

222

someone very like him, of course. Van der Secker no. But De Vries certainly seems to ring a bell. I wonder if they've used Sark before? Havre Gosselin would certainly make a very secure and unlikely anchorage for a yacht full of heroin, or whatever they're running. Anyway, let's ring the Jersey police. Have you got a phone here?'

'No, but there'll be one in the school next door.'

'Right, well, the sooner we get to the bottom of this the better I'll be pleased. I don't know what it is, but I think something isn't quite right. I'll just go and ring up. Give me the letter that came with the wanted list will you? It's got the telephone number on it.'

The Seneschal left. Within ten minutes he was back again, his face ashen. He sank into a chair.

'Cor, John. I tell you straight, we're in a right mess! Jersey police say they never sent that letter or any wanted list and they've never heard of De Vries or Van der Secker! It must be a hoax, they say, which means, John, that those two in there are probably who they say they are, Twite and Smallpeice. Come to think of it, I believe it was a Press photograph of Twite which the picture of the so-called De Vries reminded me of. Cor damme, but we're in trouble, John! Did you look at their passports?'

'No, I didn't think to look. And maybe they didn't have them with them anyway. They don't need them for here.'

'That's right, but people often do in case their aeroplane has to land in France. Have a look, John, while I think.'

John Carre was soon back. His face told the sorry tale. Wordlessly he handed the two passports to the Seneschal. The Seneschal glanced at the passports and then looked up at his senior constable.

'We're boggered, John,' he said.

'That's right, Jack, we're proper boggered,' came the miserable response. The Seneschal's brow crinkled with thought. 'Get me a cup of tea, John. We don't have to rush into this. They can stay there for a bit.'

223

The tea came and the silence lasted while Jack Hamon sipped and considered. After a while he began to think aloud, speaking to his companion but requiring no answer.

'He didn't want to come in the first place, and the Seigneur didn't want him either. So what changed his mind? Probably Guernsey got sick and tired of him. But we still don't want him or anything to do with him. We'll send him off straight away either to Guernsey or Alderney so that he can fly back to Jersey. Should I apologise for the wrongful arrest? No. To hell with him! A genuine and totally understandable mistake. Will he sue or demand reparation of some sort? Let him try. It's us who should be calling on him for a donation to the Sark Welfare Fund in exchange for not leaking the story to the Press. Is there any point in talking to him? Absolutely none. His mind is closed, though a few parting words mightn't come amiss. Do I want to hear what he has to say? No bloody fear!'

His mind made up, the Seneschal came back to full consciousness.

'John. Get a boat ready to take these two either to Guernsey or Alderney. I'll let you know which after I've telephoned Sir William. Then get a carriage here to take them straight to the boat as soon as it's ready. In the meantime they can stay where they are.'

The senior constable had gradually come to look more cheerful as the Seneschal's soliloquy had progressed, and now he positively beamed.

'Right, Jack! So we don't apologise?'

'That's it. No apologies! And you and Hilary can escort them off the island. Call it protective custody if you like. And not so fanciful at that. I wouldn't answer for some of our younger ones if they got a chance to have a go at Twite.'

By the time that John Carre returned to say that a boat would be ready at Creux Harbour in half an hour, the Seneschal had spoken to Sir William and established that

Twite should be sent on to Alderney. Sir William had undertaken to warn the President of the States of Alderney that Twite would arrive that afternoon.

The Seneschal regarded him with the ghost of a smile on his tanned face.

'You may release the prisoners, constable!'

Then, crinkling into a grin, 'Let the boggers out, John, and stand by for fireworks!'

John Carre turned the massive key in the lock, drew the bolts and, opening the door, said matter of factly: 'You can come out now.'

Twite emerged first, crumpled, unshaven, blinking in the light with his fury not only undimmmed but heightened by his night of captivity.

'I demand to see the Seneschal!' he stormed at Carre.

'I am the Seneschal, Mr Twite.'

Twite's reaction to Jack Hamon's words could not have been faulted by the most demanding of theatrical directors. He started wordlessly as though the victim of an electric shock, or three inches of darning needle in his bottom. His jaw dropped, he gulped, he fought for breath while at the same time gobbling like a turkey who, in search of dramatic effect, had overdone things a bit and cut its own throat.

Before the dam could burst and the words come flooding out, the Seneschal took control.

'You are due an explanation Mr Twite, and it is a simple one. The supposed Jersey police letter and photographs were, as we now know, a hoax set up presumably by some person or persons in Jersey who do not wish you well. Quite a wide field, I should imagine, Mr Twite. Could be any one of the 75,000 inhabitants, I shouldn't wonder. My constables were quite right in what they did and you've no cause to complain.'

'No cause to complain!' Twite found his voice in what sounded like a demented but partially strangled shriek.

'No cause to complain, you say! Wrongful arrest! Assault!

Denial of legal rights! I'll sue you for every halfpenny you've got Mr whatever your name is, Mr Seneschal, damned fool title though that may be!'

'You just go ahead, Mr Twite, though no English court has jurisdiction. You could try your luck in Guernsey, of course, but I wouldn't fancy your chances. And wouldn't the national press and all the rest of those media boys love to know you cooled your heels in Sark prison! Cor, I can just see it! And as for my title of Seneschal, you don't know much, do you, Mr Twite? Perhaps you don't even know that Sark actually belongs to the Seigneur. We're independent here, Mr Twite. We only owe allegiance to the Crown, what's represented by the Governor of Guernsey, and we answer to the Guernsey Court. We don't answer to you people at all and we don't need no lessons in democracy. The powers of the Seigneur have mostly been surrendered to Chief Pleas, that's the Sark Parliament, just like in England, and the Seneschal presides and is the chief executive. We don't have no political parties, thank God, and most of our decisions are unanimous.'

Throughout the Seneschal's uncharacteristically long statement, for Jack Hamon was usually a man of few words, Twite had been struggling to interrupt. Now, as the Seneschal paused for breath, he succeeded.

'You'll regret this Mr, Mr whatever your name is. You can think back on it when you're a tiny, remote, insignificant part of Hampshire, as you soon will be, mark my words! I'll see to it if it's the last thing I do!'

'My name's Hamon, Mr Twite, and there have been Hamons in Sark for over 400 years. And as for making Sark part of Hampshire, you just can't do that. It belong to the Seigneur. You can't take it away just like that!'

'We not only can, but we will, Mr Hamon! You may not know it, but there are at least two precedents in recent times. Immediately after the last war the Government of the day excluded Rajah Brooke from Sarawak and took over

226

the territory. Soon afterwards the same thing was done to Clunies-Ross in the Cocos Islands.'

'I don't know about that, Mr Twite, but you'll not get away with it here, I tell you flat. The people of Sark just wouldn't have it, and you can't put us all in jail!'

'If it's the law, then the law must be obeyed!'

'We'll see about that when the time comes, if ever it does. But at this minute I represent the law here in Sark, and I'm telling you, Mr Twite, that I want you out of the island in half an hour. There's a boat waiting to take you to Alderney. You can have a wash and shave in the school but I want you moving down the hill in 15 minutes.'

'And if I refuse?' demanded Twite furiously.

Jack Hamon indicated the two muscular young constables.

'You'll go just the same.'

'What! You would dare to lay hands on a minister of the Crown?'

'Yes. To save you from getting proper beaten up I'd do just that, Mr Twite. I think the word's protective custody, or some such.'

CHAPTER TWENTY ONE

Some three and a half hours later the boat carrying Twite and Smallpeice came alongside the jetty in Alderney's Braye Harbour. They were met by a police sergeant and a constable, both in uniform. The sergeant greeted Twite respectfully.

'I have a car waiting and instructions to escort you two gentlemen to your hotel, Sir. I also have a letter for you from the President of the States.'

The constable took their luggage and the sergeant led them to the car. For once Twite did as he was instructed without protest.

The boat journey from Sark, though not as horrendously rough as their crossing of the previous day, had been long, tiring and uncomfortable, and coming on top of the night in Sark jail had left him drained and exhausted. Cyril was in even worse condition.

Arrived at the hotel they were soon installed in a suite consisting of a comfortable sitting room with a fine view of the French coast with two bedrooms, each with its own bathroom, opening from it. Whoever had made the arrangements had taken some thought for their needs. There were drinks and sandwiches on a side table in case the guests had missed their lunch, as indeed they had, and a refrigerator purred discreetly in one corner.

Twite's spirits began to revive. Perhaps here there would be some acceptance, even understanding, of the need to change the medieval nature of these islands whose ana-

228

chronistic status, financial success and placid contentment was an affront to those, like Twite, who believed in uniformity and in levelling down.

This mood of wary optimism did not last long; did not, in fact, survive the first few lines of the letter from the President of the States of Alderney which Twite proceeded to open and read. The letter was not long but it was to the point.

The President started by reminding Mr Twite of something which he supposed Mr Twite would by now have come to know only too well, that is to say that his proposals, and by extension he himself, were not welcome in the Channel Islands. And that went for Alderney too. Indeed, although the President did not use the words, the letter clearly implied that that went for Alderney with knobs on.

After drawing Twite's attention to the fact that in terms of numbers the populations of Alderney and of the Falkland Islands were much on a par, and after having compared the Government of Argentina with that over which Kevin Pratt presided, to the disadvantage of the latter, the President went on to say that the island would take whatever steps proved necessary to thwart Twite and his plans. Appeal to the Court of Human Rights in The Hague, then if that failed, which was most unlikely, consideration either of a unilateral declaration of independence or of opting to revert to the French mainland part of the Duchy of Normandy.

This part of the President's letter spoke eloquently of the depth of feeling of the islanders. 'If you look out from the room in which you now are, you will see the coast of France. Normandy. Seven miles away. Although these islands have in centuries gone by formed the outer periphery of a bastion against the French, never more perhaps than in Napoleonic times, and although we give pride of place to no man in our loyalty to the Crown, we are

229

prepared, if driven to it, to continue that same loyalty to the Queen's person as Duke of Normandy, rather than as Queen of England.'

Twite's lips tightened as he read. Posturing theatrical nonsense and empty threats, not worth his serious attention.

The letter concluded with a cursory expression of regret that the writer had had to leave the island before Twite's arrival, and by giving an outline of the arrangements for the next day. These consisted of a programme of sightseeing in the company of the police sergeant, should Twite so wish, before his departure by air for Jersey after lunch at the hotel. The Jersey authorities had been informed of his movements in confidence but no announcement had been made of his presence in Alderney in view of the strength of public feeling.

Twite threw the letter on the table.

'To hell with them all,' he said, glowering at Cyril. 'They can protest and wring their hands as much as they like. Yes, and ridiculous extravagant rubbish like that letter won't help them either. They'll become part of Hampshire all right, however much they kick and squeal, you see if they don't!'

'They've been simply horrid to you, Ernest dear, I know. Oh, I do so wish this nasty visit was over, it's been nothing but one upset after another,' Cyril sighed. 'And there's another thing, Ernest. You don't want us to stay in that awful haunted Hall again tomorrow night, do you? It might be best if I was to ring Commander Point and tell him to get hotel accommodation for us.'

'Yes, do that, Cyril. We'll have to go there for dinner but I agree with you that I certainly don't want to spend another night there.'

But Twite's wishes were not to be granted.

When Geoffrey Point met them at Jersey airport the following afternoon it was to say that all hotels were fully booked and that he would once more be escorting them to the Hall.

'But that's simply ridiculous!' Twite protested. 'They can't all be full. It's just not possible!'

'I'm inclined to agree with you that there is another explanation.'

'And what's that?'

'Really, Mr Twite. If you have failed to realise by now that you have succeeded in the space of a few days in antagonising the entire population of the Channel Islands, I simply can't help you.'

'You mean the hotel managers have got together and decided to keep me out simply because they don't like me?'

'You could put it that way. I would say that you had been blackballed but I wouldn't say they didn't like you.'

'No?'

'No. Hated, loathed or detested would be more accurate plus, of course, despised.'

'They can't do that!' They can't conspire to insult a minister of the Crown!'

Geoffrey's lips twitched.

'Conspire, Mr Twite? Isn't that rather a big word? No, all that's happened, Mr Twite, is that the managers have exercised their democratic right to consult together and to decide on joint collective action. In this instance they have decided to withdraw their labour so far as you are concerned. All very routine trade union procedure and practice. Surely you're not complaining at that?'

Twite was white with fury.

'You know very well that you're playing with words, Commander! It's not like that at all and I demand that the Governor order one of these hotels to accommodate me and Mr Smallpeice for the night!'

'His Excellency has no power to compel, Mr Twite, and even if he did I very much doubt whether he would choose

231

to exercise such authority in this instance. So, if you would be so good? We're just wasting time.'

Geoffrey indicated the Daimler with the chauffeur standing by its open rear door. A reluctant and angry Twite and a petulant Smallpeice got into the car, their backs stiff with protest.

CHAPTER TWENTY TWO

During Twite's absence from Jersey two events of importance had taken place, the first having some effect on the second.

The first had been Richard and Pussy's decision, important only to them and to Ursula and Johnnie so they thought, to take the Hall off the market, this as a result of Johnnie happening to say to his mother how much better he liked the Hall than their house in England and how much he hoped that he might be able to live there one day. They had not suspected that the news would be of importance to Scratcher, and Pussy was somewhat taken aback by the warmth of his reaction when she happened to let slip the fact.

'Praise the Lord! The Lord's name be praised!' Scratcher intoned with evidently devout enthusiasm and then, getting carried away, he reverted momentarily to his missionary past. 'May the magic of blessed St Matthew make you fruitful and may your cattle multiply! May the juju of blessed St James make the testicles of your enemies shrivel and wither away!' He came to with a start. 'In a manner of speaking, that is, Ma'am,' he added hastily.

'Scratcher! Whatever's got into you?' Pussy asked, not knowing whether to laugh or send for the doctor.

'I don't know, Ma'am, I'm sorry. I'm just so very pleased that you and the Group Captain will be staying on after all. I somehow couldn't abide the thought of the Hall without you and of not working for you both any more.'

This was a side to Scratcher that Pussy had neither glimpsed nor guessed at before and she felt strangely humbled by the evident depth of his feeling.

'Well, that's lovely, Scratcher, I'm so glad,' she said somewhat inadequately, and turned away hastily in embarrassment, aware that unexpected tears were rising to her eyes.

There was an equally emotional atmosphere, or perhaps excitable might describe it better, at the second major event which was the meeting of Podger's irregulars, called by him to run through the final phase of Operation Twite.

The group had been strengthened by the addition of Arthur Crabbe, no longer disqualified by his special relationship with the Bailiff. At the same time it had in another sense been weakened by the departure of Maeve O'Cork. Though she had not even known of the group's existence her presence, as Constance knew, had made it possible for them to deploy the poltergeist as a weapon of first use.

With the great medium vanished from the scene Constance felt that nothing could be assured and that it was difficult even to guess at how the poltergeist might react, if indeed it reacted at all, to Twite's second visit. The best that could be hoped for, so she informed them, was in her opinion the spirit equivalent of a tantrum, a drumming of tiny poltergeist heels on the nursery floor of their consciousness. She was inclined to think this could be quite effective in unnerving Twite and Smallpeice if only it happened. More probably nothing would happen at all but, if it did, she promised them that the barrage of trays and rate of fall of pictures would be likely to exceed anything they had yet witnessed.

At this Scratcher's eyes, had anyone observed them, seemed to take on a speculative and calculating look. Such a pity, but there it was, Constance concluded sadly. Without the presence of the great medium nothing could be forecast with confidence, let alone guaranteed.

234

'So,' Podger said, taking control of the meeting. 'It seems clear that we'll have to leave the poltergeist to chance, but I suppose we can count on the resident ghosts in the west wing, eh, Connie?' She nodded assent.

'And on you, Scratcher, for another organ voluntary?' Podger's blue eyes twinkled.

'With pleasure, Brigadier.'

'Good. Well, now. Let's see what we've got to go on, eh, what? From what I've heard, the bounders got it in the neck hot and strong in all three islands. Old Gorey came up trumps and really laid it on in Guernsey with the Clameur; the arrest in Sark knocked the stuffing out of them and in Alderney the President's letter – you've all seen a copy, I think? – can't have improved morale. Enemy forces likely to be a bit demoralised, I fancy, what? eh?'

'Roger for dodger! Read you loud and clear. Enemy aircraft last seen heading for base and losing altitude, two engines hit, No. 3 feathered and No. 1 trailing smoke. Stand by for belly landing at the Hall!'

'While on the one hand I am, ah, er, inclined to support the proposition just advanced, namely that the, ah, enemy morale may have been to a degree perhaps adversely affected by the curious and I trust inexplicable turn of events in Guernsey and in Sark, and while I accept that it can be logically posited that what we may perhaps term the Alderney letter will be most unlikely to have detracted from this, ah, assumed diminution in morale, we should I think on the other hand not exclude the possibility that these, ah, somewhat unusual experiences may have had the opposite effect and in fact stiffened Twite's resolve. Smallpeice we can I think dismiss from the equation while at the same time, of course, remembering that his potential influence on Twite might in certain circumstances prove to be not without importance.'

Pranger, for whom this was the first experience of Arthur in action, fought back a reflex response of 'Say again. Your

transmission was garbled' and sat with his jaw slightly dropped and his brow furrowed. So far as he could tell by looking
at Arthur, this no doubt masterly analysis had been achieved
without effort. The man had merely been operating at
cruising revs. What wouldn't he be able to do at full throttle
or at max power with afterburner in? The mind simply
boggled.

Connie looked around the circle, her eyes shining with
pride. Dear Arthur, he was so clever and where, she wondered, would any of them be without him?

Podger broke the short silence.

'Harrumph! Ha! Yes, what? If I read you aright, Arthur, it's
similar to a unit that's taken heavy losses. Could have lost its
fighting spirit or could on the other hand fight with increased
determination and bitterness. A matter of training
beforehand and leadership at the time. Doesn't apply here,
of course, but I take your point. Yes, take your point, Arthur.
Good thinking, good thinking. Shouldn't count on a demoralised Twite, eh? Likely to be shaken but could be even
more bloody minded, what?'

'Precisely so, Podger. Precisely so.'

Pranger retracted his jaw and his brow cleared. 'Strength
niner with the pukka gen. Finger out and watch your six
o'clock, hey?'

'You're right, Pranger,' said Podger. 'And I think we must
all be grateful to Arthur for his counselling against over-
confidence, what? We can't take any chances over this.
We've got to make sure we tie Twite up but good, as our
American friends would say. I think we're all fairly clear on
the main plan but we'll go over it again in a moment, as
timing is critical. But what I suggest we agree first is how
much of a re-run of last Thursday we should play.'

Arthur was the first to speak and Connie beamed with
anticipatory pride while a look of fierce concentration came
over Pranger's face once more.

'I was not as you know privy to any of last Thursday's ah,

236

happenings although I was witness to some of them and know of the others in retrospect and at second hand, not perhaps the best of qualifications for offering considered advice. But, with that reservation made it seems to me, prima facie, that those incidents which might be held to have had an, er, less unnatural aspect might, if not repeated in similar form, just conceivably give rise to suspicion. On the other hand it could plausibly be argued, as I would be the first to admit, that the exact opposite would be the more likely outcome.'

Pranger's expression of concentration had been replaced by a glazed look, but his optimism remained high in spite of his lack of comprehension. There was no doubt, he told himself, that the old maestro was in cracking form, playing himself in gently but seeing the ball well. Just warming up with a few flick rolls and rolls off the top before getting into the really tough negative G stuff. His thoughts were interrupted by Podger.

'See what you mean, Arthur, see what you mean, old chap. Dogs and cats, and spooks we hope, should react in much the same way otherwise it would look fishy, what? Falling trousers and all that sort of rot, out, eh? That it, Arthur?'

Arthur, who had the grace to look momentarily surprised by Podger's claim to understanding, hastened to agree.

'Exactly so, Podger. I think one must allow oneself to be forced to that conclusion even while accepting that repetition inevitably carries with it a certain lack of impact. The risk of straying from an established pattern, though it would have the advantage of freshness and novelty must, I am inclined to believe, be discarded as too great. Though I am of course well aware that it could be argued that the benefit to be derived from that same freshness and singularity of approach might in certain circumstances be deemed to outweigh the risk.'

Podger's eyes bulged fractionally.

237

'Ah,' he said. 'Good. Well, yes, thank you, Arthur. Can I take it everyone's agreed, what?'

Taking silence to mean consent, Podger carried on. 'Now, let's see. I suggest we make it a bit simpler this time and target Dolly on Smallpeice and the cats on Twite right from the word go. That would mean aniseed strategically placed on Smallpeice together with a quick application of Puss Off. Can you handle that, Scratcher, whilst at the same time sprinkling that dried shrimp powder or whatever it is on Twite? Bit of a tall order, what?'

'I fancy I can manage that without undue difficulty, Brigadier.'

'Oh? Oh, good then, splendid! While we're about it, I rather think you overdid the shrimp powder a trifle last time, Scratcher.'

'I do so agree, Podger! I'm sure it can't be good for the darling little furry-poos to excite them quite so much, isn't that so, Ranee darling?'

The Ranee, who was senior cat-in-waiting of the forenoon watch, looked at her without expression and then turned and jumped into Richard's lap. This shocking breach of etiquette was part of a behaviour pattern intended to indicate that the Ranee was a reluctant cat-in-waiting, virtually a pressed pussy, in fact, and that her ambition was to be the sole and constant attendant on Richard. She wished to be a feline equerry and sex, she felt, should be no barrier.

'Naughty, rude Ranee-poos!' said Pussy. 'I know she agrees, really, but she's so highly strung and independent that sometimes she decides to disagree just for effect.'

'Good. Splendid,' said Podger. 'We can take it then that we've got the cat vote in favour of less powder.'

'That's the drill! Throttle back, airbrakes out, reduce the dosage as the airspeed falls off.'

'Really, Daddy!' This in a plaintive voice. 'Do you absolutely have to go on flying all the time? If your airspeed falls off any more you'll stall!'

'No danger of that, old girl! Even if you haven't got stall warners you get warning from the pre-stall judder.'

'I wouldn't count on it, Daddy, you've got a touch of the judders all the time.'

'Touch of the judders, eh? I like it! I like it!' responded what she thought of as her aged parent with all the enthusiasm of a lexicographer glimpsing a new word for the first time.

'I think we should move on a bit. Lot of ground to cover and all that, don't you know, eh?' Podger once more took the helm.

'To re-cap, we hope that the poltergeist will perform either when they arrive, or as soon as it associates them with Maeve O'Cork. Dolly and the cats we've just agreed. We've also agreed, I think, that there should be no repetition of falling trousers or Who? Me? or, in fact harrassment of any sort. That phase is over and we're into the big play of compromise. We've simply got to bring it off. It's all or nothing.'

'Shit or bust! What?'

'Yes, Pranger, if you wish to put it in that colourful way. Now, there are several critical things that we need to be quite clear about. Twite's pyjamas and other visible impedimenta must be secreted and Smallpeice's moved into Twite's room as soon as they come down to dinner. That's down to you, Scratcher.'

'Very good, Brigadier.'

'As soon as that's done, it's first curtain moving detail into action. You, Scratcher, again and you, Pranger.' They nodded.

'Before that, I forgot, we need the letter in Smallpeice's room so that we're sure that he sees it before dinner. That's you, isn't it, Richard?'

'Yes, that's right. I may need some help with the wording, but I'll see it's there in good time. The envelope is ready.'

'Good. Cameras in position, synchronised and checked out, Pranger?'

239

'I read you, and that is affirmative!'

'Master switch control rigged within sight of the bedrooms?'

'Roger. Masterswitch control rigged and ready!'

'Second curtain moving detail into action immediately Twite closes the door. Richard and Scratcher? Good. Now, timing. We know Smallpeice will go to his room before eleven, but we're not sure precisely when. We take his move as H hour and time everything else from that except that Urse and Pranger will need to be in position earlier, say at 1040, which we can guess as likely to be about H minus 5. Pussy, you're responsible for moving Twite at H plus 5. You know the rest of your bit and you, Pranger, take your timing from when Pussy and Twite pass you at, we hope, H plus 7. That's the signal for electricity failure. Second curtain moving detail, with a torch, need to be close up in rear. You, Pranger, throw the switch first time on cue from Urse, second time on altercation. The business of the necklace should be much more straightforward. You know the combination of Mr Twite's case, Scratcher?'

'No, Sir. I have established that he changes it daily and that it is known only to him.'

'Oh, I say! rotten luck, what? We'll have to cancel that bit then. Pity.'

'Not necessarily so, Sir. I have also established by what is I think known as a dry run that Mr Twite writes the current combination on a piece of paper, lest he himself should forget the precise sequence of numbers. He places that piece of paper in his wallet which he carries in his hip pocket.'

'You think, er, that is to say you, er, think, Scratcher?' Podger enquired tentatively, breaking the hush that had followed Scratcher's words.

'Yes, Brigadier,' said Scratcher.

Podger let out a long breath.

'Aah! Good,' he said.

240

CHAPTER TWENTY THREE

The arrival at the Hall started off in relatively low key.
Scratcher's reception of the two guests, while in no way
capable of being described as warm, was at least
punctilious. On this occasion he deigned to take notice of
Smallpeice and even went so far as to pluck some
offending piece of thread from his trousers.

Twite and Smallpeice were received as before by their
host and hostess and were relieved to note that there were
no animals in the room. The relief was shortlived.

Dolly and the cats were under restraint next door. Dolly
had had her puppies during the weekend, and had displayed them proudly in the corner of an outhouse made
warm by the missing woollen garments. It was resolved that
this shocking fact must be kept from Constance at all costs
lest it destroy her faith in Maeve O'Cork.

Dolly herself had been passed as fit for action and as
soon as Ursula saw that Twite and Smallpeice had been
manoeuvred so that their backs were towards her, she
opened the door.

The cats paws made no sound on the thick carpet and
the only split second warning available to Twite and
Smallpeice, had they read the noise aright, was the enthusiastic wooshing sound made by Dolly as she emptied her
lungs in anticipation of sniffing in the deep delights of the
crotch which beckoned a few short bounds away.

The Foxes' eyes did not shift from their guests' faces, nor
did their expression change. The assault, when it came,

though not as severe as that to which they had been subjected on their previous visit, had the trauma of total and complete surprise. Co-ordination could not have been bettered if Dolly and the cats had been giving a command performance.

At the exact moment that Dolly thrust her eager questing muzzle into Cyril's crotch from behind, two cats landed on Twite, one on each shoulder, with the perfect timing of Russian or Chinese gymnasts. The two shoulder cats nudged Twite with enthusiasm and evident admiration while the other five rubbed against his legs with near reverential fervour. It was obvious that in terms of feline favour he stood high in the charts.

Dolly's initial thrust took Cyril, literally, aback and it was a surprise not totally untinged with vicarious pleasure. But his initial Oooh! of surprised enjoyment almost instantly moved to a higher register and took on the shrill note of protest as Dolly lifted her massive head, leaving Cyril suspended with the toecaps of his downward pointing shoes in intermittent contact with the floor like a ballet dancer stricken by a sudden palsy.

An apparently concerned and apologetic Richard and Pussy had just succeeded in freeing their guests from the unwelcome attentions of their four-legged admirers, who had been rounded up and exiled, the cats still protesting their undying love for Twite, when the poltergeist swung into action.

The performance started with a rapid fire of trays, reaching a crescendo with a massive barrage of falling pictures. Then there was a pause while the poltergeist regrouped and reloaded before moving into a phase of steady harassing fire which in turn suddenly doubled in intensity as more pictures began to fall. The noise, multiplied by the resounding echoes of the cavernous outer hall, far surpassed anything the poltergeist had previously achieved.

242

Twite was white and shaken, Cyril clearly terrified. Pussy, long inured to ghosts, attempted to reassure them and to convince them that the poltergeist was merely mischievous and intended no harm. Indeed, what they were now witnessing was probably intended as a spirit welcome, a token of goodwill from the other side.

Richard, who alone knew the truth, listened in rapt admiration. He recalled how, at the end of Podger's briefing meeting, Scratcher had approached him, strangely diffident in his manner, and had asked for a word in private. This he subsequently explained was necessary to protect the susceptibilities of Lady Crabbe and, indeed, of Miss O'Cork, both of whom would be greatly upset were they to learn that he, Scratcher, now ably assisted by Johnnie, was in fact the poltergeist.

An embarrassed Scratcher went on to relate how he had started the deception with the sole intention of frightening away would-be buyers of the Hall, a liberty which he hoped his employer would now be able to excuse, and how circumstances had forced him to continue the deception and indeed to enlarge his repertoire.

Richard was fascinated by Scratcher's account of the ballistics involved in the precision launching of brass trays, something which he felt could well form the subject of a thesis. But it was the matter of pictures jumping off their hooks on command which baffled Richard, and he pressed Scratcher to reveal his method.

Scratcher explained that any impression that this was a precise art was mistaken. The most that could be done was to settle for an approximate timing, while constantly seeking to refine the technique to give greater accuracy. The basic method was to remove the pictures from their hooks and to hang them on pins or tacks adequate to support them in the first instance, but which would give way in time. The art, if it could be so called, lay in assessing the depth of pin required to suspend pictures of differing weights and size for a given time before the pin gave way. It was, so Scratcher said, not by any means an easy matter, but he felt it was something in which by experience he had now acquired a certain modest competence.

Listening to the well co-ordinated jump of pictures and to the impeccable rhythm of the fall of trays, Richard suddenly realised that what he was listening to was a gala performance. It was the final appearance of the poltergeist, and Scratcher was putting as much effort and artistry into the event as Sir Malcolm Sargent would have put into the Last Night of the Proms. Gradually the din diminished and then died. The poltergeist would not perform again. Its mission was accomplished.

A short while later Twite and Smallpeice, shaken but somewhat restored by strong tea, retired to their rooms to rest and to prepare for dinner. Pussy did not accompany them but contented herself with telling them that they had the same rooms as before.

'Yours, Mr Twite, as I'm sure you remember, is the second door on the right past the big curtain and yours, Mr Smallpeice, is the third.' She smiled sweetly.

On reaching his room Cyril was intrigued to find a letter propped up on the dressing table. The envelope was typewritten, addressed to him and marked 'To Await Arrival'. It bore a local postmark of the previous Friday. He opened it and, as he began to read, his heartbeat quickened and he became conscious that his mouth was suddenly dry.

'Dear Boy,' he read, 'I saw you looking at me last night and, although I could give no sign in that company, my heart went out to you.

'Unless you send a note to tell me nay, and that would break my heart, I will come to your room in the Hall on Monday night. Be there not later than 11 o'clock. Dearest one, I long to hold you in my arms.' The letter was signed 'Ernest'.

244

Cyril's pulse raced as he quickened with desire. That tanned, salt-seamed face, that hard whipcord seafaring body and, above all, the thrill of that magnificent beard. Cyril's lips, from being dry, had become wet with anticipation. For him the two hours before dinner passed in a happy dream.

Next door Ernest Twite was re-reading the document which he planned to leave with the Bailiff of Jersey the following morning. A virtually identical document dealing with the Bailiwick of Guernsey would have to go by mail because in his haste to leave St Peter Port he had forgotten to hand it over.

As Twite read, his flagging spirits bagan to revive. He could not deny that they had reached a low ebb. Although his aggressive nature thrived on opposition, and although he expected dislike from his opponents, this solid wall of hostility and something very close to hatred was something new. It had shaken him, although of course he would never admit that, even to Cyril.

He had come to the islands expecting opposition from the Establishment and relishing the prospect of what, in his younger days, he would have called putting the boot in. True, he had done that, but he had not counted on the severe mauling he himself had received in the process. He had expected support from the workers and had received none. The media were solidly against him. There had been scant respect for him as a minister and none for him as an individual.

He had been subjected to insult after insult, had spent a night in prison as the result of a hoax, seemed to have been dogged by a bizarre fall of events, not least in this damnable haunted house with its upper crust owners who, for all their good manners and show of concern must, Twite knew, despise him like the rest.

As he read, his arrogance began to re-assert itself and he began to relish tomorrow morning's meeting with Sir

Frederick. Then he would revenge himself to the full. All the cards were in his hand. There was nothing the Bailiff could do.

At length, satisfied and his spirits restored, Ernest Twite changed the combination of his expensive brief case and locked the documents away. Before spinning the dials he noted the combination on a scrap of paper which he then placed carefully in his wallet. This was a procedure which Twite followed religiously. There were papers in that case which must never come to light and Twite was determined to ensure personally that they never did.

The gathering for pre-dinner drinks saw everyone except Twite and Smallpeice, and the couple who had replaced Maeve O'Cork and Ernest of the Three Widows, keyed up. Six of them, if one included Scratcher, had a critical part to play. The other five, Podger and Prue, Arthur, Connie and Pansy, who had no allotted role, were nevertheless privy to every detail of the plan and were scarcely less tense.

Prue showed the whites of her eyes and snorted a good deal and Podger's striking rate of What! Whats! was higher than usual. Pansy Phipps was apprehensive, worried that her mate's track record was such that a cock-up could by no means be ruled out. She tried to hide her concern and prayed that this would be one of Pranger's good days.

Just before he sidled away on first Curtain moving duties she came up and, rather as a Fair Lady would have given her champion a token, whispered in his ear 'Finger out! Pranger.' 'Roger, Ma'am. And foreskin peeled!' came the reassuring reply.

Though keenly aware of what was at stake and conscious of the fact that things could easily go wrong, Arthur and Connie were more relaxed than the others. They had been the first to arrive, as Arthur wanted a quiet word with Richard. This was to the effect that the Bailiff, though totally mystified and frankly sceptical, had given instructions for the preparation of the document of which

246

Arthur, with legal advice, had been the author. Arthur felt that he could do no more, and was content to leave the hot cut and thrust of action to others.

Connie was enthralled by Pussy's account of the simply fantastic showing by the poltergeist. Maeve O'Cork would, she was sure, find this reason enough to make a definitive study of the Hall, a study in which she, Connie, would have an important place as a field researcher.

Dinner passed quickly apart from an excitable address, intended for his neighbour but, in the event, received table wide, on the latest idiocy of the Inner London Education Authority by Colonel D'Aubeney, the male half of the new couple. The Colonel now in his mid-seventies had, so it transpired, represented Great Britain in the pre-war Olympic Games in Berlin, and held strong views on the virtue of competition in sport. It also transpired that what he, D'Aubeney, held to be a lesbian-dominated, militant feminist institution, had decided that competitive games would no longer be played in I.L.E.A. schools. Were we as a nation, he demanded, going to sit idly by and let this happen? If they had their way, the I.L.E.A. would be responsible for a generation of children who were not only confused as to the occupations proper to their sex but would now, in addition, be compulsorily deprived of the stimulus of competition. 'What,' he demanded, his veined cheeks vying to match the colour of his nose, 'What was the country coming to?'

Twite attempted a reasoned reply along the lines of 'evident failure of present system to meet the legitimate aspirations of under-achievers, who only under-achieved because of racist attitudes, deprived backgrounds and chauvinist attitude of the educational establishment who, if given their head, would continue to produce recruits for an empire which no longer existed', but he knew he might as well have talked to them in Swahili. Probably better, because no doubt D'Aubeney and the Brigadier understood that tongue, while their ears were totally closed to the language of social reform.

However, good manners held sway and the Colonel, embarrassed that what he had intended as a private aside had become a matter of public discussion, did not press his view.

Conversation did not long survive dinner and the D'Aubeneys soon took their leave.

Immediately after them, the Crabbes and the Simpsons also left.

The time was 10.30. At 10.40 Cyril, Ursula and Charlie said goodnight and left together. Pranger had already absented himself, presumably, had anyone noticed, for the lavatory. At 10.43 Pussy moved over to Twite and, dramatically stifling a tiny theatrical yawn, bathed him in a brilliant smile. The cats-in-waiting, sensing that a move was afoot, came to readiness.

'I do hope you're feeling as exhausted as I am, Mr Twite, because if so, I'm sure you'll sleep well. I certainly know I shall! You must be longing to get to bed, particularly as I know you've a very busy morning. When you're ready I'll come with you, if you don't mind, because I'm curious to know whether it's a "chant" night, or whether you'll be left in total peace. Not, of course,' she added, 'that I ever find the chanting intrusive. Once you're used to it, it even becomes somewhat soporific.' She gave him another brilliant smile.

Three minutes later at 10.46 precisely, or at H plus 6, Pussy and Twite moved off, with a close escort of cats and with the second curtain moving detail close up behind.

As Pussy and Twite reached the curtain at the entrance to the west wing the lights went out.

'Oh dear! There it goes once more. I'm sure they'll come on again soon, Mr Twite. You can find your way from here easily enough – you're the second door down, as you know. I'm sorry about this, but at least you've been spared the chanting! Goodnight.' So saying, Pussy retraced her steps.

Twite allowed a few moments for his eyes to become accustomed to the dark and then, just able to see, he groped his way to the second door on the right, moved inside and closed the door behind him.

Outside in the corridor, and unknown to Twite, the heavy curtains were at that moment being moved so that in something less than a minute the room that he was now in would be the first on the right after the curtain, rather than the second.

Twite reproached himself for not bringing a torch and reproached his hostess for not providing a candle. Then he shrugged, a fairly useless gesture in a pitch dark room. What did it matter, he felt. The lights would probably come on again soon but, if they didn't, it wouldn't be the end of the world. At least there was no chanting.

He undressed and felt for his pyjamas which William would have laid out on the near side of the bed. They did not seem to be there. Oh, well! He'd slept nude before. He climbed into bed and stretched contentedly. There was something especially luxurious about having a double bed all to oneself.

Suddenly Twite tensed. He had become aware of a heat source on the far side of the bed. Probably some of those cats or, even worse, that infernal dog. He stretched his arm out gingerly, his fingers reaching to identify the type of fur which they would meet.

Instead, to his astonishment, they encountered warm flesh with unmistakable curves and, at that same moment, his bewilderment was increased by the noise and movement of someone slipping into bed on his near side. Again the warmth was intense.

Wild thoughts came into his head. Could it possibly be? Those two girls had given no sign, but they had certainly gone upstairs early and, unless he was much mistaken, he now had two girls in his bed.

Further speculation was cut short by a shrill scream from the girl on his right as she shot upright in the bed. Twite did likewise and reached out to reassure her. As he did so he felt himself clasped from behind, and the lights came on with a blinding flash. Twite had been right about one thing. He was certainly in bed with two girls. But all else was different. Not only did they not welcome his presence but, to listen to them, they positively abominated it.

What then, Twite righteously demanded, were they doing in his bed? He hadn't invited them, they'd come of their own free will and not, presumably, for tea and toast.

The response was shrill and definite. It was certainly not his bed and, indeed, it was not even his room. His was the next one up, the second after the curtain. Surely he knew that by now, and the sooner he got out the better.

A demoralised Twite did the best job he could manage of wrapping a counterpane around himself as he climbed over the girl on his left, whom he now identified as Charlie. The screamer had been Ursula.

Gathering up his clothes he prepared to retreat to the corridor, uncertain of his next move because he knew for certain that this was the second door on the right. If this was not his room then his room no longer existed and all this was a dream.

As he shut the door behind him and found that he had just left the first room after the curtains his reason all but snapped. He knew it could not possibly be so, and yet it was. Perhaps the doctor was right after all and he really had been working too hard. God, what a night! And there was that damned chanting just starting up! And the lights had failed again.

He knew he'd never sleep now, but at least he could lie down. Here was his door. One, two. The second door on the right. Make no mistake this time. Not that he had last time, and yet he must have done. It was positively uncanny. Yes, that was it, an illusion, the work of phantoms! God, but he'd be glad to get out of this cursed house.

He opened the door of his room, felt his way to the bed and climbed in. He met an eager embrace.

'Oooh! Here you are at last, darling boy.' Then, while words were still frozen on his lips and his brain struggled to surmount its image of a world suddenly bereft of reason, he felt a fumbling and something brushing his face.

'Naughty, naughty Ernest! You've shaved off your lovely beard! And you've got quite a little one haven't you? Very small for a big sea dog like you! Still, as my granny used to say, there's good things in little parcels! Oooh, you lovely, lovely boy!'

The psychological grip on Twite's windpipe relaxed sufficiently for him to jerk upright in bed and find his voice.

'Get away from me! What in hell's name is going on,' he shouted, and at that precise moment the lights came on blindingly, showing him as his eyes recovered from the flash that he had a startled Cyril as a bed mate.

CHAPTER TWENTY FOUR

The following morning found Twite and Smallpeice gaunt and hollow-eyed. They had been thoroughly shaken and disorientated by events and had spent a virtually sleepless night listening first to the chanting and then to very loud organ music. This did nothing to improve a morale already shattered by the demonstration of occult power that could change rooms at will. For nothing else, they agreed, could account for their harrowing joint experience. In the small hours they felt fear, and neither slept until the organ notes died away and the first birds sang.

Twite in particular had huge black rings under his eyes which, during the night, seemed to have shrunk and to have retreated into his skull. He had cut himself in three places while shaving, and a nervous tic had started up on the left side of his face. He was very much a shadow of the brash and arrogant Twite of two days ago.

Pussy appeared, smiling and accompanied by a police inspector.

'Ah, there you are! Good morning, Mr Twite, good morning, Mr Smallpeice. I do hope you both had a peaceful night?'

Then, lest her question should be answered, she carried on without pause.

'I wonder whether either of you can possibly help? Inspector Robinson here is investigating the disappearance of the emerald necklace I was wearing last night because, if we can't find it, the insurance company will wish to know that the police were called at the first opportunity, as the claim will run into six figures.' She gave a worried and apologetic smile.

Twite glowered. Here, if ever any had been needed, was justification for his plan to bring proper English rates of taxation to these islands. Better than £100,000 for one bauble for this one woman! And the outrage of it was that she would be able to leave it to her daughter tax free! It was nothing short of monstrous! But once Jersey was part of Hampshire, all that would change, he reminded himself with satisfaction. His glower faded with the thought.

'You were certainly wearing it at dinner,' he said. 'After that I can't be sure.'

'And you, Mr Smallpeice?' asked the Inspector.

'Mrs Fox was wearing it when I went upstairs just before 10.45.'

'You're sure of that, Sir?'

'Oh yes, definitely.'

'What were your movements, Mrs Fox, between that time and when you discovered the loss at' he consulted his notebook '11.15 when you yourself retired.'

Pussy chewed her lower lip.

'That's what makes it so mysterious. Apart from escorting Mr Twite to the west wing I didn't move from the drawing room until the other house guests went to bed, when my husband and I also went up after puffing up a few cushions and turning out the lights.'

'And none of these guests can remember for sure whether or not you were wearing the necklace when they went to bed. Is that right, Mrs Fox?'

'I think that's so, Inspector, but you'll need to ask them yourself.'

The Inspector looked at Twite and Smallpeice reflectively.

'And when will you two gentlemen be leaving Jersey?' he enquired.

253

'Later this morning,' replied Twite. 'Why?'

'Just in case you're needed for further questioning, Sir.'

'But I'm a minister of the Crown!'

'Quite so, Sir. That'll be all for now.'

By the time that Twite arrived for his appointment with the Bailiff he had dismissed the incident from his mind. He was also feeling better, partly due to the restorative effect of sweet black coffee but more particularly because he would in a few moments be serving formal notice on the Bailiff of the decision to change the status of Jersey.

Sir Frederick had aged in the last few days. He looked listless and defeated and at the same time almost bewildered, like one who found it difficult to believe the magnitude of the misfortune which had suddenly overtaken him.

He received Twite coldly and there was bitterness in his voice when he spoke.

'I do not think our meeting need be overlong, Mr Twite. I imagine you have a document which you wish to leave with me?'

'Yes, Mr Bailiff, I have it here.' Twite tapped the briefcase at his feet.

'Very well. But before you do so I have had a document prepared at the instigation of my advisor here, Sir Arthur Crabbe, which he believes you may be willing to sign.'

Sir Frederick's voice was weary. It was obvious that he did not share Sir Arthur's belief. He handed over the document, which Twite glanced through with incredulity:

'I, Ernest Twite, Parliamentary Under Secretary of State etc, etc, do solemnly undertake on behalf of Her Majesty's Government that neither I nor any other person during the lifetime of this said Government will seek to change, vary or in any way alter the constitutional relationship at present existing, etc, etc. Given this day of my own free will, being convinced that any change could only be detrimental to both parties.'

254

Twite looked up. 'Is this some joke, Sir Frederick?' he enquired. 'What on earth makes you think that I would sign this ridiculous piece of paper?'

'Not me, Mr Twite. My advisor, here,' he looked at Arthur.

Arthur coughed in a deprecatory manner.

'Ah, well, yes. It does on the face of it seem unlikely, but experience has taught me that a sudden change of heart can sometimes be effected, even when the outlook seems most unpromising.'

'Not a chance, Sir Arthur!'

'Quite so. Quite so. But I have been instructed by certain parties, who do not wish to be named, to pass these documents to you.' He held up a large sealed envelope. 'It is their belief, though I am not privy to the grounds on which that, ah, belief is founded, that having studied these documents you may wish to reconsider your position.'

Twite clicked his tongue impatiently.

'What is this nonsense about, Sir Arthur? If you want me to see those papers, please hand them over!'

'Very well. But first, Mr Twite, you are to understand two things. The first is that neither Sir Frederick nor I is cognisant of the exact nature of the contents of this envelope. The second is that copies exist. I understand that you are welcome to keep the originals. And, ah yes. One final thing, Mr Twite. My clients instructed me to advise you that you would be sensible to open this envelope in private.'

'This is absolute nonsense! Please give it here.'

Twite almost snatched the envelope from Arthur and, ripping it open, moved to a side table by the window to examine the contents. His back was to the room, so they could not see his face, which was perhaps just as well. But they heard his gasp of consternation and disbelief.

What Twite was looking at were three items, any one of which could finish his political career and one of which

255

would ensure that he spent some years in prison. The least damaging of the three was a picture of him in bed between two young women. Twite, facing the camera in surprise, appeared to be about to fondle a plump left breast which had somehow broken free from the flimsy nightdress of the girl on his right. The girl on his left, whose face was hidden by her hair, appeared to be embracing him fervently and to have no clothes on whatsoever.

The second photograph, as he knew it would, showed him and Cyril sitting close together in bed wearing just such a look of embarrassed surprise as might be expected of any male couple caught consenting in private. No one would believe for one moment that the situation was accidental and wholly innocent, especially given Cyril's well known inclinations.

But it was the third document which seemed to freeze his blood as he looked at it. It was a statement of account from his Swiss Bank which, in the hands of any competent accountant, would indicate only too clearly what had happened to £327,000 of union money moved abroad to escape the Official Receiver.

He was ashen and shaking and he could feel the cold sweat running down between his shoulder blades.

Wordlessly he stuffed the photographs and the statement back in the envelope. How could they have got hold of that damning bank statement when it was always locked in his briefcase and only he held the combination? It wasn't possible. Surely he couldn't have been so careless as to leave the case unlocked at any time? Again, hardly possible. But that could wait. His one thought now was to get that envelope with its incriminating contents under lock and key. He turned round, fumbling in his back pocket for his wallet, his face ghastly. Cyril was all immediate concern.

'Minister, whatever's the matter? Shall I get you a glass of water?'

Twite waved him aside, extracted the piece of paper from his wallet and attempted to set the combination, but his hands were shaking too much. He pushed the case and the piece of paper at Smallpeice.

'You do it, Cyril,' he said.

Cyril set the combination deftly.

'It's open, Minister.'

'Right. Put this envelope in and relock it on the same combination.' Cyril opened the case and all eyes were immediately drawn to the object which lay on top of a mass of papers, reflecting with exquisite richness the bright sunlight which flooded the room. The colours kept changing and the patterns shifted, each one more fascinating than its predecessor. But through it all the deep commanding green of the delicate stones held sway. They gazed, as though hypnotised, at the missing emerald necklace.

There was a knock at the door and the Bailiff's secretary put his head into the office.

'Excuse me for interrupting you, Sir Frederick, but Inspector Robinson is anxious for a word with Mr Twite. He says it's urgent.'

Twite started and quickly slammed down the lid of his briefcase. His mouth worked soundlessly.

Arthur Crabbe broke the tense silence.

'With your permission, Mr Bailiff, I rather fancy that if the Inspector were to be told that Mrs Fox's emerald necklace has now been, ah, recovered, his desire for an interview with Mr Twite might be sensibly diminished if not indeed, er, eliminated altogether.'

He looked questioningly at Sir Frederick who nodded his agreement. The secretary withdrew. Arthur Crabbe looked at Twite.

'A strange affair, Mr Twite, and one to which we have all been witness. Susceptible to only two explanations, I fancy. I'm sure that we can agree among ourselves to keep

257

the police out of the matter. So much better to settle things like this quietly between, ah, friends. After all, there's no harm done, is there now? Perhaps if you would be so kind as to let me have the necklace so that I may return it to Mrs Fox?'

Wordlessly, Twite felt in the case and handed it over.

While all this had been going on, Sir Frederick was undergoing a transformation similar to that of Mr Oscar Wilde's unfortunate character, Dorian Gray, though in Sir Frederick's case the transformation was in the opposite direction. He once again carried his head high above squared shoulders, the tired skin on his face ceased to sag and sat tight to the firm bone line, the deep lines on his forehead cleared away, his eyes sparkled with vitality and, as if at a stroke, their bloodshot yellow was once more whiter than white.

The Bailiff was in the pink, but he was not going to interfere with Arthur Crabbe. This, he reasoned, was very much Arthur's show and he sat back with the deep, almost unbelieving pleasure of a punter who having unwisely placed a bundle on a 66-1 outsider, sees the nag a short distance from the post with nothing to touch it.

Arthur Crabbe steepled his fingers and regarded Twite over his half-moon glasses.

'I don't know why, Mr Twite, but something in your demeanour makes me feel that the unexpected may have happened and that you have had one of those changes of heart which no one can explain but which, when they do happen, have all the depth and sincerity of a religious Conversion. Could it be, Mr Twite, that you have, er, how shall I say it, ah, seen the light in the sense that of your own free will you are now anxious to sign the document I showed you just now?'

Twite glared.

'You know damned well I'll sign. I only wish it was your death warrant, you blackmailing little bastard!'

'Come, come, Mr Twite. Blackmail is a nasty word. Actionable too, no doubt. But then we don't want any of this to come out, do we?'

CHAPTER TWENTY FIVE

Later that day Podger and Arthur were having a celebration drink in Arthur's study. Arthur looked at his friend.

'I thought you told me, Podger, that there would be no question of blackmail?'

'Quite so, Arthur old man, quite so! A dirty game indeed, yes dirty, that's the word. Wouldn't touch it with a barge pole!'

'But . . .'

Podger cut the question off before it could be formulated.

'Doesn't arise old man, simply doesn't arise. He certified that he signed of his own free will, didn't he, what? I mean to say, what, he did, didn't he?'

Arthur thought about it and, as he thought, he became aware that all was now well and familiar once again. Podger had just created an arid zone centred on his own glass.

The only thing that fell short of perfection in the way things had fallen out was Podger's rejection of his, Arthur's, so carefully redrafted opening to his novel. Was it impossible that Podger might be brought to see that his criticism, indeed his veto, was heartless, perhaps even hasty? Arthur scarcely dared to hope that it might be so, but his anguish at what he perceived to be the loss of elegance and of impact was such that he determined on one more try.

'Podger,' he began tentatively. 'I've been worrying about the opening of my novel.'

'Oh, ah?' said Podger.

'Yes. I wonder whether when we last discussed it we didn't in fact prune it too drastically. I thought perhaps there might be a compromise position whereby some of the original could be retained without offence to Fowler. Do you think that might be possible?'

Podger looked at his old friend.

'Can't see why not old man, can't see why not, what? I mean, what?'

Arthur's happiness was complete.

THE END